D0916312

Greenbrier!
VALLEY *of* HOPE

A NOVEL

Thomas H. Williams

BOOKWRIGHTS PRESS
of CHARLOTTESVILLE

Copyright© 1997 by Thomas H. Williams
All rights reserved under the International and Pan-American Copyright Conventions.

Published by
BOOKWRIGHTS PRESS
of Charlottesville

2255 Westover Drive, Suite 108
Charlottesville, VA 22901
phone: 804-823-8223
email: editor@bookwrights.com
www.mindspring.com/~bookwrights

Cover illustration from a painting © 1997 by Robert E. Tuckwiller

Prints of the original may be obtained by calling the Tuckwiller Studio at (800) 343-7386

Cover photograph © 1997 Deana S. Smith

Printed in the United States of America
1 2 3 4 5 6 7 8

Printed on recycled paper.

To my parents, Carnie and Madge Williams.

Acknowledgments

I take this opportunity to thank those who have provided assistance in the publication of this book. Thanks goes to my sister Ida May Spessard and my mother and father for reading and providing suggestions for the improvement of the manuscript. Without their help and encouragement, I would not have seen this project to completion. To my wife, Joanne, goes my love for her unwavering support and enthusiasm. Thanks, too, goes to my longtime friend Mike Williams, who promptly replied to my late night email requests for information regarding the History of Lewisburg.

Special appreciation goes to Robert Tuckwiller who painted the illustration for the book's cover. He endured my many pone calls and visits to his galleries in Lewisburg, West Virginia and Blacksburg, Virginia in developing the concept for a historically accurate painting. And, I am indebted to Mayapriya Long, at Bookwrights Press, for her patience and special expertise in the preparation of this book.

In writing this book, I have relied heavily on Otis Rice's *History of Greenbrier County* for historical detail, and on the *Methodist Hymnal* for quotes regarding song lyrics and the ritual for the burial of the dead.

A Note on Historical Accuracy

Throughout this work of fiction, I have attempted to remain true to the actual events surrounding the Battle of Lewisburg. Although I have researched the events that precipitated the battle and afterward, and at one time owned a home that was located roughly between the skirmish lines of the Union and Confederate forces, I do not claim to be a historian. I only hope to be a storyteller.

For my own convenience and to advance the story-line of this novel, I have taken liberty with certain events and places. For example, to my knowledge, there is no passage to the Greenbrier River from the sinkhole that has resulted from the waters of the spring in the center of town, as depicted in Boyd's escape from Yankee forces and the slaves' attempted escape. However, the spring house and small stream that flows from it and into a sinkhole actually exist, as did the jail near the spring. Only the foundation of the jail remains now since the structure burned some years ago.

The valley in which Charlie's home was located and Blackbird Knob are figments of my imagination, although Muddy Creek Mountain is real as is its location in relation to the Greenbrier River and Charleston.

The events related to the battle are roughly accurate. The forces involved, their leaders and relative battle positions, and the outcome of the battle are as accurate as I could make them.

Grapevine cave, in which Boyd was briefly imprisoned, is real. The opening to the cavern described in the novel exists today, although the cavern is now a commercial venture and has been renamed. An alternative entrance has been excavated.

Some of the events in the novel are inspired by actual occurrences. Following the battle, a sniper shot and killed a union soldier from ambush in town. I have attributed this event to the character Jones.

Mr. James' home and others depicted are montages of the civil war era homes that still stand in the city of Lewisburg. No single home served as a model for any described in the story.

The use of the public library and churches as hospitals for wounded soldiers is factual, as is the mass burial site near the Old Stone Presbyterian Church. After the war, the bodies of the Confederate soldiers were moved to a cross-shaped grave on the hill behind the church that is still visible today. The bodies of the Union casualties were buried on a hilltop west of town and later moved to the national cemetery in Staunton, Virginia.

Although it is implied in the novel, I am not aware that citizens were paid to care for the wounded. Many opened their homes to the wounded—both Confederate and Union soldiers—but did so for charitable reasons.

Nor am I aware that any of the Confederate soldiers who were captured during the Battle of Lewisburg were offered parole, as depicted in the story, although it was a practice that occurred elsewhere.

Thus, I have fashioned a tale that could have occurred in and around the Battle of Lewisburg: discrepancies from the historical record that may be found in this work are solely my responsibility.

Greenbrier! Valley of Hope is a work of fiction. All characters, other than those found in the historical record, are creations of my imagination and do not represent persons living or dead.

Tom Williams
Lewisburg, West Virginia

Greenbrier!
VALLEY *of* HOPE

A NOVEL

"The war is still raging it seems that we will know what war is after while."

The Journal of Sirene Bunten
January 26, 1863
French Creek, Virginia

1

They had just marched from Pearisburg to Union, Virginia, and Boyd Houston had never been so exhausted in his life. He sat on the oiled wooden floor with his back against the judge's bench in the county courthouse in Union, with other men of Confederate Brigadier General Henry Heth's command laying in weary heaps around him. The rough wooden benches used when the court was in session were stacked against an inside wall in a precarious pile. The pungent odor of tobacco, dust, and unwashed bodies filled his nostrils as the exhausted men rested and began to settled for the night and whatever sleep it would bring. There was little talk, especially from the new recruits, as the men pulled off their boots and rubbed their blistered heels and ankles. Those who had food dug it from their filthy kit bags and ate mechanically, staring blankly at the opposite wall of the courtroom. Boyd was hungry, but had too much pride to ask the other soldiers for food. He pondered the last two months of his 26 years that had led him to this place, high in the rugged Appalachian mountains of Western Virginia. What turn of events had led to his enlistment into the Confederate Army and why was he soon to be tested as a soldier in battle?

Dizzy with fatigue and hunger, he recalled how, like his father before him, he had lived the life of a fisherman. The fishing boat he inherited had reluctantly yielded a meager living, and he realized that to remain a fisherman would slowly drain his strength and desire to succeed.

Four years of backbreaking work with nothing to show for it was

1

enough to convince him that there was no future for him there. He sold the boat and cottage for twelve hundred dollars, put the money in coin in his money belt and walked ten miles to town to join the army. He had no family, no ties to the community, and no desire to stay in the hot, mean piedmont country. He had not thought much about the War before he joined, but couldn't think of anything better to do.

Now, as he sat among soldiers, raw recruits alongside veteran fighters, he began to seriously consider what it would be like to fight other men, very much like him, to the death. Would he run like a hog from a yellow jacket's nest, or would he have the courage to stand and fight despite the flying bullets? A dove's mating call, from the sugar maple trees just outside the open window above his head, broke the stillness.

After the men had rested briefly they began to move about, talking quietly to their friends with grim determination on their faces. Even the veterans were apprehensive about the coming battle. Boyd could hear the sounds of many soldiers outside—the hawking of phlegm from dusty throats, the rattle of mess kits and sabers, the clunk of boots on the sidewalk, the muted conversations of tired men. The smell of wood smoke and boiling mutton followed the warm, May breeze through the window. On the march from Pearisburg, many of the men had foraged far and wide for food and anything else of value. The General had warned the men not to raid the farmers along the way, but some had—despite his orders. Boyd had to admit that the food smelled good even if it was stolen.

"So you sold the family farm and joined the army, did you?" a tall, skinny soldier in a dusty uniform asked. Boyd judged him to be about thirty-five years old and he spoke with a distinct accent, probably from this mountainous area. He had talked to the soldier several times in the last few weeks—never about anything personal—and the two of them had become friends.

"Well, you're going to see plenty of action soon, feller. Ole Colonel Crook'll see to that, you can bet yer life. Him and almost two thousand Yankees are sittin' in Lewisburg just waiting fer us. Heth thinks we'll surprise 'em, but in this country, word spreads faster than a brush fire in May," he paused, waiting for a response from Boyd. It was obvious that he wanted to talk. Hearing no immediate reaction, he continued, "I grew up on Muddy Creek Mountain, just west of Lewisburg, so's I know what I'm talkin' about. Most folk livin' around here have some sympathy fer our cause, but if they's one thing sure, country folk like to talk. Word'll get back that we're comin' all right. I've lived here too long not to know what folk'll do. I live on the mountain so's I'm not like one of those town men from down below, ridin' in their buggies and all. My folk tend to stick to themselves and prefer to ride good horseflesh. I'd give most anything I own to have one of my horses under me right now." The man lying next to Boyd snored loudly and twitched in his sleep.

"Where'd you say you come from?" the tall man asked.

"Down on the coast in South Carolina," Boyd replied warming at once to the friendliness of this strange soldier. "Does it get any better than this? I don't mean to complain, but, I don't think I've ever been this tired before and I haven't eaten for two days now. I don't think I can go much farther." The tall man looked at him from the corner of his eye and laughed.

"Nope. There's one thing fer sure about a foot soldier—he's always tired and hungry. Here," he dug into his mess kit, "have some of this." He extended a dirty hand with a piece of blackened, roasted meat wrapped in newspaper. Boyd accepted gratefully and using his folding knife, cut off a generous slice. Asking was one thing, but being offered food was different.

"Thanks, I am surely grateful," he said. While chewing the meat he wondered what kind of animal it had come from. Although it was dark and a bit stringy, with a powerful odor, it tasted about as good as anything he had eaten recently. Come to think of it, he hadn't eaten much of anything lately. He slid his hand down under his belt. There was a lot more room in there than when he was issued the breeches.

"The trick is to eat when it's available and never turn down food," the tall man advised, "You never know when you'll get to eat again, and always drink lots of water. It keeps your body goin'. My uncle Harry, he went to sea on one of them schooners, and they ran out of food. He went for thirteen days without food, but couldn't hardly go for three days without water. Finally had to drink sea water, but that made him more thirsty than ever. He said he'd rather go anytime without food than good water. The water hereabouts is 'sposed to be real good, but some of it's awful hard. Up on Peter's Mountain they's springs that have the best water anywhere," the tall man said. "Good water is mighty important on a farm. You can't 'spect to raise good crops and stock without good water, or my name ain't Charlie Howard Taylor. I'm named fer my grandfather. He was one of the first to settle in this area. After this fightin's over I reckon I'll never leave these mountains again." he said, finally winding down.

The soldier rose and stretched, raising his fists high above his head. His clothes hung from his lean frame like a shirt on a ladder-backed chair. He had a high forehead with a rapidly receding hairline; the wisps of damp hair on his head were plastered down on his brown scalp after spending the day's march under his hat. His nose was prominent with a mighty hump in the middle. He had intense, brown eyes that peered out from under shaggy eyebrows. His beard, dark brown with stray, gray hairs was cropped short. He was lean and brown, and some had whispered that he wasn't to be trifled with. The other men said he was a vicious fighter.

Dusk was falling rapidly as the sounds of the army bedding down for the night wafted through the windows. There was hushed laughter, the clank of metal, loud snores from those already asleep, and the occasional sound of birds also preparing for the night's rest. Other men were garrisoned in the church on main street, and in a school building close by. Pickets were set to the west of town along the road that led from Union to Lewisburg, some twenty miles distant.

"You'd better get some sleep, Boyd, tomorrow's march will be a killer. It's only about twenty miles to town, but Heth'll want to move quickly so that he can sneak up on Crook. It can't be done, but he'll try anyhow," Charlie said. "You stick by me in the battle. We'll see what the fightin' has to offer together."

Boyd slid down from the back rest of the judge's bench so that he could stretch out, pushing gently against the man in front of him with his feet. He cradled his musket in his arm, and felt under his coat for the money belt, running his fingers over the smooth leather. It was reassuring to know that it was still there. What am I doing here, he wondered? Will I fight like a soldier, or will I run? He rolled over toward Charlie and studied the back of his uniform jacket. A louse scurried down the jacket and under his armpit. Charlie was already breathing steadily, sound asleep. There's another thing that a good soldier does, Boyd thought, he sleeps when he can. The court-room was quiet save for the snoring of the tired soldiers. Light from a cook fire outside flickered through the window made dancing patterns of light on the ceiling, while the comforting smell of wood smoke reminded him of the fireplace at home. The veterans were sleeping, the recruits were still awake, staring into the dark.

Colonel George S. Patton stood in the courthouse doorway with his hands on his hips, legs apart. His gaze took in the ragtag soldiers sprawled across the floor in assorted poses. Muskets, clothing, and packs were scattered about. Several men, walking wounded, wore blood darkened bandages—others were red-eyed and sick. West Point hadn't prepared him for this kind of war, with battle-hardened soldiers interspersed with raw recruits. All were poorly equipped and hungry. The local citizens were mostly Confederate sympathizers, but they were quite vocal about having to "donate" their cattle and horses to the passing army. Tomorrow, it might be the Yankees to whom they had to provide provisions.

The Colonel was proud of these men who, except for the recent recruits, were battle-tested and had yet to experience defeat. Yet he worried; their morale was low from hunger and exhaustion.

"Up men, up and at 'em," he roared, walking quickly among them kicking their feet and roughly shaking them awake. "Roll out, roll out, we're on our way to another victory. Just a short march to Lewisburg. Come on now."

They came awake slowly, coughing and spitting. Boyd rolled to his feet, rubbing his bones where they burned from the long night on the hard wooden floor, and looked about for Charlie. But he was gone, along with his gear. Over to the side of the courtroom, just in front of the jury stand, a dirty soldier failed to rise from his make-shift bed. The Colonel nudged him tentatively with the toe of his shiny boot. There was no response. Rolling him over on his back, the Colonel straightened abruptly when he saw the man's bloody, bandaged chest.

"He's dead, Colonel," a soldier, who couldn't have been more than sixteen, said. "I heard him coughing in the night and he was moaning something terrible. Then he got real quiet. I reckon he just couldn't go no further." The young soldier stood white-faced looking out of the window.

The soldiers stared at the dead man and shuffled their feet, each seeing in the corpse his own destiny. A green fly buzzed around the room, sensing a new source of food. It lit on the dead man's face and searched for a beginning place.

"You men there," the Colonel whispered, "pick him up and carry him out to the church. They'll take care of him there. Come on now, it ain't like you haven't seen a dead man before. Get moving." They watched somberly as the body was carried away.

The men limped out of the courthouse into the morning sun

and mustered into rough formation—the 22nd Virginia Infantry under Colonel Patton; the 45th Virginia Infantry led by William Brown, the Boy Colonel; the 8th Virginia Calvary on foot; and two newly recruited battalions under Lt. Colonel William Finney and Major George Edgar. As the army assembled in the main street of the small mountain town, six artillery pieces were being hitched to horses. Smoke hovered in the still air as breakfast was cooked over open fires. Twenty-three hundred men prepared for a long march and the sobering prospects of battle.

Thirty sick and wounded sat on the steps of the courthouse and sprawled on the grassy lawn while others, less fortunate, lay out of sight in the vestibule of the church awaiting burial. General Heth gave the order to leave them behind to be cared for by the local citizens. With great respect, the wounded were loaded into farm wagons or helped into the homes of the townspeople, or left to be cared for where they lay.

"Boyd. Boyd, over here," Charlie called to him.

Boyd trotted over to him, his gear rattling. He was surprised that he had the energy to walk, much less run.

"'Pears you survived the night. You look right perky, considerin'," Charlie drawled, looking him up and down as if on inspection. "Colonel Patton wants us to scout ahead. We expect there'll be pickets down about the Greenbrier River. We'll knock them out so's not to spoil the surprise," he said with a sideways look. "Besides, we don't want 'em to fire the bridge on the James River and Kanawha Turnpike, else we'll never get the cannons across."

"I'm ready, Charlie, just as soon as I get some of that breakfast I smell cooking," Boyd said.

"Never you mind about breakfast. I've got all we need to eat right here, " he patted his kit bag fondly. "We don't have no time to waste, so come on."

They strode along the street, heading west out of town, dodging among troops preparing to move out. Just outside of town, in front of a large brick home standing at the end of a long carriage lane they joined a small squad of men led by a tall straight soldier in a crisp, clean uniform.

"Who's that?" Boyd asked jerking his head toward the officer.

"Why, that there's Captain William Bahlman. He says he just can't wait to get to Lewisburg to dance with every pretty lady there. Reckon he'll have to ask permission from ole Crook first. He's a pretty fair soldier in spite of his fancy ways." Charlie whispered.

The Captain gave orders quickly and returned to the main street of town to his command. How did he keep himself so clean, Boyd wondered. Everyone else looked and smelled terrible.

A pretty young girl stood on the porch of the brick house with her right arm wrapped around one of the white columns that supported the massive front porch roof. Several soldiers sat down flat on the porch floor with their backs against the house. They were quiet and listless with dirty white bandages wrapped around their heads and bodies. The girl stared at the departing soldiers curiously, then waved to them slowly with her handkerchief. Her gingham dress, darkened by blood on the front, rippled in the morning breeze. The home had a rundown look and had obviously not fared well in the war. A large matronly woman waddled through the door, took the girl's arm, and gently drew her inside, causing the screen door to bang loudly. Boyd looked longingly at the house wondering what these people thought of the soldiers and the war they waged.

Charlie, Boyd, and ten other men set off at a fast clip down the dirt road that wound among the soft rolling hills. As they moved quickly along, the land unfolded under the rising sun. There were cleared fields with gray stone outcroppings that looked to Boyd's amateur eye like rich, productive farmland.

"Charlie, where are the cattle? This looks like good grazing, but there's no stock in sight. I guess they've hidden them," Boyd said.

"Hell, if you was a farmer and you heard that a hungry army was a comin', you'd probably find some reason to move yer stock to the back forty too," he drawled. "'Sides, they was probably some prime beef in those cooking pots you smelled this mornin'."

"Oh, yeah, I guess you're right. The boys don't seem to mind appropriating a cow now and again," Boyd responded. "Speaking of food, where's that breakfast you promised me when we left town?"

"Here you go, Sonny. Eat up." He handed over the package wrapped in the same filthy newspaper. More of that dark smelly meat. Boyd chewed on the rank offering, frowning at the grinning tall man. At least it made his stomach stop growling.

They moved quickly through countryside dotted with small farms. There were strange land formations that Boyd had never seen before. Funnel-shaped depressions dotted the fields. A few had standing water in their bottoms, but most were dry. They ranged in size from the width of a carriage to depressions large enough to hold several large houses. Others, larger still, had small streams running along their bottoms that disappeared into holes at the lowest point. In one field, the depressions were arranged in a curving line, as if mortar fire had dropped in a sweeping curve.

"Charlie, what in the world caused these holes?" Boyd asked in amazement.

"They're sinkholes. They're made when water runs down into caves below. This whole land here has caves underneath. Some of the caves are big enough to ride a horse in. They mine saltpeter from the bat shit in them and make gun powder outin it," he grinned. "Some places it's ten feet deep."

"How do these sinkholes get started? It looks like some of them have been here longer than others."

"Well, a geologist feller from over at Lexington tole me one time that the limestone sort of dissolves in the rain water. Sooner or later the water runs into the cave below and carries some of the dirt with it. The hole gets bigger and bigger. It's like when sand runs through a hour glass. You know how it makes a funny dimple in the sand up above. Why, one time after a hard rain, a whole street in town fell in.

Left a big sinkhole right smack in the middle of court street. It took most of a summer to haul enough dirt and rocks to fill it up. Reckon some day it'll go agin."

"Where does all that water and dirt go? Sooner or later the cave must fill up."

"Why boy, you've got more questions than Matt, my least youngin'. He asks questions daylight to dark. The caves lead out at the river, or thereabouts. Most are filled with water and you can't get back in 'em. Down at Fort Spring on the Greenbrier, they's a whole stream that comes out of the side of the mountain. Other cricks go into the mountain on one side and comes out on the other side. Reckon you could walk right through the mountain if you could hold your breath long enough," he laughed.

As they topped the higher hills, they could catch glimpses of the main body of the army as it advanced far behind them. Boyd was surprised at the speed with which the force now moved, spurred on by Colonel Heth, no doubt.

A few miles out of Union they stopped briefly to fill their canteens in a spring near a white frame farm house set on a knoll beside the wagon road they had been following. They dropped down into a deep, narrow sinkhole and filled their canteens from the spring flowing from beneath an outcropping at the bottom. The water was sweet and cool. A foot path led from the spring to the farmhouse. Boyd thought that he'd like to stretch out in the shade under the huge black walnut tree that grew from the side of the sinkhole and sleep for a year, but the scouting party quickly moved on.

Soon they crossed Second Creek with a beautiful farm spreading away from the road, both upstream and down. A farmer dressed in worn work clothes rounded a sturdy barn in time to see them. He stopped abruptly, squinted his eyes against the sun's glare, recognized the dirty gray uniforms, and smiled broadly. Charlie broke from the group and walked briskly toward the man, greeting him. They shook hands warmly as Boyd and the other men watched. With much animation and arm waving, the two men talked. For once Charlie was brief and soon returned. The farmer hadn't seen any recent sign of the Yankees. He said that the road was probably clear all way down the draft to the river, but he couldn't be sure. After a brief respite, the small force began the long trek up the hill toward Organ Cave.

The noonday sun found them crossing a narrow ridge whose sides fell sharply away. The road wound through a dense woods, following the ridge.

"Right down there." Charlie pointed down into the trees, "That's Organ Cave. You can see the stream at the mouth of the cave. Some fellers took torches and walked back in there. Said they's rooms in there as big as the grand ballroom at the Greenbrier Hotel at White Sulphur Springs where all them fancy folk go to sit in the sulphur water—they say it cures what ails them. I wouldn't know about the sulphur water or the room in the cave; I ain't never been in either one of them and don't have no plans to."

Just past the cave, the road sloped downward. They had reached the headwaters of the draft that led directly to the river and the covered bridge. The men began to walk faster now as the road wound down along the branch with its tumbling white water. The small, steep valley narrowed and they had to cross the stream repeatedly as it followed a serpentine path downward toward the larger river. The dark, narrow valley was shaded by ancient hemlocks and sprawling red oaks. Straight yellow poplar trees reached for the sky and the shorter shade-loving dogwood graced the sides of the gorge with bright white, flowers. On the northern slopes of the narrow valley trilliums covered the ground with white blossoms, accented with an occasional purple wake robin flower. Bright orange flame azaleas cascaded from the banks above the road. Boyd, reminded of home by the dogwood, longed to stop and loiter under the magnificent canopy of new leaves. Instead, the small force moved, almost at a trot downward, ignoring the beauty around them, intent on their task. As he fought to keep up, fears of battle crept again into his thoughts. Could he do it? Would he be brave? If he ran, what would his new friend think of him? Could he kill another man?

Finally, the road lost some of its steepness and the stream flattened out, flowing quietly through the trees, signaling their approach to the larger river. The men moved cautiously now, removed their canteens and kit bags, and stashed them along the side of the road. Any metal object that might make noise was also removed and left behind.

"Careful now men," Charlie whispered. "Their pickets have to be posted here somewhere. When we get to the end of this holler, the draft will empty into Howard's Crick. Just there, see?" he pointed toward a larger valley intersecting with the draft. "Then a few hundert yards down it empties into the Greenbrier." Crouching, he led the men quietly from tree to tree. "I'll scout ahead. Y'all stay right here and for God's sake don't make no noise. I don't want to get myself shot." He slipped quietly into the shallow, clear water of the larger creek and waded across. Beyond him was another larger valley.

Boyd stooped behind a clump of brush. Peering intently in the direction that Charlie had taken, he stood as still as he could, fearful that any movement would make too much noise. A male cardinal called sharply in the tree above him, its brilliant red plumage in stark contrast to the clear blue sky. Time passed slowly. Boyd's back began to ache and he realized that he had chosen a poor position. He would have to get down lower on the ground and find a more comfortable posture. Slowly, he lowered himself to the ground, making considerable noise as the dry leaves and twigs crunched beneath his weight. The soldier next to him glared and put his finger to his lips. He shook his head and Boyd could hear him mutter something about 'dumb-assed fisherman."

His position was better now, but he couldn't see as well. With brush rising all around, the enemy would be on top of him before he knew it. Where was Charlie, anyway? It seemed as if he'd been gone for an hour already, although it was probably only a matter of minutes. A slight sound directly in front alerted him that someone was coming. What if it wasn't Charlie? What if the Yankees had caught him and they were coming this way now? His heart pounded wildly and his mouth was dry.

"Was that you wallerin' around in the leaves here?" Charlie asked, making him jump. Where had he come from? Boyd hadn't heard him approach, only that whisper of sound from the trees. Charlie grinned at him. "You sure have a lot to learn about sneaking up like an Injun, Sonny."

"Sorry, but I just had to move. I couldn't stand it any longer."

"That's alright, but next time find yourself a spot you can live with and stay put, you hear?"

"Okey boys, here's what we're goin' to do," Charlie whispered. "The Yanks are picketed on this side of the river. That's a mistake for them. They shoulda stayed on the other side to force us to cross the river in the open or attack across the bridge. Either way they'd have a considerable advantage, but we won't complain none. You two men," he pointed a dirty finger at two soldiers, "you hike it back up the draft and meet Heth. Tell 'em that we've located the pickets and will move in on 'em as soon at it gets full dark. That'll be in about an hour or so. Soon's we hit 'em, have Heth move the men up quick-like."

The two soldiers moved quietly away, keeping low to avoid being seen. Charlie and the remaining men settled for some rest. Boyd, now in a comfortable position, dozed as did the others. Charlie stared intently toward the river, cocking his head to hear better like a great skinny dog.

Cool air flowed silently from the narrow valley at their backs, and the temperature dropped quickly. Birds, of many sizes and forms called in the trees and brush around them. A gray squirrel, chased by another, ran noisily between two of the soldiers. They watched the squirrel's progress by moving only their eyes, the whites showing in their dirty faces. Somewhere, down near the bridge, a rooster began to crow and a dog barked. A heavy wagon rumbled by on the turnpike, moving west toward town, and crossed the wooden covered bridge. The men waited for darkness to fall.

After what seemed like an eternity to Boyd, Charlie gave the signal to check their muskets, and moved quietly into the stream. Boyd and the others followed, the icy water rushing into their worn boots and numbing their legs. They moved along the draft road, keeping in the middle of the wagon path to avoid making noise. It was so dark that Boyd could only follow the gray uniform in front of him. When they reached the turnpike, they turned west following it toward the bridge only a few hundred feet away. Then, well ahead they could see a campfire. There would be guards closer to them away from the fire, so they spread out and approached as quietly as they could.

Suddenly, just in front of Boyd, a form rose stiffly from the shadows and a frightened, boyish voice yelled shrilly, "Halt, who is it?" Boyd froze in terror, unsure of what to do. A shot would awaken the other pickets and some were sure to escape across the bridge and warn Crook's troops in town. He raised and cocked his musket, pointing it toward the Yank. Heartbeats thundered in his ears.

♪ ♪ ♪ ♪

Nellie sat on the three-legged stool with her coarse dress drawn up over her brown knees. She leaned forward and pressed her head against the brown cow's side as she pulled jets of warm milk from the cow's swollen teats, first with one hand and then the other. The milk splashed against the metal pail's bottom. The rhythm reminded her of the music the orchestra had made at the dance last week. What a time that was. Townsfolk walked from all around to arrive at the big house up on the hill. They had left their carriages and horses hidden away for fear that the Union soldiers, now camped up on the hill to the west of town, would take them for food or mounts. All the young girls, and some not so young, had eyed the Yankee soldiers wistfully, unsure as to whether or not they should be interested. Most folk hereabouts didn't have much sympathy for the soldiers in blue uniforms, but as Susie Aims had said, "A man's a man." You can't be too choosy with all the local young men off fighting for the South. Only a few had enlisted with the Yanks. She liked the music and had listened attentively from her bed in the attic of the slave quarters. Mister James had denied her request to go listen from the road outside the house.

Nellie sighed and beat a fancy rhythm on the side of the bucket, tapping her foot in tune to her milk music. Jake, the barn cat, crawled from beneath the manger and sat licking his chops as he stared at her. He mewed plaintively. Nellie shot a stream of steaming milk at him and he licked frantically to catch it in his pink mouth. To make the game more enjoyable, she counted the milk squirts carefully and shot Jake every tenth one. She could count easily to one hundred and knew how to read, not well, but just enough to understand what was written in the newspaper headlines from papers used to wrap meat and such. Bessie, the cow, grew impatient with her game and stomped her rear feet and swished her tail. The pail, almost full now, had a mighty head of foam on top. She stripped the last of the milk from each rough teat, moving clockwise, as Jake cleaned up. Sitting with his brown tail tightly wrapped around his feet, he licked the back of each front paw and used them to clean his face, head and ears, pausing frequently to watch Nellie. Deciding that there was no more milk to be had, he crawled back under the manger.

Nellie picked up the heavy pail and placed it on a shelf attached to the wall of the barn. Leaning over to avoid the cow's sharp horns, she released the stanchion allowing the cow to back up, swing heavily around and walk out the barn door. Humming the latest Virginia reel, Nellie walked toward the back of the huge brick house while swinging the pail. She knew that she could swing the pail in a loop-the-loop if she did it fast enough, but didn't dare in case she spilled the milk like she had before. Mr. James had been powerful mad because the soldiers paid well for fresh milk. What, she wondered, kept the milk in the bottom of the pail when it was directly overhead? If she stopped at the top of the swing, it would come cascading down on her.

The evening was cool and she could hear the peepers down in the spring that flowed through the huge sinkhole in which most of the town of Lewisburg sat. The water flowed into a sink at the east side of the depression. She liked the sound as she liked the flowers and fresh smells that the month of May brought each year.

The house, made of hand-formed and fired brick, sat along the turnpike that cut east to west through the center of town. The front porch roof reached all the way to the second floor and was supported by four square wooden columns. Behind the house was the smaller brick kitchen, a one story structure with a fireplace and chimney at one end. Its small, covered porch faced the back entrance of the house only a few paces away. She carried the milk into the kitchen and placed it on the wooden table that dominated the center of the room. Her sister, Mazel, would strain the milk through a clean cloth and store it in the cellar house just behind the kitchen. She had three sisters besides Mazel, but they were sold long ago, and she didn't know where they were now. She had never known her father, and her mother had died twelve years ago, when she was only eight.

Henry, tall, strong and in his mid-forties, slept in the shed attached to the carriage house. He did the heavy work, cared for the horses, and tended the vegetable garden at the back of the lot. Nellie and Mazel slept in the kitchen house that also served as the slave quarters. At one time there were three other slaves, but Mr. James had decided that he didn't need all that help with his family grown and married and had sold them to a farmer over in Lexington.

Mr. James was a widower. His wife had died a year ago from the coughing disease. All the marching back and forth by both armies hadn't done her much good, with the excitement, dust, and all.

"Mazel," Nellie asked, "what do you reckon it would be like to go to a real dance in a fancy dress and all? I bet I could dance as well as any of them town girls, an' I bet I could gossip and flirt with the boys just like they do."

"Don't do you no good to wonder, sister. You ain't never goin' to get to go," Mazel replied wearily as she continued to work without looking up.

"Oh, I don't know, one day we might get to do just that."

"What makes you think you's ever going to get to do a thing like that?" Mazel asked with a frown. She looked at her sister curiously.

"You know that I can read some, don't you? Well, the newspaper said something about Mr. Lincoln 'mancipatin' the slaves. I don't know zackly what that means, but I heard Mr. James talkin' about it to a stranger ridin' through town and he said that it meant 'freein'. I think it means that if the Yanks win this war, we'll be freed. If the Rebs win, we'll stay the way we are." she said, looking at Mazel intently. "What do you 'spose Mr. James would think of that?"

Mazel became quiet, staring at the backs of her dark, work-worn hands. The thought that freedom might be hers was exciting, but frightening at that. How would the whites react? Where would she live? Where would she get enough food to do through the winter? These were fleeting thoughts. Freedom would be beyond all that she could imagine. But, no, she couldn't let herself think of such a thing. Disappointment would be too much for her to bear.

"Nellie, you best forget about such things." Quickly changing the subject, Mazel said, "You go into the house and check on the soldier man. See if he's any better. Last time I checked, he didn't look any too good. Here take a dipper of water for 'im." She handed Nellie a silvery, long handled dipper after filling it from a jar full of spring water. The grey-tan stone jar had a matching lid and was embossed with raised, blue lettering on the front. Frowning, Mazel ran a calloused finger over the lettering—her illiterate lips moving randomly.

Nellie quietly closed the back door behind her as she tiptoed into the parlor where a bed had been set up for the patient. Now that dusk had fallen the only light came from a lamp trimmed low, on the stand at the foot of the bed. The heavy drapes were pulled over the tall windows as was the custom for the sick. The soldier's head was wrapped in a yellowed bandage, spotted with crusted blood that had seeped from his wounds. Other bandages, under the blankets, wound around his middle. He had been stabbed in the chest with a bayonet and a minnie ball had taken a chunk of his scalp and part of his ear as it grazed his skull.

She stood quietly looking in pity at the soldier. He was a Yank. She knew because she had seen his uniform as she had undressed him and helped bathe and bandage his broken body. His dark blue uniform had been crusted with mud and blood. Many of the homes near Lewisburg held wounded soldiers from both sides. This Nellie couldn't understand. If the two sides were so angry at each other that they fought to kill, why did they take such good care of each other's wounded? Till the day I die, she thought, I'll never understand these people. So vicious one instant, and giving the shirt off their backs the next.

She looked intently at the soldier. A Yank! If his army won, she might be free to dance to the music. She smiled. What a wonderful thought. Freedom! Could it ever be?

"Soldier boy," she whispered, moving closer for a better look in the dark room. "Soldier boy. You 'wake?" No answer. The room was totally quiet. "Hey, mister," she tried again, "why don't you answer? You a goin" to be all right. Just you wait an' see." Closer and closer she moved. Tentatively she extended a slender hand to touch his pale cheek.

"He can't answer," a voice boomed behind her. "He's dead."

Nellie's breath sucked into her in one great gasp as she jerked her hand back suddenly. Her heart beat furiously.

"Mr. James, you like to scared me to death, you and your big, loud way of talkin'," she rasped.

"You never mind about that," Mr. James said angrily, "you run and get Henry. We've got to carry him outside. Oh, and tell him to hitch up the carriage. We'll have to take him down to the church. That's where they're taking the bodies. You hurry now."

Nellie was only too happy to leave the room, and hurried out to the carriage house where she found Henry sharpening an axe. She quickly told him what had happened, he hitched up the buggy, and walked the horse around to the back of the house.

Nellie stood, holding open the heavy oak door. She could hear the two men grunting with their task inside, and then the sound of a heavy body hitting the floor came to her. Henry's back appeared in the hallway leading toward her. He shuffled backwards, holding the body under the arms and dragging its feet. As he passed, the distinct smell of death floated up to her and she closed her eyes and bit her lower lip. With great effort Henry and Mr. James loaded the soldier's body into the front seat of the buggy, setting him up as if alive. Henry climbed onto the seat and held him in place by putting his arm around the dead man's slumping shoulders. Mr. James clambered up on the other side of the body, slapped the horse twice with the reins and set off down the main street toward the Presbyterian church.

As Nellie watched the grim procession, Henry turned back toward her, grinned and waved merrily. Just three of the boys off to town. Nellie stood quietly as the ghoulish procession moved away, and the warm May evening closed about them. Deep inside her breast a burning knot formed, threatening to take away her breath. A sob rose in her throat. Who was she crying for? A dead Yank, or dying hopes?

"You just better forget what's in your silly head," Mazel said softly from the darkness. As always, she read Nellie's thoughts before they were fully formed. "I've lived long enough to know that we ain't a goin' nowhere that Mr. James don't want us to, so's you had better just go on about your business and keep sech thought outin' your head."

A whippoorwill called from its perch along the road, the shrill song urgently penetrating the darkness. Wood smoke drifted from the Yankee camp on the hill across town, and laughter rose to mock her and her unbearable sadness. Good luck, you Yanks, she thought. Do your best and one day maybe I'll be free like the 'poorwill, then I'll sing at the top of my voice too. Nellie turned and walked softly through the night, back to the kitchen behind the big splendid house, and returned to her work. Daylight and breakfast would come soon enough and there was much work yet to be done. Mr. James would soon return from his ghoulish task and it wouldn't do to be caught dawdling.

♪ ♪ ♪ ♪

"Mr. James, tell your darkie to get on back home. I want to talk to you," the blond man said roughly. He was tall and thin with light yellow hair and a red moustache. His jaw was scabbed here and there where the razor had scraped his sensitive skin. Mr. James frowned briefly, then turned to Henry and instructed him to take the buggy and return to the house.

"What do you want with me now, Jones. I'm on my way to the tavern for a drink, so hurry it up."

"You know damned well what I want, 'Mr. James'," he mocked. "You still owe me for that last bunch of goods I delivered to you. Fifty dollars. If you don't pay me soon, I'm goin' to tell everyone just what kind of business you're in—sellin' supplies to whichever side gives you the best money. And, I know for a fact that some of that stuff is stole from the folks here in the valley. You won't see tomorrow if word gets out."

"Now look here, Jones, you're in this as deep as me. Some of that stuff you sold me had the delivery tags still attached, so I know where it came from. You just lay off and you'll get your money soon enough. You're not going to push me around," he retorted. In spite of his bluster, Mr. James' forehead was noticeably damp, even though the night air was cool.

"Well, I'll give you another day or two, but if I don't see some cool, hard cash soon, I'm going to come for you personal like," Jones said angrily.

The two men stood in the dark staring at each other. One, tall thin and blond, the other short dark and soft. Jones, a newcomer to town was staying in a second floor sleeping room upstairs in Mrs. Welch's house. His streetfront window allowed him to keep tabs on who was coming and going. He figured that there had to be a way to make some money with the two warring armies marching back and forth through town. Lewisburg had changed hands several times in the first years of the war. Somewhere, somehow in all this excitement, he should be able to pry a few dollars loose. Humph, a few dollars—he wouldn't settle for just a few. He was here to make a fortune. But how...

Mr. James turned without another word and waddled toward the tavern. It was just up the hill along the turnpike at the edge of town. This Jones, he thought, is no one to fool with. If he lets the cat out of the bag, I'll have to skip town. I've worked too hard to get what I've got to let some skinny nobody take it from me. I'll have to come up with the money or get rid of Jones. The tavern, a brick house just behind the hospital, loomed before him. He could hear the moaning of wounded soldiers through the raised windows of the hospital building. The stench of blood, urine, and disinfectant reached him on the night air. Another smell lingered in his nostrils—the smell of death and mangled bodies?

He needed a drink. Good thing his wife was dead and gone. She didn't approve of men drinking, much less the underhanded way he made his living. Good, too, that she had never suspected that the wealth she was so proud of, and the position in the community she enjoyed, was the result of years of theft and underhanded dealings. That drink of whiskey seemed more and more attractive.

"What'll it be, Mr. James?" the barkeep asked respectfully. The room was well lit, with tables against the walls and straight-backed chairs scattered in some disarray around them. A single lantern burned from a holder high in the center of the room. Only three other men were in the room. Jim Martin, short, stout with a barrel chest and gray, bushy eyebrows, beckoned Mr. James to come sit with him. He wasn't in any mood to talk to anyone, yet he had to keep up pretenses. With a whiskey glass in his hand, Mr. James took a chair across the table from Martin. The other two men resumed a subdued conversation at a table in the corner.

"Just the man I want to see," Jim boomed. "Tell me what you know about this battle that everyone says is comin'."

"I don't know any more than you do. Except that they say Colonel Heth's marching this way from Pearisburg. I don't expect that Crook'll let Heth and his troops get any too close with the Union camp on the hill above town and all. Crook made a flying trip back from Covington when he heard that Heth was headed this way," Mr. James replied.

"Yeah, yeah, I know all that. Now tell me something I don't know. Like, how close is Heth? Has any of your drivers seen anything?"

"Only drivers I have out now are on the turnpike from Lexington. They aren't likely to hear or see anything, since Heth's down to the south," he said wearily. It was always the same. Everyone expected him to know where every Jack-soldier was located. "What do you know?" He asked Jim.

"Well, this I know. The next feller I see at night in my pig lot, or chicken coop will likely still be there the next day. I'm gettin' damned tired of havin' to feed every soldier in two counties, 'n' I think everyone in the valley feels the same way. Harry Wilson over near Meadow Bridge tole me he's lost every head of stock he had. They've plumb wiped him out. Don't know how he'll feed his youngins this winter," he shook his head sadly. "I hate to say it, but the Yanks seem to have some money to pay fer supplies, but the Rebs don't an they just take what they want. My ole dead daddy would skin my hide if he heard me sayin' anything bad about them."

Mr. James squinted across the table at the ruddy man before him. Cigar smoke hung like a shroud around the ceiling lamp and made his eyes burn. "Jim, what have you heard about us becoming a separate state from Virginia? Do you suppose those fools in Wheeling will actually go through with it?"

"Yeah, from what I can tell, that damned Pierpont is determined to pull out. Some governor he'd be. Some of those Yanks at the convention even tried to name the new state 'Kanawha.' Can you imagine that? We already have a county with that name." Jim leaned back in his chair and continued, "But, they finally decided on 'West Virginia.' Now, they're tryin' to get Lincoln to sign it into law."

"Yes, yes, I've heard all of that. What do you think the chances are that it'll finally happen?" Mr. James asked irritably.

"Well now, I can't rightly say. It all could depend on how soon this war is over. Only time will tell."

"And, what do you think they'll do about the slavery issue? I've got a couple of darkies that are worth a pretty penny. If those meddling Yanks go and secede from Virginia, they'll go with the Union for sure." Mr. James had worked himself into a sweat. He mopped his brow with a dirty handkerchief.

"It could go either way. I read in the paper that one thing they were considerin' was not to allow any new slaves brought into the state—free darkies couldn't enter either. Some of the other delegates wanted to abolish slavery outright. But, my best guess is that they won't make you give up your slaves. They want the southern counties to vote for the constitution," Jim said.

"That's all I need. Ever since my wife died, nothin' has been going my way," Mr. James whined. His head began to throb, and he took another shot of the soothing liquid from his glass.

"Well, I wouldn't worry too much about it if I were you. It'll probably be years before all of this mess is ironed out. No one in this valley would vote for any constitution that separates us from Virginia," Jim said.

"I best be getting back to the house, Jim. That wounded Yank they left in my house died today. I brought him down to the churchyard. I suppose they'll bury him there."

Mr. James walked along the main street of town. It was the same everywhere he went. Folks were tired of the war. The streets were deserted except for a few Yankee soldiers on guard duty. He walked wearily up the main street to his house on the hill. He had worked hard to provide a fine house for his wife and expensive educations for his children, and now they were gone. His wife had died and the children had moved away. But now, it was his turn to live a little. Maybe he'd move over to Richmond after the war and find a rich widow to court. God knew there were enough of them to go around because of the war. But first, he had to make just a little more money. He'd stashed away some, but most of it was invested in land, supplies, and manpower. Just a few more months, he thought. Just a little longer and he'd have all he would need to make his move. If only that Jones feller would go away.

✐ ✐ ✐ ✐

The musket slammed against his shoulder, recoiling with a deafening roar and a scarlet flash of fire. From the brush just in front of him he could hear someone screaming and thrashing around in the leaves.

"Hot damn, Boyd, you've done it now," Charlie yelled from his right. "Come on boys, let's get the ones at the bridge."

Boyd could see the flashes of musket fire from the bridge and hear the crack and whiz of bullets as they clipped the leaves and twigs over his head. He dove for the ground, cringing from the screams of the wounded man as much as from the musket fire.

"Get up offen the ground, sonny, and come on and help out with these other fellers," Charlie yelled.

They rushed the bridge and the Yank's camp in the face of sporadic firing. After the first volley, the Yanks had to reload, and trying to pour powder and ram a ball into the muzzle of the musket was very difficult in the dark, especially with yelling Rebs heading their way. The Yanks broke and ran for the bridge, but their retreat was cut off. They dropped their muskets and put their hands over their heads. It was over as quickly as it had begun, and Charlie quickly gave orders to tie them to trees.

"Well, boys, I reckon ole Crook'll know we're comin' now. Someone up on the mountain is sure to hear all that shootin'. At least they didn't fire the bridge and we'll be able to get the artillery across," Charlie said.

Boyd squatted before the fire that only minutes before had been encircled by Yanks and stared into the flames. What had he done? Why had it been his luck to be the one challenged by the guard?

Two of the soldiers came from the darkness, dragging a body behind them. They dropped him in the circle of yellow light cast by the fire. The soldier, just a boy, moaned softly and rolled his bloody head from side to side. Pink foam formed at the side of his mouth and grew into a bubbly froth at his nostrils. Boyd, Charlie, and the other men stood in a circle, looking down at the dying boy.

"Oh God, help me," the boy sobbed, "it hurts."

Boyd stooped, cradled the boy's head in his arms and made his second terrible mistake of the evening—he looked into his eyes. The young soldier's bloody hand gripped the sleeve of the Boyd's tunic, attempting to pull him down to his face. The pale blue eyes, rimmed with tears, stared up at Boyd as a questioning frown creased his forehead. As Boyd leaned down to hear what the trembling lips had to tell him, the hand suddenly released its grip and slid limply to the ground. The open eyes lost their glimmer and only tears remained.

Boyd gently laid the dead man down, straightened his limp legs and placed the dirty, bloody hands on the chest of the dark blue tunic. He rose wearily and stumbled into the brush, retching uncontrollably. He had taken a man's life. He couldn't even remember pulling the trigger. He heaved until there wasn't anything left but the bitter taste of bile burning his throat and nose.

"Get up, Sonny. We've got more work to do. Look what you've done, you've gone and puked up all that good food I've been givin' you. Now, yer belly'll be growlin' so loud ole Crook'll know we're comin' fer sure," Charlie said not unkindly. "Mike, you and Everett, there, go and set up a picket a few hundert yards across the bridge. If you hear anyone comin' don't challenge them. Come on arunnin' back to this side. We'll face 'em here."

Charlie quickly assigned two other men to go back to the main force to report what had happened. The prisoners were guarded where they sat, tied against the trees. He kicked the fire apart and used the side of his boot to scrape sand and dirt over the burning embers. The darkness crept in upon them.

Boyd sat quietly with his musket across his knees. In the dim starlight he could see the prisoners' pale faces and the shining whites of their eyes. What will become of them, he wondered. Whatever happened, they were lucky to be alive.

Well, Boyd, he told himself, you didn't do so well did you? You were scared to death. Killing that young soldier was an accident. He could just as easily have killed you. And, throwing up in front of the men...

"Don't be too hard on yerself, Sonny. Look at it this here way—Yer still alive," Charlie whispered from the darkness. "All a soldier can ask is to make it through the next battle in one piece."

A lantern, bright at first to his unaccustomed eyes, was lit nearby. As his eyes adjusted to the light he could make out the dim form of a house just off the road. The lantern, swinging from side to side approached.

"Don't shoot, men," a nervous voice behind the lantern whispered, "I'm just a civilian. I live in the house, yonder. My old lady told me to go see if anyone was hurt and needed help."

"No one here needs help, thanks," Boyd said. "The only person to get hit won't ever need help. He's dead." His voice shook.

Charlie stepped from the darkness, his brown face a mask. He questioned the man expertly and quickly learned that the pickets had been at the bridge for the last two days and that Crook's main force was still camped on the west side of town. After getting all the information he could, he sent the man back to his big brick house on the banks of the Greenbrier River.

The night dragged on, with bullfrogs booming in the river. Higher voices, piping and calling to one another, came from leopard frogs. An occasional heavy splash marked the demise of a frog as a predatory, smallmouth bass took them from the water's edge. From the house, a dog barked tentatively at the troops.

It was well past midnight before the main body of the army arrived. With considerable commotion they crossed the wooden bridge. The still valley echoed as men tramped across the bridge with cannons rolling hollowly behind them. The valley being only a quarter mile across, the army soon began the long climb up the pike to the town. With a vertical distance of over seven hundred feet, the road wound up and around the mountain, following a small stream. They crossed the brook several times, the men grunting and cursing from the weight of their packs and weapons. The horses, toiling wearily to pull the cannon, snorted and threw their heads. They squatted and pulled their heavy burdens with quivering muscles.

Somewhere up at the front of the column Boyd could hear sporadic gunfire as a small Union force sent to reconnoiter was pushed back before them. Word swept back down the advancing column that Crook was retreating, but Charlie, fighting fatigue beside Boyd, said not to believe it.

"It's just their advance pickets, Sonny. Ole Crook'll still be sitting there awaitin' when we reach town."

At last they reached a bench near the top of the mountain where the road leveled out a bit and the officers urged the men quickly forward. And then as they crested the last hill, the dying fires of the Yankee camp were clearly visible across the shallow valley before them.

Boyd stood looking in awe at the fires. Between them lay the sleeping town. The pike, on which they stood, dipped down to the center of town and then rose again in a flat vee to continue to the west toward Charleston, a hundred miles distant. The enemy camp was west of town and just south of the pike. Behind him, a faint flush of dawn could be seen just above the ragged mountains. To Boyd, a native of the flatlands of the coast, it was like being on top of the world.

The army dropped down to the edge of town before spreading to the right and left of the pike in skirmish lines. Officers, some on horseback and others on foot, gave orders quickly. Boyd found himself behind a low split-rail fence on the northern flank. Far to his left, soldiers quickly set up an artillery battery. The rattle and clank of the army suddenly, eerily, was silenced. The mountain air, still and cool, hung like a great sodden blanket over the land. A heavy dew coated the grass and quickly soaked the men's shoes and pants. A rooster crowed from somewhere down in town and a chorus of birds began their waking songs. Boyd, with dread in his heart, gripped his musket tightly with both hands and clinched his eyes tightly shut. He heard what he thought was hoofbeats behind him, but was startled to realize it was the drumming of his heart. As he peered between the rails of the fence, a soldier beside him chanted under his breath, "Oh, God... Oh, God... Oh, God..." Boyd looked fearfully across the shallow valley, across the rooftops, to the camps beyond.

"Steady now, boys," Charlie whispered. "Steady."

2

The still morning air shattered as the Confederate artillery opened fire on the Union camps across town. The cannon on a hill to Boyd's left fired; its concussion spread over him like a giant wave. He could feel the blast in every particle of his weary body. Across town, the blue-clad soldiers swarmed from their camp like ants to form up their regiments. Great gushes of dirt and smoke rose skyward as shell and canister fell among them. Toward the center of town, Boyd saw a chunk of a church wall blasted loose in a swirl of red dust and brick chards. Another shot fell short among the Confederate soldiers.

"Charlie, they're hitting our own men," Boyd yelled.

"Easy, Sonny," he replied, "they've got the range now. Just you worry about your own hide, never mind what those fellers are up to."

The cannon-fire rolled in a solid, even roar in the shallow valley. Musket fire opened down the line, but Boyd couldn't see anything at which to fire. The terrain in front of him dropped away gently; it would be difficult for the Yanks to charge up the grade toward their position. There were only a few houses scattered along the town's streets.

The Union army attacked on three fronts: a small force moving east along the pike, and larger forces on each side. Confederate forces, also fighting on three fronts, were arrayed in almost matching order. Boyd, hunkered behind his fence, could see blue-clad troops advancing along the pike to his left.

The roar and thump of cannon fire was head-splitting. The

smoke from burning powder was carried by the wind toward him, burning his eyes and causing him to cough. He gripped his musket and waited.

⸿ ⸿ ⸿ ⸿

Mazel was shocked awake by the cannon-fire on the hill behind the house. She jerked upright on her pallet, feeling the shake and jolt of each explosion.

"Nellie," she screamed, "God Almighty, they're akillin' us"

Nellie in her night shirt stumbled down the ladder from the loft, eyes wide in terror. "What'll we do, Mazel. What'll we do?"

"Quick, we got to get in the cellar. It'll be safer there."

They looked cautiously out of the kitchen house door; the way seemed to be clear. Flinging the door open, they ran across the dog trot between the two buildings and rounded the corner of the house. It took only seconds to open the door to the cellar, but to Nellie it seemed like time had frozen. Finally, they were inside and had slammed the door behind them.

Dust sifted down through the beams over their heads and the cobwebs swayed and jiggled with each new blast.

They sat in the musty darkness, side by side, with their knees drawn up to their chests. Mazel rocked gently back and forth and hummed her favorite hymn. Nellie could feel her flinch at each cannon blast. As their eyes adjusted to the darkness, the familiar cellar took shape. One tiny window served as an air vent in the limestone foundation wall, and bright spring sunlight streamed through the narrow cracks around the door.

At the back of the cellar was a large potato bin made of slats of wood spaced to allow air to circulate. A few shriveled potatoes littered its bottom. In one corner lay parts for the family buggy, and Henry's tools stood in some disarray in another.

One side of the cellar was occupied by boxes of dry goods—huge wooden boxes with lettering stamped on their sides stacked from floor to ceiling. Out of curiosity Nellie spelled out the words on the sides of the boxes, mouthing each letter as she read. S-A-M-U-E-L-S. Samuels. Samuels! Hadn't she heard something about Mr. Samuels' load of farm supplies being stolen? Wonder what...

The sound of running soldiers brought her attention back to the conflict outside. They could hear men cursing and running, their equipment banging together on their packs. Were they Yanks or Rebs? The streams of light filtering into the cellar danced and flickered as the men's shadows fell on the door. Nellie huddled against Mazel, shaking with fright. The footsteps receded. Musket shots rang out just behind the main house. It sounded as if they were fighting from the back yard.

Mazel straightened suddenly and said in a rough whisper, "I'm goin' out there and tell them fellers to get out of my yard. You don't reckon they'll take all of Mr. James' food from the kitchen do you?"

"Don't you worry about that, sister, you'll get yourself shot if you so much as stick your head outin the door."

"Yes, but if they take the food, you know who Mr. James will blame for it. Us, that's who."

"I know sister, but we have to just stay put until one side or the other wins. Then we'll come on out."

The two young women sat in the semidarkness quietly, each deep in her own thoughts. "Nellie," Mazel whispered hopefully, "didn't you say that if the Yanks won we'd be free?"

"Yes, but this is only a battle. The Yanks have to win completely before we'll be 'mancipated. Just this here one little battle don't mean nothin'."

"Ain't there something that we can do? I mean, ifin we just sit here and do nothing, the Rebs might win. What'll we do then? Oh, Nellie, I hope you hadn't tole me about this...this... what'd you call it...I mean "freein". It's all I been thinkin' 'bout. Ifin the Rebs win it'd be better if you had never tole me 'bout it."

The beams over their heads shook and rattled as another salvo was fired over their heads. Suddenly, someone was scratching at the cellar door. Mazel and Nellie froze, their eyes rolling in their heads. They clung together like Siamese twins.

"Who is it?" Nellie shouted. No answer. Again, whoever it was scratched on the door. "You better not come in here. I got a gun," she bluffed. Still no answer. Then, they heard a faint whining.

"Why, it's that ole dog of Mr. James,'" Nellie whispered in awe. "I's agonna let him in."

"No you ain't, neither," Mazel retorted. "Someone might see you and come on in here and shoot us. 'Sides, that ole dog stole a ham I was makin' for Mr. James' wife just before she died. Remember? He blamed it on me. Said I had taken an' hid it. He took me out in the kitchen, closed the door and kicked my legs and shins until I was black and blue all over."

"I remember, Mazel, but what ifin it was you out there. Wouldn't you want me to let you in?"

"Yeah, but I ain't no meat stealin' dog."

"I'm agoin' to let him in," Nelly said firmly.

"Oh, all right, but ifin you get your fool head shot off, don't come cryin' to me." The two girls looked at each other in silence for a moment and then began to giggle.

"Ifin I get my head shot off, Mazel, I'm agoin' to give you a great big bloody kiss." With that both girls began to laugh and covered their mouths with their hands.

Nellie opened the door a crack and peeped cautiously outside, then opened the door enough for the dog to rush in. A common mutt, the dog quivered and shook.

"Get on over in that corner, you thief you," Mazel hissed. "Go on, you get now!"

Tucking its tail between its legs, the dog slunk into the corner and sat down, staring at the two women. It licked its lips and tossed its head as if trying to tell them something important.

They sat in the dank and gloom whispering to each other as the fighting continued. They jumped as a cannon, now positioned closer, roared, the shock waves making the door rattle on its hinges. The dog had crept closer and leaned against Nelly's leg. She could feel it shaking under its rough fur.

Suddenly, the door was flung open and a soldier ran into the cellar, slamming the door behind him. The dog, frightened into action growled, its lips curling back from its teeth. The solder whirled at the sound, raising his musket and pointing it first at the dog, and then at the girls. Nellie yelled at him, "Stop, don't shoot."

He squinted at them, trying to see as his eyes adjusted to the dim light. "Who's there," he whispered. "Don't move, or I'll shoot," his voice quaking in the darkness. The dog growled again and as Nelly touched its head she could feel the hairs standing on end on its neck and back.

"It's just us darkies, mister. You'll don't have to be afraid," Nellie whispered. "We won't hurt you."

The solder relaxed and stood upright from the crouch he had assumed.

"Just y'all stay where you are 'til I get a good look at you; I'll not hurt you," he said hoarsely. "I ain't goin' back out there—a man could get killed..."

Mazel shifted slightly and whispered a single, menacing word to Nelly: "Reb." Nellie slid her hand behind Mazel and knotted a handful of her coarse dress, pulling it up tight, tugging slightly to let her know that she was being restrained.

The Reb began looking around the cellar, ignoring the girls for the moment, his fear receding now that he was safe inside. Mazel watched him closely, her eyes shifting in her dark face. The soldier turned back to them.

"There's enough food and stuff in here for a year. What do you reckon the owner's goin' to do with it?" He was young and stocky, with curly blond hair creeping from under his campaign hat. "Who's the owner, anyway?" he asked. Neither girl replied.

"What's the matter, cat got your tongue?" he spat, as an evil grin crossed his face. "You darkies better answer or I'll take the belt to you." He took a step toward the girls, looming tall above them. The dog, threatened by the advancing man, leaped, locking its jaws firmly on his arm. The Reb screamed and jerked his arm back, pulling the clinging dog toward him.

Mazel sprang from her seat in the corner and leaped onto the startled solder's back. The musket discharged with a deafening roar in the confined cellar as the solder swung the barrel around, striking Mazel across the forehead, knocking her into the corner. The dog released its grip and ran under the potato bin. The soldier advanced menacingly toward Mazel. "I'll fix you, darkie," he rasped. He pulled his bayonet, its keen edge glistening in the dim light, keeping his eyes on Mazel. "You'll never attack a white man again," he vowed as he attached the razor sharp blade to the musket.

The blow came from his left side, causing him to drop like a rock. Nellie stood in the darkness staring at the inert soldier. She held the end of the ax handle in both hands with the other end resting at an angle on the dirt floor. She stood straddle-legged and wide-eyed as she gasped for breath. A huge blue goose egg rose on the side of the man's head. He wasn't dead—she could see his chest rising and falling—but what about Mazel? She dropped the ax handle and rushed to Mazel's side, feeling her face and chest, searching for some sign of life.

"Why don't you quit feelin' around on me," Mazel snapped, "it ain't decent."

"Oh, you're alive, praise God, you're alive," Nellie whispered.

"Of course, I'm alive," Mazel said indignantly as she struggled to her feet, "It'll take more than a knock on the head to do me in. What about the Reb?"

"He's over there, out cold. I hit him with Henry's ax handle. What'll we do with him?"

"Don't you worry none, sister, I'll take care of him. I'm agonna slit his throat just like Henry does the hogs at butcherin' time."

"Oh, no, you can't, Mazel. He's just a boy. He don't know what he's doin'."

"He tried to kill us. He's just like the rest of em. They don't even think we're women and men like them. Did you hear the way he talked to us?" Mazel stood unsteadily, swaying slightly from the blow, as a trickle of blood ran down the side of her face.

The Reb, groaning slightly, began to stir and wave his arms as if to grasp some unseen support. His eyes, wild and rolling in their sockets, came to focus on Mazel and Nellie.

"You hit me," he said with a shocked look on his face. "I'll teach you to hit a white man. I'll get you..." he began. But, suddenly, in one swift move, Mazel picked up the rifle laying on the earthen floor and plunged its glistening bayonet into the soldier's chest, pinning him to the hard packed dirt floor. He arched his back as his heels moved against the black soil trying to gain a purchase, but could not move from under the great weight that held him against the floor. With a shuddering sigh, his tortured body relaxed and lay still. A cannon blast jarred the house and dirt sifted down into his unblinking eyes.

♪ ♪ ♪ ♪

"Attach your bayonets, men, we're goin' to need 'em, I'm afeared," Charlie shouted over the roar of the cannons. Down the slope before them, on the road that ran parallel to their lines, they could see the Yank forces forming up, just out of rifle range.

"Now, you follow my lead, Boyd. You do whatever I do and for God's sake, keep your head down. These Yanks are right smart shots."

A long line of blue-clad soldiers began the charge up the slope toward their position. Boyd watched, fascinated, as they came on in the face of withering musket fire. Here and there a man fell, but the officer in front yelled for them to keep up the charge. He waved his sword and urged the line of men forward.

"Fire," Charlie yelled. A volley roared from their position behind the fence. Boyd hardly noticed the heavy recoil of the musket as a cloud of white smoke briefly hid the screaming men charging up the hill. Fleetingly, Boyd wondered if he had hit the man in his sights. He began reloading as quickly as he could, but his shaking hands dropped the load and he had to search his pocket for another. As the spring breeze carried away the smoke, Boyd could see the advancing men again. He couldn't see any effects of volley on the Yanks.

Charlie's musket roared again at Boyd's side and a Yank soldier crumpled to the green spring grass on the field of fire before them.

Now the advancing line was close enough to see the men's faces. Boyd quickly chose a man directly in front of him and sat the musket sights on the man's chest. Funny, he thought, how a man's fate is decided. I could have chosen the man beside him instead. He touched the trigger and the man fell, clutching his chest. A terrible scream poured from his dying throat.

"Stand and hold," Charlie screamed, his voice raising an octave. "Don't let the Yanks flank our men." Who was he yelling at, Boyd wondered, as he reloaded. Why was the musket fire slowing from the Confederate position? The blue line drew nearer and Boyd drew a bead on another screaming Yank and touched off the charge. The heavy recoil of the musket punished his shoulder.

Oh God, Boyd thought, they're not going to stop. They just keep on coming.

"They're running, Boyd. Our men are running like dogs," Charlie yelled. But it was too late to retreat with them. The Yanks swarmed over the split-rail fence, slicing and cutting the few remaining Confederate defenders. Boyd, fighting for his life, stuck the first man over the fence in the chest with his bayonet. The falling man knocked Boyd onto his back still clutching his empty musket before him. The next man over the fence impaled himself on Boyd's bayonet, twisting it from his grip. The wounded Yank screeched in anguish, falling behind him.

Screaming, frightened out of his wits, Boyd grabbed another Yank's throat with his hands and sunk his thumbs into his windpipe. To his side he was aware of Charlie fighting with only his hunting knife. A Union officer stood calmly across the fence and took aim on Charlie. A gout of blood flew as the minnie ball plunged into his chest. Charlie was thrown backward beside the men he had been fighting to save; a look of horror and pain was stamped on his face.

A bullet struck Boyd in the leg, just above the knee and sent him spinning, dislodging his grasp on the Yank. Screaming incoherently, he struggled to his feet only to be struck immediately by a second bullet causing a searing pain to sweep through his left shoulder. He fell, semiconscious, onto his side as the Yanks overran their position. A soldier, in pursuit of the fleeing Rebel force behind them, tramped heavily on the side of Boyd's neck. As he lay among the bodies of both Confederate and Union soldiers, he stared into the face of a fallen Reb. There was a neat blue-black hole in the soldier's cheek.

"Oh," he moaned, "why has this happened?" A red flood of pain crossed his eyes as all became darkness.

✿ ✿ ✿ ✿

"Oh, God, Mazel. You've kilt 'im. You done went and kilt 'im," Nellie waled. "What are we gonna do now?"

"You just hesh up, sister. He's just a stinkin' Reb."

"Yeah, but Mr. James'll skin all the hide offin us if he find out."

"Mr. James ain't never goin' to find out, so you just sit down over there with that stinkin, meat-stealin' dog while I think of a way to get rid of him."

Nellie had never seen Mazel like this before. She was usually quiet and did what she was told, but she was suddenly different. All that talk about freein' had changed her. What would she do next?

"Nellie, get ahold of his feet. We're goin' to drag him outside."

"But they'll find him and know that we kilt him."

"No, they won't," Mazel insisted, "They'll think some Yank done stuck him. Come on, we've got to hurry, 'fore the battle is done."

"But, they'll shoot us, too," she complained.

"No, now you do what I tole you. Get his feet. Come on, get his feet!" Mazel said forcefully.

Nellie gingerly picked up the man's feet as Mazel lifted him by the shoulders. They dragged him through the door and up the cellar steps. The fighting continued, but had moved up the hill to the east.

They dropped him in the side yard around the corner from the cellar door. Quickly, they ran back into the cellar and sat in a corner.

"Thank God, they didn't shoot us," Nellie whimpered. "We're lucky they didn't see us and shoot us dead."

"Stop your frettin' sister. Nobody ain't never goin' to find out. We'll just sit an' wait until they stop shootin' an' then we'll come acrawlin' out."

"Oh, my God, his gun. Lookey there, Mazel, his gun. What'll we do with his gun?" The musket lay in the dirt where they had dropped it after Mazel had pulled it from the Reb's chest; the bloody bayonet was still attached.

"You just sit there, sister. I'll take care of it. I'll just have to take it back out there an' put it with him."

Mazel picked up the empty musket and again slipped quietly out the door. She ran quickly, bent over at the waist as if that somehow made her less visible, to the body and threw the rifle down next to him. Turning quickly, she began to run back to the cellar. As she rounded the corner, she ran headlong into a Yank soldier. Both were sent sprawling, and Mazel squalled as if shot. Without a word, both regained their feet and ran on; the soldier frowned over his shoulder as he ran up the hill to join the battle. As she ran, her skin crawled and she could almost feel the bullets ripping into her plump body. She ran down the steps and through the door, slamming it quickly behind her. Her breath came in great, racking sobs. It was done.

They returned again to their corner. Time dragged. As they sat in the cellar, Nellie's eyes grew large as she saw the huge bloodstain on the dirt floor and a bloody trail toward the door and steps. They spent the next quarter hour scraping dirt over the stains and scrubbing the steps and door with pieces of Mazel's petticoat.

Later in the musty dimness of the cellar, Nellie whispered to Mazel, "Do you reckon it's safe to go out now?"

"I reckon it might be. I don't hear no shootin' and there hain't been no cannon fire for some time now."

"Who do you reckon won—this battle I mean?"

"I don't rightly know, sister," Mazel replied.

"Mazel, I'm agoin' out to see what happened."

"I reckon its over now, but we got to be careful," Mazel mumbled. Now that the action was over, reality began to set in. Mazel knew full well what the Reb's death meant to her. She was committed. There was no way to turn back now.

Quietly, cautiously, the two girls, one tall, slim and pretty, the other shorter, plump and dark, crept from the cellar. The dog followed, its tail between its legs. It lifted its muzzle to sample the strange mix of smells—blood, gunpowder, and man-fear.

The battle was over. Blue coated soldiers stood in small groups and talked excitedly. The Rebs had run from the battlefield, all the way down to the bridge across the river and in their panic had burned it to prevent pursuit. They had left many dead and wounded behind. Nelly and Mazel walked to the front of the house and watched the Yank soldiers returning down the pike to the center of town. A few were wounded and several had been killed, but the men seemed to be in good spirits from their decisive victory.

Henry, grinning broadly, appeared beside the girls.

"Where you been, Henry," Nellie asked.

"I hid in the manger in the barn with Jake," he smiled. "I just covered myself with hay and stuff and waited until all the shootin' stopped."

"Well, you're one lucky darkie. You coulda been shot, and that's the truth," Nellie said, happy to see that he hadn't been hurt.

"You there, Henry," Mr. James shouted from the pike, "Come here and help me. The Colonel wants us to help haul the dead Rebs to the church. Come on, now. They're payin' good money."

Mr. James, looking no worse for the battle, had spent the morning in the tavern on the west side of town. Early warning had allowed him to move to safety.

"You, Nellie and Mazel, get to work. Don't just stand there gawking. I want my breakfast as soon as I get back. Get to work now," he said harshly.

Nellie and Mazel hurried around the house to the kitchen. As they passed, two soldiers picked up the dead Reb in the side yard and carried him heavily to the front of the house to be picked up along the pike like so much cord wood.

Nellie clinched her eyes tightly together, tears streaming down her smooth cheeks. Why was she crying? The Yanks had won. That was good—wasn't it?

She stood in the warm morning sun as robins searched the close-cut lawn for worms, and looked sadly at the crumpled spot on the side-lawn where the man Mazel had killed had lain. So many deaths. And what would become of Mazel? Nellie felt as if ten years had suddenly been added to her young life. At the instant that the cold steel of the bayonet had sliced away the Reb's life, everything had changed. With that violent act her childhood had been swept away and now she and Mazel were suddenly old.

As Mazel rattled pots in the brick kitchen building, Nellie began to do her morning chores. Mr. James wanted his breakfast of ham and eggs first thing upon his return. Why did he have so much to eat when others in the valley were going hungry?

With a deep sigh, Nellie brushed the wrinkles from her dress, picked up the bucket from the kitchen table, and walked sadly down the foot path toward the barn to milk the cow. The morning was warm and cheerful and there were bright blue Johnny-jump-ups along the way, and a dead Yankee lying in the path.

♪ ♪ ♪ ♪

Troy Jones watched the fighting from the upstairs window of Mrs. Welch's two story brick house along the pike. He wasn't afraid, even though the two opposing armies exchanged cannon fire over his head. He watched in amusement as the Confederate forces crumbled under the daring frontal attacks by the outnumbered Union forces. Colonel Crook had ridden back and forth on a huge black horse encouraging his men and giving orders to his aides. He had directed the battle calmly and expertly from his carefully selected vantage point.

Jones watched with great interest as the battle concluded. Heavy smoke and dust hung in the air over the town. He fingered the musket in his hands and watched for an opportunity. Troy Jones hated the Yankees even though his dealings with them had been very profitable. He had no objection to doing business with them when possible, but he hated them nonetheless.

His mind drifted back to the preceding summer in another town down to the south. The Yankees had been in that vicinity only for a short excursion, but they had caught him stealing food from one of their heavy wagons. Not just enough food to eat, but he had tried to steal a buggy load in the middle of the night to sell back to one army detachment or another. It didn't matter much to him which side he sold to. He had been dragged before a captain who was little more than a boy and had been summarily whipped for his trouble.

Now, as he watched the Yankees celebrate their victory, he fingered the coarse welts that would permanently grace his back and shoulders. He would get them for whipping him, he thought. Even though the captain who had ordered his punishment was long gone, it didn't matter in his mind; a Yankee was a Yankee.

He watched from his window with great concentration. Somewhere in this conflict there should be a way of making a few dollars. He set the musket in the corner of the small room he rented from Mrs. Welch and pulled out his pistol. He rotated the cylinder and checked the caps on each chamber. He had taken the pistol, one of the newer models, from the dead body of a Confederate soldier a few weeks back. Yes, a man could pick up some valuables from this war, he thought.

Jones stepped from the house and walked easily up the pike toward Lee street where the Confederate line had been. Union soldiers carried bodies, both blue- and grey-clad, and began to transport them toward the center of town. The Union wounded limped and struggled along as best they could. A group of six dirty Confederates sat along the street under a tree with their heads down. One had a huge gash along his arm. A Union soldier stood guard over them. From their appearance, no guard would have been needed. They were thoroughly defeated.

Jones strolled along the street looking for a body to rob. Other civilians were gawking at the carnage and walking freely among the soldiers. There were too many people around. He turned suddenly, left the street, and walked over the brush-covered hill toward the center of the huge sinkhole in which the town sat. The houses and small out buildings of the town were arranged around the steeper center of the sink like the spokes of a wheel, with a spring house and tiny stream forming the hub. The stream meandered across the floor of the sink and then disappeared into a dark opening.

Away from the street, he soon found a body lying in a clump of bushes. Looking around carefully, and acting as though he was checking the man to see if he was alive, he quickly rifled the man's pockets. He found only a few coins and an old pocketwatch, but nonetheless slipped them into his pocket. He was nervous about robbing bodies in broad daylight since, if he were caught, he would be lucky to receive only a whipping.

He emerged from the brushy hillside lot and continued down Lee street. Apparently this was the site of some of the most vicious fighting because both sides of the street were littered with bodies. A group of civilians were carrying a wounded man from a split-rail fence toward the street. Jones felt over the man's body discreetly, searching for valuables, as he helped them struggle with the dead weight. The young Confederate soldier groaned with pain but did not open his eyes or regain consciousness. The grim workers placed the wounded man carefully with the others along the street, stemmed their blood flow as best they could, and waited for wagons to transport them to the hospital or private homes to be cared for.

He quickly became bored with helping the wounded men and wandered back toward the center of town and Mrs. Welch's house. He sat for a while on the front porch and watched, but soon returned to his room and stuffed his meager belongings into a carpet bag on the rickety bed, picked up the musket, and walked to the open window. As a column of men marched back through town toward their camp on the hill, Jones rested the musket on the window ledge and took aim on the broad back of the nearest blue-clad soldier.

3

"Yea, though we walks thro' the valley..." the voice droned on through the darkness. "We shall fear no...no...no, Oh, Umh! evil."

Boyd, through the pain and confusion, could not open his eyes. There was the rustle of clothing and the sudden slamming of a book, then silence except for the loud ticking of a clock.

Some undetermined time later, Boyd pried his eyes open just a crack. They were matted and he could feel a trickle of tears running from the corner of each eye. The room was darkened by heavy, drapes pulled over the tall windows. He lay perfectly still looking at the cracks in the ceiling. He could hear birds singing in the trees outside of the house, or whatever type of place he was in, so it was likely morning.

His gaze moved from the ceiling to the wing chair by the door. A servant girl sat with her head laid back, and held a huge family Bible on her lap. Her eyes were closed, but one scuffed shoe tapped a rhythm on the hardwood floor. Boyd, propped up on overstuffed pillows, was covered to his chin with a down comforter. He could see her clearly, even in the dim light. She was lovely, tall and slim. Her coarse, black hair fell to her shoulders. She sat comfortably, her ankles crossed, and absently fingered the scarlet ribbon that streamed from the closed book. Her breasts rose and fell rhythmically as she breathed.

She frowned, opened her huge brown eyes and began to fumble with the Bible as if to resume reading. Then she saw him watching her.

A mulatto, he thought. Probably more white than black. But, still a negress.

"Oh," she gasped, "you're alive. The last soldier boy we had here died." Why did she have to say that?

"You just wait here. I'll go an' get someone. You just stay here," she said nervously, and rushed from the room. The Bible tumbled unnoticed to the floor.

The room was quiet again except for the sound of the grandfather clock in the hallway. It gave him time to think. He tentatively tried moving first one hand and then the other, then one leg and the other. His left leg was heavily bandaged and hurt badly when he moved it. But worse, there was a deep, throbbing pain in his chest and shoulder. He shifted his weight and sent a sharp, piercing pain through his body. Best to lie still, he thought, until he knew for sure what his injuries were. He closed his eyes to rest, just for a moment, but fell asleep again.

He awoke next to hear a whispered conversation in the hallway outside the room. He could hear clearly.

"Whoever it was shot the Yank right through the heart. Shot him square in the back. Henry said he dropped without so much as a twitch," Mazel whispered. "He shot from ole Mrs. Welch's house there along the pike an' the soldiers searched and searched. They didn't find nothin'.'"

"Is that when they burned her house?" Nellie asked incredulously.

"Yeah, ole Colonel Crook said he was agoin' to teach these here people a lesson, so's he ordered his men to fire the house. It's still smokin' from what's left of it," Mazel frowned. "Some of the men in town were powerful mad, but they's nothin' they can do 'bout it."

"Wonder what Mrs. Welch will do now, with no place to live an' all."

"I don' reckon I know, sister, but it serves her right for havin' some Reb in her house. Maybe next time she'll think twice 'bout it," Mazel complained bitterly.

As they stepped through the door, Boyd asked hoarsely, "Where is this place?"

Mazel replied shortly, "You's in Mr. James' house, Reb."

"Oh, I see," Boyd replied, ignoring the acid in her voice. "How long have I been here?"

"Well, the fightin' was day 'afore yesterday mornin' an' its almost supper time now," Nellie replied, somewhat more kindly than Mazel who stood ramrod straight, her arms crossed over her ample breasts. She glared at Boyd. What's got her all upset, he wondered.

"What happened. Who won the battle?" he asked.

"You Rebs got your tails whooped. Ran all the way 'cross the river an' back to Union," Mazel smirked. "Burned the bridge an' folk hereabouts are all upset 'cause now they's no way to get wagons 'cross an' the stage can't run 'til the river goes down some. You's agoin' to prison if I know what I hear. Henry, he hears everythin' folk in town say 'an he say it true."

"Mazel, you hesh up," Nellie challenged, "You mustn't talk to him that way." To Boyd she added, "She's been all upset with the war an' all."

"That's okay, I understand. Nellie. That's your name isn't it? Did you see any of our men who were killed or wounded?"

"No, sir, we ain't 'lowed to go off the grounds 'less we tole to by Mr. James. Who you lookin' for?"

Boyd described Charlie, then told them about seeing him take a minnie ball in the chest.

"Please ask around to see what happened to him. He was nice to me and he had a wife and kids. Lived up on Muddy Creek Mountain," he said weakly.

"Charlie his name was? From up on the Mountain? Was his last name Taylor?" Nellie asked wide-eyed.

"Why, yes. Charlie Taylor. Tall, bearded man with a high forehead, about thirty-five. Likes fine horses, he said."

"Everyone in Lewisburg knows the Taylors. They don't mix much.

Only come to town a few times each year. People whisper that they'd rather fight than eat brown beans an' cornbread," Nellie replied.

"Most likely he's down at the church awaitin' to be planted six feet under," Mazel grinned.

"You just hush, now, Mazel. Is that any way to treat a wounded man?" Nelly frowned.

"We can't stand here talkin', sister. Mr. James'll want his supper soon," Mazel fussed, tugging at Nellie's sleeve, "Come on, this 'hero' prob'ly needs his rest."

"Nellie, will you come back and talk with me soon," Boyd asked. "I need to rest now, but I want to know what happened."

"Yeah," she readily agreed. "I ain't agoin' nowhere."

In the kitchen house, Mazel stood sharpening her kitchen knife. She drew the blade forcefully over the lip of a large stone jar, turning it with each strike to sharpen first one edge and then the other.

"Nellie, what's the matter with you? You act like that Reb in there was your best friend. You watch what I do. I'm agoin' to slip in there some night and let some blood. Just you wait an' see. He won't never fight again to keep us from bein' freed, you can bet your life he won't," Mazel spat.

Nellie looked at Mazel from the corner of her eye. "Oh, no you mustn't, sister. He's just a feller who's fightin' for somethin' he thinks is right. 'Sides, if Mr. James ketches you he'll take you to Sheriff Brown an' you know what he'll do. He'll hang you up on the pole like he did ole Uncle Reuben."

"Well, I ain't agoin' to stand by and let them Rebs win. I'll do him in just like I did that other Reb," Nellie bragged as she tested the edge of the knife blade with her thumb.

"Shush, Mazel, don't talk that way. Someone might hear you." Nellie looked quickly out of the kitchen door, fully expecting to find Mr. James there listening. She didn't know what had happened to Mazel. She had changed so much in the last few days. What would come of her?

Another thought caused her to frown. What was she feelin' for the Reb in the big bed in the living room? She should feel like Mazel about him; after all, he was a Reb and a stranger at that. She had never felt like this before. Sure, she had been attracted to the Martin's boy, Hank, but she had only been able to see him once a month or so, and then for only a few minutes. What was there about this man? He hadn't said anything much to her, yet there was something... But she couldn't allow her thoughts to progress, with him being one of them and all.

⋆ ⋆ ⋆ ⋆

Boyd sat propped up on the bed. The last two days had passed in a blur of sleep and wakefulness, with only Nellie there to provide for his needs. He had a vague recollection of a terrible dream in the dark of night about blue-clad soldiers coming at him with bloody bayonets, marching row upon row. He could still see the terrified face of the soldier he had shot at the bridge, and the same face had returned in his dreams. But who was that person who had soothed him during his dreams? Who had mopped his sweaty face and had crooned soft, reassuring words to him? Had she really held him in her arms and rocked him back to sleep?

As much as he wanted to know, Nellie had not been able to tell him anything new about Charlie. All she would tell him was that she wasn't allowed to leave the "property," which meant that she and Mazel were confined to an area of about two acres.

How would he react if he couldn't leave an area that small? How could anyone endure being confined to such a small world? He thought about his work on the fishing boat with his father. All that open space. He could almost smell the salt air and feel the deck heave up and down beneath him.

Neither he nor his father had owned slaves, but many of his friends had. A few held slaves to work the fishing fleets or cut and dress the fish that the boats brought in daily, but most of the slaves worked on the plantations near Charleston. Both he and his father kept to themselves and rarely went into town, preferring to stay close to their home. What with working from daylight to dark, there just wasn't much time for socializing. He had not chosen to own slaves, but had not objected to his friends who did.

He had joined the Confederate Army because he had no better plans after selling the boat and cottage, and because the talk had been that the States shouldn't be told what to do by the Federal Government. Now that he found himself in this mountain town, so different from the seacoast, he wasn't sure what he believed.

A dainty rapping on the etched glass of the front door claimed his attention. Nellie opened the front door and Boyd could hear female voices in the hallway, but couldn't make out what was being said.

Nellie tiptoed into the room and whispered, "Mr. Boyd, are you up to seein' company? Mrs. Saunders and her girl Lexus is out visitin' the wounded."

"Yes, I guess I could talk to them a bit. Here, help me sit up so I can see them better." He struggled to rise as Nellie placed pillows behind him. He was winded with the effort and the pain was almost unbearable.

Nellie brought the visitors into the room. Mrs. Saunders was a short, plump woman with dark hair, except for few strands of gray that sparkled in the dim light. She was neatly dressed, but her clothing was worn and Boyd could see stitching on one shoulder where a tear had been mended.

His attention was quickly captured by her daughter. She stood quietly just behind her mother with hands clasped before her. He had never seen eyes so blue. Her ash blond hair fell in tight curls to her shoulders. She was slim and straight and Boyd thought he had never seen a girl as pretty as the one standing before him. She looked boldly at him, judging him as only a pretty woman can do. Did he meet her approval? He felt suddenly unkempt, a growth of dark beard covered his face. He had never felt this way before. He self-consciously pulled the comforter closer around his chest.

Mrs. Saunders patted Boyd gently on the hand and talked with him quietly, sympathizing with him about the Confederate defeat. It was such a shame, she admonished, that Boyd's unit had run from the field. The whole force had retreated rather ungentleman-like, but oh, she wasn't talking about Boyd. He had fought valiantly, had been wounded—almost killed—and had served the South well.

"You just lie there and get well, now, Mr. Houston, and you'll be back on the field of honor in no time," she said with a southern drawl. "Come Lexus, we've several other houses to visit, and the hospital is full of wounded men. Most of them are southern gentlemen, and we must visit them too."

Their charitable visit over, the two ladies moved through the door into the hallway. Nellie looked at Lexus appraisingly, then at Boyd, and then turned away, showing them to the door. Lexus paused and looked over her shoulder at Boyd, a small smile briefly lit her pretty face, and then she was gone.

Boyd lay on his sick bed and listened to the ticking of the clock in the hallway. They thought he was some minor hero because he had been wounded and had not run away as the other men had. If they only knew how scared he was. He had been too busy surviving to think about what he was doing. If at any time after the battle had started he had tried to run, he would have been shot down or stabbed in the back with the cold steel of a bayonet. His skin crawled at the thought. No, he wasn't a hero. He had been scared to death, and that fear had given him the strength to fight. He had survived only because he had fought with the strength generated by an unreasonable fear.

Could he fight again? It was unlikely that he would get the chance to find out. What Mrs. Saunders hadn't realized was that he was a prisoner. He had heard the soldiers talking to Mr. James in the hallway. As soon as he could be moved, he would be sent to a Yankee prison camp. Colonel Crook wasn't about to leave men behind who were able to fight. His future, Boyd realized, didn't look very good just now. Oh, what he wouldn't give to be back aboard his father's fishing boat, hauling those silvery bluefish over the side. And he hadn't had a decent meal since he had joined the Army—he could eat a bushel of hot, steamed blue crabs about now. Leaning back on the pile of soft pillows, he closed his eyes and drifted. He could smell the fresh sea air now and hear the ring-billed gulls as they fought over the scraps of fish.

꙳ ꙳ ꙳ ꙳

It was dark behind the tavern as Troy Jones waited impatiently for Mr. James to arrive. If he didn't get his money soon, there would be hell to pay. If Mr. James thought that he'd work for nothing, he was sadly mistaken. All he had to do was find a way to blow the whistle on him without implicating himself. He'd have to think about that, but one thing was for sure—he wasn't about to let this pass without taking some action.

He took a small dark cigar out of his pocket and struck a match. The flare of light highlighted the lines of his cruel face briefly before he cupped his hands around the flame. He drew the acrid smoke deeply into his lungs, savoring the sharpness, and tossed the match aside. Damn, he thought, why didn't these farmers have smokes worth stealing? He had searched all through the plunder he had stored in the shack up on the hill, but these cheap cigars were all he could find. Thank goodness they had better taste in liquor than smokes. He had a nice cache of whiskey. Enough to last him through the summer and more to sell to the soldiers.

He shifted nervously, looking around the corner of the building. If these farmers knew who was stealing their food and stock, they'd be sure to string him up on the first white oak available. He smiled nervously and stroked his red moustache. But, then, part of the attraction of being a thief was the danger of being found out. Although he was nervous, he didn't have any intention of being caught. He was just too smart. They'd never catch him.

The back door of the tavern opened and a man stepped out. The door closed quickly, shutting off the light that had streamed from inside. The man stood quietly, letting his eyes adjust to the darkness. He adjusted his belt over his ample belly, and hawked and spat on the ground.

"'Bout time you showed up, 'Mr. James'. What's your last name anyway? I ain't heard anyone call you by anything but 'Mr. James' since I got here," Jones said contemptuously from the darkness.

"I brought your money," he replied, ignoring Jones' question.

"Well, now, it's about time. I was about ready to come lookin' for you. Another day and you would have regretted tryin' to snooker me."

"I wasn't trying to do any such thing, Jones. I'm just a little short on cash right now."

"Okay, okay, lets see the money."

Mr. James pulled a leather money belt from under his coat. It was too short to be fastened around his considerable girth, so he had simply run it through his belt loops over his own belt. It was heavy, and he handed it to Jones.

"There. You can count it if you want to, but it's all there. All two hundred. I told you I was good for it. Now, maybe you'll get off my back."

"Yeah, well, it had better be here. I don't like anyone tryin' to snooker me," he repeated. "I'll just keep the belt for a place to stash the money. I'm sure you won't mind."

"Be my guest," Mr. James smiled in the darkness. "It's one of my old ones that I've outgrown," he lied.

"Since you paid in gold an' all, I don't see no reason not to continue our arrangement. I'm scouting another farm to raid right now. You still interested?" Jones asked.

"That depends on what kind of stuff you get. I don't want anything that can be easily identified."

"It'll be mostly food. Cured hams and dried meat, mostly. Maybe some good corn whiskey. That stuff'll be worth its weight in gold to the Yanks. But we'll have to hurry. I heard that they may pull out soon. Make up your mind, man. You know where to find me if you want me to deal you in."

Jones faded into the darkness. Mr. James stood quietly, scratching his belly absently. The evening was cool and pleasant and he could hear the frogs peeping in the swampy place below the town's spring. Could he trust Jones? Probably not, but as long as he had proof that Jones was a thief, he should be safe. Jones couldn't squeal on him without implicating himself. Yet something about Jones worried him. He definitely couldn't be trusted. With a sigh he reentered the tavern. There were only a few men there drinking quietly. He ordered whisky and sat at his favorite table. As the bartender served him, he fingered the remaining gold coins in his pocket.

♪ ♪ ♪ ♪

The days dragged by until finally, after weeks in bed, Boyd was able to sit first on the edge of the bed, and then walk cautiously about the room.

Nellie had helped him walk to the front porch to sit and watch the traffic go by on the pike. Only the wagons that could ford the river travelled the pike since the Rebs had burned the bridge. Occasional patrols of Union soldiers marched up the road, to return later in the day. They paid no attention to the wounded man sitting alone on the porch.

His wounds were healing quickly. The bullet that had struck his leg had passed through without hitting the bone or severing an artery, but it was terribly sore and he limped badly. The wound in his shoulder was much more serious. Nellie told him that the doctor had dug out the minnie ball, but some internal damage remained. It was likely, the doctor said, that whoever shot him had failed to load the musket properly and the ball had not hit him with full force. Otherwise he would undoubtedly have been killed. Nelly had saved the minnie ball for him, and he now sat turning it over and over in his hand.

Boyd looked across the pike to the house opposite. It was made of the same red fired brick as Mr. James', was large and had a full porch across the front, with high white columns supporting the two story roof. There was wealth in the town, or at least there had been before the war. This quiet town sat at the crossroads of two major roads, the pike that ran east-west and one that ran north-south.

There were wagons and buggies on the pike most hours of the day. Nellie told him that the valley had prime farmland and that before the war cattle and horses were the main sources of income. Merchants received their supplies from the East Coast, some two hundred and fifty miles away. This small mountain town was in close contact with Lexington, Richmond and Williamsburg. The location, he knew, was the source of the Confederate sympathy that prevailed here.

The next day Boyd limped down the pike to the center of town. Henry was given permission to assist him by a reluctant Mr. James, and he was surprised to see that with Henry's help he could walk without too much discomfort. His shoulder didn't hurt too badly if he held it very still. His left arm was wrapped tightly against his body.

A heavily loaded army wagon rumbled along the pike toward the Yankee camp on the west side of town. The driver looked at him with minor interest, taking in the tattered Confederate uniform. Although he had left his jacket at the house since the day was warm, his gray uniform pants were a dead giveaway. He shuffled down the street, enjoying the warm June sunshine.

He limped along the main street of town, looking at the shops that lined both sides of the street: a hardware store, the newspaper office, the general store, a barber shop, and several clothing establishments. The sound of iron on iron rang clearly from the blacksmith's shop one block off the main street.

Many of the buildings were made of brick; others were wooden with high false fronts. Once a prosperous little town, its buildings were well built and nicely arranged along the street. On this warm, spring morning, there were many people on the street and they smiled sympathetically at him as he passed.

"Where you wantin' to go, Mr. Boyd," Henry asked.

"First thing I want to do is go to the hospital. Nellie said there were wounded soldiers from my unit there. I hope I can find Charlie."

" I hope you find him too. It ain't no good to lose a friend. I 'member when they hung Uncle Reuben..." Henry's voice trailed off and he looked away.

Boyd wondered who Uncle Reuben was and why he'd been hung, but decided not to ask. Henry quickly changed the subject.

"The hospital's right on up the street here. The pike goes right in front of it. Used to be a libary, with books an' all, but they cleared it out so's the soldiers could have a place."

"Henry, I'll have to stop and rest a mite. I sure get tired quickly."

He sat on a bench in front of the barber shop and listened to the pleasant drone of conversation inside. Henry stood respectfully at the end of the bench. Passersby called fondly to Henry and he grinned and bowed to each of them. It seemed as if Henry was a favorite among the townspeople.

"Sit down with me, Henry, and tell me about the people here."

"No, suh, I mustn't. Folk hereabouts want us to keep our place." He stood quietly, embarrassed, waiting for Boyd to decide when to move on.

After Boyd had rested for a few minutes, they began to walk again, Boyd limping along slowly and Henry, a step behind, talking excitedly, told him about the town and its inhabitants.

They reached the hospital at last. It was a large, brick, two-story house of the federal style that fronted the pike. The windows were open and Boyd could smell the illness and misery inside. A soldier in a blue uniform stood guard at the door.

"Just a minute, Reb," he challenged. "You have business in there? What're you doing out unguarded anyway?"

"Don't look like I'm likely to run off, now does it?" Boyd retorted.

The guard looked carefully at him, then a softer expression swept across his face. "Naw, I don't guess you will. Well, I guess you can go in. Who're you lookin' for? Someone in your unit?"

"Yeah," Boyd replied. "Charlie Taylor, you know him?"

"No, I just got assigned this duty, so I don't know anyone in there, except those from my own unit."

Boyd stepped through the door. Cots were arranged in rows with narrow walkways between them, each with its own miserable burden. Some of the patients were awake, others were very quiet, their eyes closed. Over in one corner a soldier was delirious: he thrashed back and forth on the cot, yelling for his wife. He had thrown his rumpled bedclothes onto the floor. A nurse rushed to his side to quiet him.

Boyd and Henry stepped aside as two soldiers carried a limp body out the front door. Boyd couldn't tell if he was a Reb or Yank, but it wasn't Charlie. Just to the right of the main entrance, a wounded soldier sat on a stool drawing a picture of a paddle boat on the whitewashed wall.

"Miss, Miss," Boyd called to a woman who was serving as a nurse. "Is Charlie Taylor here?"

"Don't know. I don't have time to talk, mister," she turned and began to change a soldier's bandage. Boyd limped up and down the rows of cots looking carefully at each face, but Charlie wasn't there. Henry stood in one corner, watching patiently, not seeming to be disturbed by the pain and agony of the mutilated men.

Terribly discouraged, Boyd turned away and moved slowly toward the door. The nurse had completed her task and carried a pan full of foul-smelling, blood-soaked rags toward the door.

"Please, Ma'am, I didn't find my friend. Are there other soldiers being nursed anywhere else in town?" he asked hopefully.

"No, all the Rebs are being guarded here, except for those captured unhurt and they're already on their way to prison. If he isn't here, he's probably down at the church. They've buried the dead there in a big, common grave."

"Oh, no, I had hoped to find him here."

"Maybe they took him to prison with the others," she offered.

"No, I saw him get hit. He's wounded...or dead," Boyd said sadly.

"Sorry, young man, but there's a lot of men dying on both sides."

Boyd turned again toward the door and began to leave.

"Soldier, did you look upstairs? There's more men up there."

"No, no, I didn't," he said hopefully.

The stairs were narrow and he had to stop at the landing halfway up to rest. When he reached the top, he saw more rows of cots and more wounded soldiers. Even though the windows had been thrown open, the heat under the low ceiling was stifling.

Charlie Martin Taylor lay on a cot by an open window. He stared outside, his face ashen and drawn. Boyd could see heavy bandages around his chest.

"Charlie, Charlie," Boyd said loudly. "Thank God I've found you. You're alive."

"Glad that you noticed," Charlie said. "Takes a mite of doin' to kill a Taylor." He grinned weakly at Boyd.

Boyd stood by his cot and looked down at his friend. He was very thin, even thinner than before, and his eyes didn't look good. Boyd's mother—he could just barely remember her—could always tell if he was ill just by looking at his eyes. Charlie's eyes didn't look so good.

"Are you goin' to make it, Charlie?"

"Well, now, the doc tole me that I'll live ifin I just rest up a mite.

But, Boyd, they're fixin' to take all of us wounded Rebs to prison. Said they'd haul us in wagons ifin they had to."

"You're in no state to ride any distance in a wagon, Charlie. You won't make it."

"Well, we'll see. There is another choice, but I don't like it none. Crook's sayin' that he'll give us a parole if we swear not to fight no more," he whispered. "I tell you I don't like it none, but I reckon that's what I'll have to do on account of Kate and the youngins. I've been away too long as it is an' I got to get back to the farm. What do you reckon you'll do?"

"I don't know. I'll have to think about it some."

Boyd's eyes wandered around the cramped room. The walls were lined with empty shelves—the books had been removed for safe keeping until the war was over. Cots were crammed in together, almost side by side. The air was heavy with the stench of blood.

"That man over there, Charlie. Is that Captain Bahlman?" Boyd asked.

"Yeah, that's him. He was wounded along with us. I reckon he'll have to heal up some before he gets to dance with the women like he bragged."

Boyd waved to the wounded officer and received a weak wave in return.

Charlie's eyes began to droop. He opened them again with great effort, focusing on Boyd's face with that hawk-like look Boyd had come to know.

Charlie grasped Boyd's sleeve and pulled him down so that he could hear the soft-spoken words that Charlie had to say to him. "You done good, Sonny. Them others ran, but you didn't. I seen you fightin' right good. Too bad we had to lose the first fight you were in. First time the regiment was beat. They ran like dogs, Boyd, like dogs," Charlie said sadly. "But you done good."

Boyd squatted as best he could by Charlie's cot with his head hung down toward the floor and whispered, "Charlie, I was scared.

Real scared. I only fought to save my skin. I was so scared that I was afraid I'd wet my pants." He twisted a corner of the thin, soiled sheet that covered his friend. He couldn't look into Charlie's eyes. "They say I fought like a soldier, but I just fought to save my skin," he repeated.

"Sonny, what do you 'spose soldiers do? They just fight 'cause they're too scared to do anything else. People think solderin' is all glory an' all, but it ain't." Charlie closed his eyes again. Boyd waited until he reopened them a moment later. "They's been many a time that I thought that I'd wet my pants during a battle. Why, they's nothing wrong with that even if you had.

"Boyd, you 'member when the Yanks first started up the slope towards us? When the shootin' started an' they got closer an' closer, I could see their faces. One of the Yanks I shot was Clyde Martin from up on the Mountain. I'd heard that he'd joined up with the Yanks. He was my second cousin's boy. Now I got to go an' tell his old daddy that he's dead an' I shot 'em. That's what this here war is about—folk fightin' their own folk. I reckon I've had enough to last me a spell."

Charlie's eyes closed again and his breathing took on a regular rhythm. He was asleep. Boyd tucked the sheet under Charlie's chin and rose to leave. He watched his friend for a few minutes more, then turned toward the stairs.

Outside, Boyd and Henry walked back along the pike toward the center of town. A heaviness, more than a man could normally bear, settled on his shoulders.

"Where we goin' now, Mr. Boyd?" Henry asked. He didn't seem to be in any hurry to return to the house and his work.

"To the church, Henry. I want to see where they buried the men."

They walked slowly along Church Street to the Presbyterian Church. It was large, square and tall and made of rough-squared limestone. The graveyard was out behind. They walked around the corner of the church and before them was a large mound of red-brown soil. A large mass-grave. An old man leaned on a shovel and looked up at them as they approached. A stubble of gray whiskers covered his chin, and his soiled clothes hung on his skinny body.

"Just tidying up where they buried them. They's ninety-five Reb soldiers layin' under that heap of dirt. They buried the Yanks on a hill west of town. You got men you know in there?" he asked, nodding toward the terrible mound.

"Yes I guess I do. I'd just joined up and hadn't got to know too many of them, but they were good men."

"Yes, well, what I heard was that they ran when the real fightin' started. Now, if I was younger I'd be out there fightin' too." he bragged. "Bet I wouldn't let any Yank run me off. Heard that you had 'em outnumbered two to one," he looked hopefully at Boyd, anxious for an argument.

"I don't think these men ran, friend, else they'd be alive now," Boyd said defensively.

"Don't be so touchy, soldier. Folks say you did all right. You're that Houston feller, staying up at Mr. James' ain't you?" He chuckled. "Don't look so surprised, this is a small town and there's nothing goes on here that folk's don't talk about. Hell, when there's nothing else goin' on we talk about one another," he grinned.

The tension broken, the older man chatted pleasantly with Boyd about the town, pausing occasionally to spit a stream of dark tobacco juice on the trampled grass.

Boyd stood quietly, looking at the grave that held his comrades. The air was still and he could smell the sweet fragrance of iris growing on a gravesite nearby. Robins searched the grass-covered graves for worms and insects, and explored the edge of the newly-turned soil. The mournful call of a dove drifted down from the hillside in front of the church. Boyd closed his eyes and forced back the sob that rose in his throat.

Later, Boyd walked back through the town to Mr. James' house, but had to lean heavily on Henry to walk up the last hill. He collapsed wearily in the bed and lay for a long time looking up at the ceiling, thinking about the battle and that red pile of dirt down at the church.

What would he do? Should he try to continue to fight, or should he take the offer of parole? What would the Yankee prison be like? Could he slip away and get back to his unit? He drifted off to sleep as the afternoon bird chorus began to tune up for the evening serenade.

He awoke at dusk and lay quietly for a few minutes listening, trying to recall where he was as he shook off the fog of sleep. Hearing the scuff of boots, he drew aside the heavy drapes and looked out onto the porch. A Yankee soldier stood guard.

Nellie woke him the next morning and told him that the guard outside said his orders were to take him to see Colonel Crook first thing.

"The Colonel wants all the Reb soldiers to be at the hospital this mornin'. Mr. Boyd," she asked wide-eyed, "what do you reckon he wants with you?"

"I don't know, Nellie. Word is he's ready to ship us out to prison, or offer us parole." He carefully explained to her how parole worked.

Nellie was concerned about Boyd's future. He could tell by the way she looked at him that she liked him. She was only a negress, but a very attractive one.

"What you goin' to do ifin they offer you parole, Mr. Boyd?" Nellie asked. "You'll take it, won't you? They say the Yankee prison is terrible, just terrible." She helped him pull on his boots, being careful not to hurt his wounded leg.

"I don't know yet, Nellie. I really don't. I guess I'll have to make that decision soon, though." Boyd sat gingerly on the edge of the bed, holding his left arm against his body. The walk to town and back yesterday had tired him, yet the exercise had seemed to help. He felt a bit stronger today. His wounds were healing with no signs of infection. The fever that had left him weak and hot in the weeks after the battle was gone.

Nellie touched his face with her work-rough hands, looking thoughtfully into his eyes. What will happen to this man, she asked herself. No, Nellie, she told herself. You must not let your heart carry you away. What you're feeling inside just can't be. It can't happen.

Boyd looked at her tenderly. This woman had served him hand and foot while he was sick. She had defended him against her own sister: He had heard her admonish Mazel in the hallway, telling her to leave him alone. He took her hand in his.

"Nellie, thank you for nursing me back to health. I'd have died if it wasn't for you." Tenderly, without thinking, he drew her head down and lightly kissed her lips. Oh, he thought, if only she wasn't...

"Lets go Reb" the soldier yelled impatiently from outside, "You've got a date with the Colonel."

ᵔ ᵔ ᵔ ᵔ

They all crowded into the hospital. Colonel Crook stood by the door, an aide by his side. He was tall and strong, and there was no doubt he was in charge. The Colonel emanated control and confidence. Without introduction he addressed the men assembled before him.

"You men have a unique opportunity before you. All of your comrades who were captured uninjured are on their way to prison. I don't envy them. But those are the perils of war. You, on the other hand, had the misfortune of being wounded. Maybe it's your good luck. I'm giving you this choice: Be transported to prison or sign parole. Parole means that you swear never to take up arms against the Union again. We'll even let you keep your arms, since most of you need them to hunt food. But hear these words of warning: If you're caught fighting against the Union again, you'll be executed in the blink of an eye. You can go home and live peaceably, or you can continue your struggle aginst fate. It's your choice.

"My orderly here has the papers. You'll get a copy of your own to carry with you in case someone questions you. So there it is, men. It's up to you. Sorry that you were hurt, but we're happy that it's you and not us," he grinned.

With that said, he left the hospital. The aide walked from one man to the next asking their names and where they were from. When his turn came, Charlie, with a shaking hand, signed the papers. Finally it was Boyd's turn.

"You there, Reb what'll it be? Parole or prison?"

"I, I haven't decided quite yet," Boyd stammered.

"Well, now there's nothing much to decide. Do nothin' and you'll be on your way to prison first thing tomorrow morning. Come on now, I don't have all day," the aide said not unkindly.

Boyd looked again at Charlie who nodded his head almost imperceptibly. Unsteadily, Boyd took up the pen, dipped it in the inkpot and signed his name to the parole sheet. It was done. He was honorbound to stay out of the war to its end.

Later, in the quiet of the evening, Boyd sat on the edge of Charlie's cot.

"What do we do now?" Boyd asked. "It looks like we're out of it."

"Can't say I'm sorry, Sonny. I've done enough killin' to last me a lifetime. I'm agoin' home. Just as soon as I can, I'm agoin' home an' you're acommin' with me. You can stay with us 'til you're healed and back on your feet."

"No, I can't do that. My father always said that a man shouldn't be beholden' to anyone."

"Don't be silly, Sonny. Ifin a man can't help a friend, who can? We'll start out first thing in the mornin'. I've already sent for a wagon. Hell of a thing—a man goin' home from the war in a wagon," Charlie groused.

"How did you get word out to send for a wagon?"

"Boyd, I was born an' raised here in Greenbrier County, my daddy was born an' raised in this county, and his daddy before him. There's not much that goes on here that my folk don't know about. They knew that I was fightin' for Heth, so they just naturally came alookin'. My oldest boy has been talkin' to me through the winder. We'll leave first thing in the mornin."

"Charlie, thanks. Without you I'd have never made it," Boyd began.

"Don't you go an' get all soft on me, Sonny. Us Taylors don't cotton to soft men," he grinned. "You be here at the hospital first light ifin you don't want to walk to the top of Muddy Creek Mountain."

Henry helped Boyd back up the pike to Mr. James' house. When he entered, Mr. James was sitting in the parlor across the hall from Boyd's room.

"Hey there Reb. I heard you've signed parole papers," he said. "Colonel Crook is pulling out in a day or two, so I'm not obliged to keep you here. Besides, you look fit enough to take care of yourself. Your stuff's there in the kit bag," he gestured toward the heap on the floor. "You'll have to find another place to stay tonight. Sorry." To Boyd, he didn't look very sorry.

"Yes sir," Boyd replied. "I'll be out in a few minutes. I just want to say thanks for..."

"Never mind. Just get your stuff and get out."

Boyd picked up the kit and walked as straight as he could out the front door, not looking back. In the yard, a voice from around the corner of the house said, "Mr. Boyd. I's sorry. He's kinda mean at times. But I's glad you're feelin' better an' you found Mr. Taylor. Maybe I'll see you again," Nellie said hopefully.

"Yes, Nellie, maybe you will. I'm going on up the Mountain with Charlie in the morning, but I'll be back in town upon occasion," he said formally.

"You take care now, Mr. Boyd Houston," she whispered, "you take care." Then she was gone.

Boyd stood in the deserted street and listened to the cool mountain air whisper around him and through the new summer leaves.

He walked quietly toward the center of town and stopped by the tavern. Light from the lanterns inside streamed through the windows onto the street, forming rectangular pools of yellow light. He opened the kit bag and looked inside. All of his meager belongings were there—except his money belt.

⚘ ⚘ ⚘ ⚘

Boyd was waiting for Charlie in the front yard of the hospital before the first sign of light the next morning. He had slept, or at least tried to sleep, in the doorway of a shop just off the main street of town. The doorway, set into the building, had given him some protection from the dew, but he awoke frequently during the night shivering in the cool night air. If he only had a blanket he would have been comfortable enough to sleep, but as it was the night had been long and miserable. The least Mr. James could have done was to give him some warning so that he could have found a room for the night. He had fretted about his lost money, trying to remember the last time he had seen the money belt.

As best he could recollect, he had the belt when the battle had begun, but had not even thought about it afterward until he had looked into the kit bag. Anyone could have taken the belt after he had been wounded. Nellie told him that it was after noon the day of the battle before they had taken him to Mr. James' house. He had been hauled in a wagon by Union soldiers, so there was no telling what had happened to the money. What would he do now? He had no home, no money, no job, and little prospect of any means of employment. He searched his pockets carefully and found a twenty dollar gold piece. It wasn't as much as he had when he came to town, but it was better than nothing.

He stood in the hospital yard and waited for someone to come and pick up Charlie. He absently rubbed his shoulder where the bullet had struck him. It throbbed with the cold and damp, and he had considerable trouble working out the stiffness from his night's sleep. As he gingerly rotated his left arm, he could feel the tightness and pain in his shoulder where the damage had been done. How much use would he regain in his arm? The doctor didn't know and had indicated that only time would tell.

He pulled up his pants leg and looked at his wounded leg in the dim morning light. The wound had begun to bleed again. He was beginning to feel sorry for himself, standing there in the morning damp, with the pain and hunger settling in the pit of his stomach, when a wagon rattled down the pike from the west. It had passed the Yankee camp on the hill above the hospital and slowed to stop before the hospital entrance, its brakes squealing loudly.

"'Peers like that brake needs fixin, Jacob," a voice drifted down from the window above.

"Is that you, Dad?" the young driver said. He was tall and thin and wore patched breeches and a light jacket. His hawk-nose and high forehead left little doubt in Boyd's mind that he was Charlie's son. He looked to be only sixteen or so, but was already tall and would fill out to make a powerful man.

"Who do you reckon you've been talkin' to through this window the last few days? If only I could stand, or even get out of bed, I'd be able to see over the window ledge," he bantered. "Keep your eye out for a tall, gangly lookin' feller with a big shock of brown hair an' all shot up. He'll be 'bout as ugly a man as you're likely to see."

"I'm here, Charlie, if it's me you're talking about," Boyd answered.

"I reckoned it was you out there shufflin' around. You never could keep quiet much," Charlie chuckled.

Jacob went upstairs to figure out how to get his dad down the steps and loaded into the wagon. The guard had left after all the wounded men inside had signed parole papers. Boyd waited outside since he would be of no help, and after much shuffling about and mumbling and muttering inside, Jacob and another young man emerged carrying Charlie on a stretcher. They gingerly loaded Charlie onto a cornshuck mattress in the back of the wagon that had been brought along especially for that purpose.

As Jacob expertly turned the team and wagon, Boyd carefully looked them over. He didn't know the first thing about horses, since he was a fisherman, but they looked much better than any of the army horses that had pulled the cannon. They were sleek and seemed to be well-fed.

"You'll have to climb up here and sit with me, Mr. Houston, there's not much room in the back. Hope the ride won't be too bumpy. Where's your gear, I'll throw it in," Jacob said.

"Everything I own is in that kit bag. I don't even have a musket since it was lost in the battle," Boyd said wistfully.

He climbed carefully up on the seat beside Jacob and the team began to move up the pike. They headed west out of town, along the well traveled road winding through the low, rolling hills of the valley. Union soldiers on picket watched the wagon pass without comment. A heavy blanket of woodsmoke from the encampment fires slid down the hill on the cool morning air to cover the town.

Boyd looked back at Charlie riding on the mattress. He was silent, with beads of perspiration on his high forehead. His teeth were clenched tightly together. Jacob looked back too, concern written on his face.

"I'll go as slow as I can, Dad. But, we're bound to hit a few ruts 'tween here and home. Just hang on and I'll stop and let you rest every few miles."

As they traveled through the green farmland, Boyd could see a long row of smoky-blue mountains rising off to the southwest. The mountain chain extended as far as he could see in both directions.

"Is that where we're headed, to those mountains over there?" Boyd asked.

"Yep, that's where we're goin' alright," Jacob replied. "Some of the best farmland anywhere."

"You mean here, in the valley," Boyd stated.

"Yes, here in the valley, but up on the mountain, too. Once we get up there, you'll see. It flattens off up on top. You can see forever once you get up there—all the way to the ocean on a clear winter's day," he teased. "Tom Jefferson once wrote that the mountains over at Charlottesville looked like waves coming in to the beach. I can see why he'd think that, because from up there," he waved a hand toward the mountains, "they look just like an ocean full of waves."

They stopped a few miles out of town under a sprawling maple alongside the road. Jacob fished out a jug of water and gave both men a drink. Boyd hadn't eaten since the noon meal yesterday, and was beginning to get hungry. As if with the same thought, Charlie stirred on the mattress and began to fumble in his kit bag.

"Here you go, Sonny," he grinned, handing Boyd a familiar lump wrapped in dirty newspaper, "help yourself."

Boyd unwrapped the dried meat and began to hack off a chunk. He offered the meat to Jacob who said, "Er, no thank you. I just had breakfast before I came into town. I think I'll wait until I get back before I eat. I don't want to spoil my dinner," he grimaced, looking in wonder at the meat.

"How about you, Charlie?"

"No thanks, Sonny, I'm sick enough the way it is," he chuckled.

Boyd looked at the unappetizing lump and wrapped it up in the newspaper again without comment.

They continued along the road, passing several forks, and soon approached the foot of the escarpment. They crossed a tiny covered bridge over a small stream, and Boyd stared at the grist mill that sat just off the road. He had never seen a mill powered by a water wheel before.

"That's Hern's mill, there. That's where we take our corn 'n' all to get it ground," Jacob advised.

The road became more narrow and began to climb the mountain. There were occasional switchbacks dug into the mountain, and though the horses crouched into their harnesses, they seemed to pull the heavy wagon with ease. Boyd looked out over the valley as they passed occasional openings along the heavily wooded mountain slope. He could see a shroud of smoke hovering above the town where the Yankee army prepared its morning meal and the sun glistened on water in the small stream below.

As they reached the top of the mountain, Boyd could see that the trees were different from the ones lower down. The road wound among ancient white pines that covered most of the land. As they passed beneath the pines, the horses' hooves were muffled by the thick litter of needles that covered the road. What beauty, he thought. How different from the ocean and beach, but every bit as beautiful.

The horses, sensing they were nearing home, began to trot, causing the wagon to jerk and buck. A groan from Charlie prompted Jacob to speak sharply to the horses. They slowed, but immediately began to pick up the pace again.

They traveled along the mountain's ridge, leaving the main road behind. After a short distance, perhaps a mile, the track they had been following dropped into a small, beautiful valley. There was a snug log cabin tucked against the south-facing slope and farther along, a low barn and sheds. A wisp of blue smoke rose from the stone chimney.

4

The wagon bounced down the rutted road to the bottom of the valley. Charlie groaned in pain in spite of himself. Boyd's shoulder ached and his wounded leg bled through his heavy army breeches. If they didn't get where they were going soon, neither one of them would make it. Finally they reached the valley floor where the road was smoother. The horses, nearing home, were hard to keep in check and Jacob worked to keep them from running.

As the wagon approached the cabin, Boyd could see a woman standing on the porch, her hands wrapped in her apron. She was tall and straight, strikingly pretty with bright red hair. She looked nothing like Boyd had imagined Charlie's wife would look. She was young, looking almost childlike at a distance, but as they approached he could see that she was maybe thirty or so.

Jacob stopped the wagon in front of the cabin flush with the floor of the raised porch. Charlie's wife looked sternly down at her husband lying on the mattress. At first, she said nothing. The horses stomped their hooves, impatient to be unharnessed and free to roll in the dirt. Charlie's wife frowned.

"Charlie Taylor, what did I tell you about going off to that silly war of yours? I told you that you'd get your stubborn head shot off, didn't I," she answered her own question. "If you go marching off again, I'll leave you for sure. You hear me, Mr. Taylor?"

"Yes ma'am, I reckon I hear you all right," he grinned.

"I mean it, Charlie, if you go gallivanting off again, don't expect

70

me to be here waiting for you when you get back." She stood with both fists on her hips, relief beginning to show in her pretty face. Boyd looked at her with his mouth open. What kind of a welcome was this?

Her gaze moved to Boyd, sitting on the wagon seat.

"Hello, I'm Kate Taylor, she smiled pleasantly. "You're Boyd Houston, aren't you? Jacob told me all about you, but only from Charlie's description. I expected you to be wearing a halo, according to what he said," she winked. "I want to thank you for standing by Charlie during the battle."

Turning back to Charlie she asked, "Well, how are you? It looks like you got yourself shot up pretty bad. Let me see." She stepped off the porch onto the wagon and began fussing with his bandages, inspecting him from head to toe. She touched his cheek tenderly, looking deeply into his eyes. Boyd felt he shouldn't be sitting there watching, but didn't know what else to do. Tears flooded her eyes but she turned away briefly to hide them. When she turned back, the tears were gone and she began to take charge.

"Come on Jacob, help me get your father into the house. We'll have to get Matt to help us, too. He's down at the creek. Run and fetch him," she said quietly.

Within a few minutes, Jacob had found Matt and they ran back toward the house. Matt, a younger version of Jacob, was delighted to see his father; he chattered happily and climbed into the wagon bed with him, but became quiet when he saw the bloody bandages and noticed how thin and pale his father looked.

The three of them together moved Charlie into the cabin. Boyd stumbled along behind, trying to carry Charlie's kit bag. Inside, the cabin was neat and clean. The logs were hand-hewn and fitted tightly together—the sign of an expert craftsman. Only a little chinking was necessary to keep out the winter winds. The main room was large and had a stone fireplace at one end. There were sleeping rooms toward the back, a built-in kitchen with a hand pump, and a sleeping loft above for the boys. On the hearth there were children's toys in some disarray; dolls, with cornshucks for hair and tiny, hand-carved furniture and a doll house. Obviously there was a daughter around somewhere. It was a snug, warm home, made so by much work and care had made it that way.

After Charlie had been put to bed, Kate sat on the front porch with Boyd and spoke quietly of their life in the mountains. Kate, as a young lady, had visited Lewisburg from her home in Lexington. She had been taken by Charlie's charm and sincerity and, had married him despite her parent's objections. She had never regretted her decision. She rode the stage occasionally to see her parents, and they had reluctantly come to visit a few times. There were three children: Jacob, the oldest, was sixteen: Matt the middle one was ten years old now; and Colleen was six. She was staying with the Coopers down the valley for a few days and would be disappointed that she hadn't been home when her daddy returned from the war.

✐ ✐ ✐ ✐

Two days later, with Charlie propped up in bed, Kate had asked Jacob and Matt to take the wagon down the valley to get Colleen. Boyd, deciding that it was time for Charlie and Kate to have some time together, asked if he could ride along.

The valley opened wider as they made their way toward the Cooper's farm. Matt kept up a continual chatter, and Jacob laughed and grinned at his antics. Boyd was enjoying himself, even though the jolting wagon caused him some discomfort. The morning was bright and warm, and the birds were noisy in the trees. Boyd could recognize only a few: mourning doves, robins, cardinals, and others. Matt happily told him the names of each; evidently someone had taken pains to teach him. The family dog, a hound, trotted alongside the wagon, making occasional forays into the brush on each side of the road. A wild turkey, flushed by the dog, darted across the road in front of the wagon with a flock of young, blue-headed poults just behind her. Their shiny heads glistened in the sunlight.

"Durn," Matt shouted, "I wish I had my gun. Mom would like to have one of them turkeys to cook for supper."

"You wouldn't be able to hit it if you did," Jacob chided.

"Oh, yes, I would, I'm a good shot," he argued.

They arrived at the Cooper's farm just before noon. The cabin was old and well kept, but the barn and out-buildings were not so well maintained. Colleen ran out to meet them. She had red hair and was a miniature version of Kate. She became quiet as Jacob told her of her daddy's wounds, but smiled broadly when she heard that he would recover. She took Boyd by the hand as if she had known him all her life, and led him into the house, smiling up at him.

Mom and Pop Cooper welcomed them to their home and Mrs. Cooper insisted they stay for dinner. Pop, stocky and bald-headed, was browned from the sun. Boyd chuckled when Pop removed his hat—the top half of his head was lily white. As Mom began to prepare the meal, Pop questioned Boyd about the war, hungry for news. Boyd told him about the march from Pearisburg and the battle in Lewisburg. Pop was especially interested in Boyd's life as a fisherman, since he had never seen the ocean, and asked endless questions about what it was like to sail upon the sea.

"My great-grand daddy sailed here from England," Pop Cooper proclaimed. "He built a house right up there on that knoll. You can still see the old chimney from here. The Indians came one night and killed him and my great-grandma. They're buried up there under that big ole' oak tree. The Indians burned the home place to the ground and my grand-daddy built this cabin, an' I remember sittin' in that room there," he nodded toward the front room with his bald head, "with my grand-daddy and my daddy talkin' an' all. I've lived here all my life—seventy-five years, an' I plan on bein' buried up there on the knoll with my daddy and grand daddy."

Mr. Cooper had lost an arm, and had only a stump just below

the shoulder. Matt whispered that the Indians had cut it off as a warning to the other settlers, but Boyd wasn't sure that was true. Pop waved his good arm and talked loudly as he told Boyd about his life. Boyd was surprised that he talked so openly. Everyone had said that mountain folks kept to themselves and didn't have much to say to strangers. Maybe it was because Boyd had arrived with the Taylor children that he was accepted so readily by this couple.

"Pop," Mrs. Cooper called from the kitchen, "come in here and help me open this jar of beans. You know with my sore wrist I can't hardly do nothin' for myself."

Pop walked into the kitchen to help, and Boyd could see them, standing together by the table, as they worked. She held the jar with her good hand and Pop worked the lid loose with his only hand. Between them they had one good pair of hands. They talked quietly as they worked. How lucky they are, Boyd thought. Even with their infirmities, they have a good life together.

The food was wonderful. Kate was a good cook, but Mrs. Cooper was even better. There was cured ham, gravy, dried beans, fried chicken, and potatoes. The mountain farms had survived the ravages of the war much better than those along the major roads. The armies hadn't pillaged this far into the mountains. There didn't seem to be a shortage of food in these self-sufficient farms.

On the way back to the Taylor cabin, Colleen and the boys talked incessantly, and Boyd enjoyed witnessing such childhish exuberance. Colleen had asked many questions about Boyd's wounds and wanted him to tell her all about the war, but most of her questions were about the town and the people there. She wanted to know how other people lived, what they wore, and what the children were like.

When asked about the Coopers, Jacob laughed and said, "They're like family to us. They always come to visit, and we often go down there to see them. Pop makes the best cured hams around and he sells them down in town. Town folk especially like them."

"Did Pop take you out to the smokehouse?" Matt giggled.

"Why, no he didn't, Matt," Boyd answered, a questioning look on his face.

"Cured hams ain't all Pop's known for," Jacob laughed. "Him and Dad usually go out to the smokehouse after supper an' when they come back, they laugh and giggle a lot."

Colleen frowned and asked, "What do you mean, Jacob?"

"Why, Colleen, Dad and Pop gets into the corn liquor and they get all silly. Mom and Mrs. Taylor won't allow liquor in the house, so's they keep it out in the smokehouse," Jacob grinned. "Maybe next time you come fer supper, Boyd, Pop'll take you out to the smokehouse, too.

Colleen hunched her shoulders, rolled her eyes and giggled. Her red hair shone like a new copper penny in the sun.

₰ ₰ ₰ ₰

Boyd sat on the front porch of the Taylor cabin and looked out over the farm before him. The fields were being overtaken with greenbrier brambles and weeds. Here and there a red cedar sprouted from the rich meadowlands. The farm had been neglected for the last several years. There were cattle and horses grazing in the fields, but they didn't eat the briers and brambles and wouldn't touch the cedar. Only periodic mowing would keep back the unwanted growth. The barn was beginning to deteriorate, too: a loose shingle here and there, and a door hung on one hinge.

Only the house had escaped neglect. Kate and the children had worked hard to keep the roof in good repair, and the chinking maintained to keep out the cold winter winds. Jacob had worked hard just to keep the family in food. He had hunted regularly and had butchered an occasional steer to keep them in meat. But most of his time had been occupied cutting and stacking firewood for the winter. It was a backbreaking task, especially alone, but he had managed.

Through it all, Kate had kept the family together, waiting impatiently for the occasional letter from her husband. Although he was home for good, she still worried about him. His recovery was slow. Now, in midsummer he movedcarefully, and his wound, tender and raw, mended slowly. How he had survived such a dangerous wound, she couldn't tell.

Boyd stretched and moved his shoulder. It was still stiff, but didn't hurt much now. He just couldn't move it as extensively as he had before. His leg was almost healed and he walked with only a slight limp. It was time to get to work. Time to repay the Taylor's for their hospitality. He and Jacob would begin work in earnest in the morning. He had helped with the chores as best he could, but now it was time to tackle the harder work. They would have to work quickly because the summer would be over before they knew it.

Boyd found that repairing a barn wasn't much different from repairing a fishing boat. He used Charlie's tools to fix the shingles, and using a leather strap, got the door to swing properly. With Jacob's and Matt's help they spent several days cutting hay. Matt drove the team while Jacob and Boyd forked the dried hay into the wagon. They stacked the hay around the tall, locust posts set into the ground for that purpose. Matt especially liked to tamp the hay down tight, walking around and around the post while the hay was pitched onto the stack. After the stack was head-high, Jacob climbed onto the stack and when Boyd tossed the hay up, he caught it with his fork and placed it just right. Then he tamped it down. They made the stacks cone-shaped to turn the rain and wet, so that they looked like giant beehives dotting the bright green hay field.

The days passed quickly and Charlie, recovering now, drove the team while Boyd and the boys worked. It was pleasant, even though it became very hot in the afternoons, and the work went quickly. They drove the team into the woods to cut firewood and Charlie gave them all a lesson on selecting the best wood.

"Beech is the best," he said, "it burns the hottest, an' don't leave much ash. Maple and red oak's good too, but white oak don't split clean. Some folk won't allow white oak in the house on account of bein' superstitious, but I don't think they's nothing to that."

Just before quitting time, Charlie told the boys to cut a small black-gum tree and they cut it into short blocks with the crosscut saw. The boys grinned broadly as they worked and couldn't stop giggling.

When it was time to split the wood, Jacob began first with the maple and showed how it split clean and white inside. Matt took a turn next and demonstrated how to split the beech. When Boyd's turn came, Charlie set a block of black-gum on the splitting stump and handed him the axe. All three stood back away from him and grinned.

Boyd, determined not to be shown up by mere boys, took a mighty swing at the block. The axe struck it dead center, but bounced off as if the block were made of stone. His hands tingled. Charlie and the two boys stood looking at him with poker faces. Another swing and the axe again bounced off, making his hands tingle even more. He looked at Charlie in frustration, and they erupted in laughter. Jacob slapped his thigh and laughed, bent over, until tears ran down his face. Matt laughed and pointed at Boyd, and Charlie, trying to keep from laughing, held his side and chest, obviously in pain.

"Gum don't split too good, does it?" Charlie laughed in understatement, putting his hand on Boyd's shoulder. "I 'member learnin' that same lesson from my daddy."

Boyd stood looking at Charlie and the two laughing boys and grinned dumbly.

⨎ ⨎ ⨎ ⨎

Boyd asked to borrow one of Charlie's saddle horses, and rode off the mountain and into town. He had some difficulty controlling the spirited horse; it seemed to sense that its rider hadn't much experience.

It was late August and the Yankee camp was deserted. The town had returned to normal and he stopped first to pick up the Taylor's mail. With it safely tucked into his pocket, he made a stop at the general store to pick up some supplies for Kate. As he stepped into the store, his first sight was of Lexus, standing at the counter. She looked radiant to his hungry eyes.

"Hello, Mr. Houston. I see you've recovered well from your wounds," she said with a friendly tone in her voice.

How did she remember his name, he wondered. The town had been full of wounded soldiers and she and her mother had probably visited them all.

"Good morning, Miss Saunders," he replied.

They chatted pleasantly as the salesman filled their orders. The shelves were well stocked, but there were few people from the valley who could afford to buy more than the basest necessities.

"How long have the Yankees been gone?" Boyd asked casually as they stepped out onto the sidewalk.

"Oh, they've been gone for some time now, but will probably be back soon. They come and go, depending on where our Confederate forces are. I wish we could get rid of them for good," she said with a slight frown.

"Well, maybe it'll work out soon."

"I hear Captain Finney is to be drummed out of the service. He's the one whose unit started that awful rout by runnin'. Some say he'll be demoted and stuck somewhere out of action, but I hope they discharge him," she said angrily.

As they stood in the late summer sun talking comfortably, Boyd saw Mr. James making his way down the street toward them. Nellie trotted behind carrying a stack of packages wrapped in brown paper and bound by white twine. As they passed, Mr. James looked at Boyd disapprovingly but passed without comment. Nellie looked first at Boyd and then at Lexus; an uncertain smile appeared for Boyd. She could only nod and continue to follow Mr. James.

Lexus noticed that Boyd was watching Nellie as she continued up the street. Touching Boyd's arm, Lexus expertly brought his attention back to herself.

"We're having a small get-together at our house the evening after tomorrow. Just a few close friends," she smiled. "Would you like to come?"

Boyd was surprised that she would be so forward but quickly said, "Oh, yes, I'd be very pleased. But I'm afraid I don't have anything very nice to wear."

"You mustn't worry. Folks understand, you being a war hero and all..."

She told him how to find her house and then said, "I must go now. I'll be looking forward to seeing you at the party." With that she said good-bye and walked up the street.

Boyd watched her go. What a pretty girl, he thought. A woman, actually. And, she had invited him to her home. He'd have to ask Kate to help him. He didn't know much about parties and all, especially in a remote mountain town like this. He looked at his reflection in the store window. Not much to see, really; just a tall skinny man with a shock of unruly light brown hair and a quick smile. He still wore his Confederate pants and boots, and a plain cotton shirt Kate had given him. He was bareheaded, having lost his cap in the battle. If only his money belt hadn't been stolen—he'd buy a nice suit of clothes. That was out of the question. He had only a twenty dollar gold piece that he'd carried in his pants pocket. He'd need all of that just to get along.

He shifted the sack of goods he had purchased for Kate to his good hand. His shoulder still ached when he used it too much. His leg was slightly stiff, but didn't bother him much.

Fastening the sack to the saddle horn, Boyd untied the horse. He would talk to the Sheriff about his missing money belt, he decided suddenly. He didn't know what help he could expect, but it wouldn't hurt to try.

Leading his horse west along the main street, he turned north on Court Street and walked the few blocks down to the courthouse. He tied the horse to an iron ring imbedded in the sidewalk and entered the foyer of the courthouse. The double entryway of the brick building opened into a large vestibule. Several benches sat against the wall opposite the entrance: one was occupied by two old men. They looked at him curiously as he approached.

"Howdy, Reb," one of the loafers called, "you lookin' fer someone?" He was tall and skinny with a ring of gray hair just over his ears. His piercing blue eyes evaluated Boyd carefully. He wore wool pants and a heavy, longsleeved shirt that was buttoned tightly to his throat despite the heat. A narrow-brimmed Stetson hat sat at a jaunty angle on his head.

"I'm lookin' for the Sheriff," Boyd replied.

"Well, his office is just down that hall," the loafer said with a friendly nod. "He just went in."

"Thanks," Boyd said.

"What you need with the Sheriff?"

Boyd laughed, "You're not very shy about asking about someone else's business, are you?"

"Just tryin' to be helpful, young feller," he grinned, "Don't mean no offense."

"None taken, pop," Boyd said. "I wanted to report a theft. Someone stole my money belt—had all my money in it."

"I never did hear of a foot soldier havin' money."

"This soldier did. I'd sold my boat and cottage before joining the army. It was all I had."

"You're not the only one to complain of bein' robbed. Two or three of the other wounded soldiers said they lost money, too."

"Thanks for letting me know," Boyd said with some relief. If others had been robbed, it was unlikely that Mr. James, or someone in his house had taken the money. Maybe someone had robbed the dead and wounded soldiers following the battle.

He found the Sheriff sitting at a small desk in the corner of the office. He was a man of medium height, powerfully built with reddish-brown hair. He wore a full, closely trimmed beard. This man, Boyd thought, is not one to tangle with. His thick shoulders and muscular arms explained why Charlie had said that no one cared to cross Sheriff Brown.

He questioned Boyd briefly, trying to pinpoint the time that Boyd had discovered his money was gone. He shoved a paper across the cluttered desk and thrust a pen into Boyd's hand.

"Here, Mr. Houston, fill out this complaint. If something turns up I'll let you know, but since you can't tell me just when the money was taken, it'll be hard to help you. I'll try, though."

"I hear that others have been robbed, Sheriff. Do you have any leads from them?"

"No, I don't," he confessed, "but if I find him, you can bet he'll spend the best years of his life in my jail. I don't take kindly to someone in my town robbin' folks. Especially folks who were wounded or killed fightin' for the South."

"Well, thanks Sheriff. Let me know if you find anything."

Boyd stood outside the courthouse and watched the traffic go by. The Sheriff seemed to be honest enough. Maybe something would turn up. If the money was still in the belt, he could identify it. He had given the Sheriff a detailed description. Boyd had found it convenient to use the belt, maybe the thief would too.

He caught up the horse and returned to the main street. He mounted the animal carefully, holding his sore shoulder stiffly, and turned toward the mountain.

The horse trotted along the pike west out of town and knew he was going home. His pace quickened. The day had turned hot and the well-traveled road was dusty. The hooves kicked up dust with each step.

Boyd rode comfortably, relaxing in the hot sun, his good hand holding the reins in firmly. The horse pulled at the bit trying to work some slack for his head.

The pike wound around the rolling hills of the valley and Boyd recalled the trip to the mountains with the wounded Charlie only a few months ago. A ruffled grouse flushed with a sudden roar from the brush alongside the road, and Boyd jumped at the sound as if shot. He could see another grouse farther along the road dusting itself in the powdery soil in the road, then it, too, burst away at his approach.

The horse tossed its head and pulled at the reins, anxious to move faster. "I'm going to let you go, boy. If you run some, maybe you'll settle down." Boyd dug his heels into the horse's flanks and gave it its head. Hanging on for dear life, Boyd relished the speed as the trees and bushes whipped by.

Suddenly, the horse and rider rounded a bend in the pike and ran headlong into the middle of a detachment of Yankee soldiers. They had heard him coming and waited, muskets ready, on each side of the road.

"Hold up there, Reb," a sergeant yelled, "You ain't goin' nowhere."

As Boyd pulled up the horse, he could hear muskets being cocked.

"You step down there, now," the sergeant said, his musket pointing menacingly at Boyd.

"Easy, now Yank," Boyd replied. "I'm not with the Rebs any more. I'm on parole."

"Let's see your papers, Reb."

"Just take it easy now. I'm going to step down," Boyd said, and eased himself to the ground. As he looked at the small detachment of men, he began to realize something was wrong. There were boxes stacked along one side of the road and there was a tall, thin man in civilian clothing with white hair and a red moustache standing beside the boxes. Wagons with teams of army mules waited.

"What's going on here Sergeant? It looks like you're doing some trading."

"Well, now, Reb. Maybe you've seen more than you need to," he said to Boyd. Then to the tall, white haired man, "It's done now, Jones," he called, "what're we goin' to do with a Reb who knows more than he's supposed to?"

"Simple. Kill him," Jones said matter-of-factly from the side of the road. "Kill him and throw his body into Grapevine Cave. Nobody'll ever find him in there. "

"You say you've got papers?" the Sergeant asked, turning back to Boyd. "Let's see 'em."

Boyd took the papers from his pocket and handed them to the soldier.

"Thanks, Reb. These might be worth something to some poor deserter," the Sergeant said with a sneer. "Tie his hands, Hank."

A dirty soldier with a pocked face stepped forward and quickly bound Boyd's hands tightly in front of him. The ropes bit painfully into his wrists.

Jones grinned at him from amidst his plunder. The soldiers relaxed now that Boyd was tied and began looking over his horse.

"Not bad horseflesh. Where'd you get him?," the pocked faced man asked. Boyd stood silently looking contemptuously at him.

"You hear me, Reb. Where'd you get him?" Still no answer from Boyd. The man struck Boyd with the coil of rope he held. "You speak when I ask you a question."

"Hold on there, Hank," the Sergeant said. "No use fooling with him. Someone else'll come along if we spend too much time here. Let's get this stuff loaded and get out of here."

"Let me have him, Sarge. I'll take care of him," Hank pleaded.

"No, now, take him over to the cave and drop him in. It's five hundred feet to the bottom. That'll take care of him."

"Okay, you heard him, Reb. Let's go." Pushing Boyd with the tip of his bayonet, Hank forced him off the road and across an old field overgrown with greenbrier and red cedars. Two other soldiers followed along to see what would happen. They walked across the field with Hank prodding Boyd with his musket. In his free hand he held a long coil of thick hemp rope that had surely seen better days.

They soon came to a small grove of trees set on the slope of a shallow sink hole. A small, dark hole loomed before them.

"Go ahead, Reb, have a look in. This here's Grapevine Cave. Over five hundred feet to the bottom, like the Sarg said. Drop a rock in. Go ahead, drop a rock in and listen fer it to hit bottom," Hank said with an evil grin.

Boyd picked up a small rock and, with their muskets pointed at him, dropped it over the edge. For some time nothing happened, then, far below he heard it strike bottom and explode into tiny fragments.

"Here, boys, tie one end of this rope under his arms. We'll just let him down a ways," Hank directed, enjoying his new-found authority. They tied the rough rope under Boyd's arms and made a large knot in the middle of his back.

"We'll let you down real easy like, Reb," Hank bragged. "Maybe someone'll come by and hoist you back up out. Go on boys, put him in the hole."

Boyd struggled as the two men grasped his arms and began to drag him toward the dark, ominous hole. Oh, God, he thought, they're really going to do it! He fought the two men, clubbing them with his tied hands. Hank stepped forward and struck him across the head with his gun barrel. Boyd's knees buckled and he sagged in their arms.

They dropped him over the edge and he came to a lurching stop as the rope cut into his chest and armpits. The wound in his shoulder felt as if it were being ripped open. The three men held onto the rope and began to lower Boyd, hand over hand, down into the darkness. The opening, now receding above his head, grew smaller and he could hear the men grunting under the strain. The cool air inside the cave was refreshing at first, after the heat of the August day. The sensation was short-lived. Boyd looked down between his legs, but could see only blackness below.

Suddenly, his descent stopped and he rotated slowly at the end of the rope. Oh, no, he thought, they're going to leave me hanging here in the darkness like a ham in a smokehouse.

"Hey, Reb," a voice from above said. "How're you doin' down there? We've tied your rope to a tree so's you don't fall," he giggled. The other two men laughed.

Boyd reached up over his head with his bound hands and grasped the rope. If they left him here, he might be able to get his hands free and climb back up the rope. Thank God they hadn't tied his hands behind his back.

Hank and one of the other men lay on their stomachs on each side of the opening and, grasping the rope, slowly began to swing Boyd back and forth. He increased in speed until he was swinging wildly from side to side.

"How'd you like your ride, Reb," Hank taunted. "Not quite as smooth as that fancy horse of yours, is it, now?" Boyd continued to swing with pain shooting up his arms.

"Oh, Reb," Hank taunted in a singsong voice, "Guess what I've got here in my hand."

Boyd scissored his legs so that he turned to see the opening. Far above he could see Hank's head and shoulders outlined against the bright sky. Two other heads were outlined on the opposite side of the opening. In his hand Hank held a long narrow object.

"It's my bayonet, Reb. See here, its my bayonet. It's sharp, too. And guess what I'm goin' to do. Lookey here. I'm goin' to cut the rope. That way you can see just how deep this hole is. Then you can let us know, you hear," he laughed hysterically.

Ominous vibrations began to travel down the rope to him. The bayonet cut into the rope and the first strand let go. The rope sagged slightly.

Boyd held his breath. If they wanted him to beg for his life, they would be disappointed. No matter what happened, he wasn't going to beg. Besides, they were going to kill him no matter what he said.

Another strand broke and the rope sagged even more. He continued to swing like a stone on a string. He scissored his legs frantically trying to keep his eyes on the opening.

"Just one more strand, Reb," the voice from above taunted, "and then you're goin' to meet your maker." Laughter erupted from above.

Boyd hung limply from the rope, turning slowly as he swung. His arms and shoulders had gone numb; he could hardly feel them. Several minutes passed.

All was quiet above. He could hear water running somewhere far below and distinctly, he could hear the chirp and squeal of bats disturbed by his presence. Maybe Hank and the two men had changed their minds.

And then, suddenly, a hand holding the bayonet quickly appeared and neatly cut the final strand. Boyd hurled soundlessly into the darkness waiting below, his mind screaming desperately.

✵ ✵ ✵ ✵

Jones sat on his horse looking down at the farmhouse in the valley below. He could see a well-kept cabin, but the barn and outbuildings looked neglected. This was not the Taylor farm, he was sure. They lived farther up the valley and he was very careful not to disturb them. Charlie Taylor would hound him to the ends of the earth if Jones offended him, and taking his food and livestock would probably offend him, he had decided. Jones shuddered when he thought of those eyes and the way they bored into a man.

Well, this cabin didn't belong to Taylor. He looked again at the cabin as an old man gingerly walked toward one of the smaller outbuildings. It was built of hewn logs as the house was, but had a vent cover built into the roof. It was probably a smokehouse. The old man was only in the building for a few minutes, then emerged, wiping his mouth on the back of his grubby shirt sleeve. Even at this distance, Jones could see the old man's grinning face. Well, he thought, I'll bet I can guess what's in the smokehouse besides smoked meat.

Jones smiled to himself. Moonshine was in great demand among the soldiers—was now and always would be. He waited patiently for darkness to fall before approaching the cabin.

♪ ♪ ♪ ♪

Nellie followed along behind Mr. James as he walked swiftly back toward his opulent home along the pike. She carried his packages and truck as he walked empty handed along the street. Men on the street looked longingly at her, both white and black men, as she walked. The thin shift she wore moulded itself to her breasts and thighs. Mazel was right. She'd have to talk Mr. James into giving her another dress soon.

Nellie didn't mind the hard work she was required to do so much as the restrictions placed on her. Her pulse had quickened when she saw Boyd this morning, but she couldn't even stop and talk with him. Although she had considerable freedom to decide how to accomplish her work, she certainly had to get it done or be punished severely. She had been born here in the valley, but had never traveled more than ten miles from her birthplace. She felt like a hound chained to its kennel.

And that Lexus Saunders! She had latched on to Boyd's arm when she saw him watching her. Henry had told her that the Saunders' were going to have a party and all the young people would be there. Well, not all—only those from the upper crust. Nellie didn't mind not seeing the people, but she sure did miss hearing the music and seeing all the dancing. Maybe she could figure out a way to sneak close enough to hear it, but Mr. James would surely whip her if she were caught.

At last they reached the house and Nellie entered the kitchen to find Mazel trimming a ham that would be baked in the brick oven for Sunday's dinner.

"Mr. Joseph was here while y'all were gone," Mazel announced.

She looked closely at Nellie, examining her face for signs of reaction.

"What he want, now, Sister," Nellie asked apprehensively.

"He say they're goin' to have a meetin' soon to decide what to do."

"You know someone's agoin' to get themselves kilt, don't you? The masters will hang them for sure if they find out," Nellie exclaimed. "You know its again' the law for more than three slaves to meet anywhere at one time."

"Won't nobody find out, sister. We'll just slip out late at night an' meet in the church cellar like we did before."

"What you mean 'we', Mazel," Nellie asked sharply, concern etched in her voice.

"'We', Nellie, 'we,'" Mazel hissed. "I'm agoin' to be there with them. I went once before, an' I'm agoin' again."

"How'd you slip out without Mr. James an' me knowin'?"

"Mr. James was off on one of his trips an' you was up in your bed snorin' up a storm. Weren't nothin' to it," Mazel said proudly. She sliced the green, moldy rind off of the ham, carefully cutting away the fat and the dark-amber, glistening hide. The smell of the smoked ham was sharp with salt and grease. Mr. James' dog appeared at the open kitchen door, sat on his haunches, and licked his chops. Nellie could hear Jake the barn cat mewing from the path that led to the barn. The dog woofed softly at Mazel and she tossed him a piece of rind; he caught it deftly in his mouth, trotted into the yard, lay down on his belly, held the prize between his paws, and began to gnaw.

"Mazel," Nellie asked softly, "what's agoin' to happen? What's agoin' to happen if you get caught?"

"You know as well as I do, sister, but whatever comes, it's better than bein' trapped on this island of misery, waitin' hand and foot on a fat ole white man who only'd care if we weren't never born if his dinner weren't fixed on time."

"Oh, God, Mazel," Nellie whispered, her hands wringing in her lap, "why were we ever borned?"

♪ ♪ ♪ ♪

Boyd's body shook with cold as he lay on his back in the partial darkness. He opened his eyes, feeling the pain in his leg and shoulder. His head hurt badly and he couldn't remember where he was. The rope, coiled like a snake, had fallen on and around him.

He lay on his back and looked up at the disk of light above him. A ray of sunlight slanted down through the opening and motes of dust danced and moved upward slowly, like tiny balloons rising slowly into the air. Near the opening they sped up as they escaped through the hole.

He sat up slowly, taking stock of his body and limbs. Nothing seemed to be seriously hurt, but he ached all over from the fall and there was a large lump on the back of his head. He felt it carefully with his fingers. He rolled over cautiously to stand up, but suddenly his legs slid over the edge of the rock on which he rested and he began to slide. He grappled frantically for any purchase. Rocks and debris clattered down into the void below him. At the last second, he caught a stump-like rock and stopped his descent. The rock was wet and slimy beneath his hands, but he quickly scrambled back onto the center of the large rock upon which he had landed. Where was he anyway? He crouched in the center of the rock and allowed his eyes to adjust to the darkness.

He dropped to his knees and began to feel for the edge of the drop-off. He easily found it, almost sliding over its sloped edge again. His hands were numb from the rope that bound them together. How to free them? He worked the rope back and forth on his wrist, able to gain only a little freedom.

The dim light allowed him to see his immediate surroundings, but over five feet in any direction all was darkness, except for a patch of light striking the rocks far below. He groped carefully around to find that he was on the top of some sort of stone abutment rising high above the floor of the cave. As his eyes adjusted to the darkness, he could see that this was indeed the case. He sat atop a huge stalagmite. It had caught him before he fell all the way to the bottom of the cave and certain death.

At first he could discern no sound at all, but as he sat with his legs drawn up under his chin, he could hear running water again, far below and then, nearby, the plop, plop, plop of water drops falling, one after another, into water. He looked behind him, on his perch, to see the stone stump that had saved him from sliding over the edge. It was hollow at the top, like a rotting stump, and a small pool of water stood in the depression. He carefully placed his lips to the cool water and drank. Drops of water, falling from far above, struck him on the top of the head. At least, he thought, I'll not die of thirst. And then the idea came to him.

He soaked the rope that bound his hands in the precious water falling from above. By working the rope again on his wrists, he was able to slide a loop over his left hand. The rope loosened and fell from his red, raw wrists. He rubbed his hands to encourage the blood circulation.

He sat, later in the day, in the gloom of the cave and shivered. It would be dark soon, and if he didn't figure out how to get out he'd have to spend the night in the cave. That thought caused a wild panic to well up inside of him. He yelled, "Help! Help me," at the top of his lungs.

A sudden roar rose around him as thousands of bats, frightened by his panicked yelling, rose around him. They circled around and around him squealing shrilly, and beating the air, yet none touched him. He covered his head least they become entangled in his hair—he had heard they'd do that—but soon realized that he was in no danger.

Fascinated, Boyd watched as the bats spiralled upward, slicing through the shaft of light, and then poured through the hole and into the evening sky. The light flickered, as if from a huge, dying candle, until all the bats were gone.

Quiet returned to the cave and Boyd could again hear the drip of water into the stone stump and the tinkle of water below. He was lucky to be alive, but that was little consolation. What was it Charlie had said? You could go for weeks without food, but water was the most important. Okay, so he had water. He would surely die of starvation if he didn't get out soon. He didn't relish the thought of slowly starving to death in this hell-hole.

As he sat, the sunlight falling through the opening slowly changed angles, and then disappeared altogether. The outline of the hole became dimmer and dimmer, and finally total darkness surrounded him. He dozed off, but jerked awake suddenly and caused a cascade of rock and pebbles to tumble into the void below him. Afraid that he would roll over the edge in his sleep, he tied himself to the rock stump with the end of the rope, being careful to loop it under his arms, lest he slide over the side and hang himself. He slept fitfully through the night, waking periodically from the cold. Once, as he looked upward, he could see stars shining brightly through the hole.

After an eternity, light once again began to filter through the hole as dawn approached. The hole, so dark and sinister when he had first seen it from the outside, was now his only source of inspiration. It was his only connection to the outside world. How you see life really does depend on your point of view, he thought.

"Thank God," he said aloud. A twittering of bats sounded around him in protest of his presence, but they didn't fly.

Maybe they had a hard night, Boyd thought wryly. He hadn't heard them return.

What now? He wondered. Do I sit and wait for death? The wet air and gloom of the cave enveloped him.

5

Boyd stretched luxuriously in the sun as it streamed down on him. He lay on a slab of rock on the cave's floor but he had to move frequently to follow the spot of precious, life-giving heat. He turned so that the front of his body was perpendicular to the light. This position gave him the most benefit of the warmth. Just like a 'gator sunning itself in the sun, he thought, remembering his home in South Carolina and the heat of the summer there.

After spending the night on top of the stalagmite, he had easily slid down the rope to the bottom of the cave, leaving it tied securely to the rock stump above. He hurt all over, and the sun's heat relieved some of the stiffness and pain.

After warming himself, he began to look around his subterranean prison, taking stock of his situation. He could hear running water nearby, so he wouldn't have to climb back up the stalagmite to drink, but his stomach grumbled violently. How long had he been in here? Likely he hadn't been unconscious more than a few minutes after they dropped him in, so that meant he'd been here for less than a day.

Surprisingly, he could see better here at the bottom of the cave than at his former position above. The sunlight reflecting off the rocks cast an eerie glow around him.

He walked toward the sound of water, clambering over the rubble that had fallen from the roof ages ago. Surprisingly there were few bat droppings here. They must sleep farther back away from the light, he decided.

He found the water flowing down over the wall of the cave and into a huge pool at the base. A delicate ring of limestone formed the lip of the rim pool. There was a series of pools around this one, each with its glistening white limestone border. Boyd stood in awe. Stalagmites arose all around him like a frozen stone forest, reaching for the cave's roof. Extending down from above were matching stalactites, dripping water rich in dissolved limestone. Just beside him a column of limestone reached all the way to the top of the cave, joined halfway thousands of years before. The base was as thick as a large wagon. It must weigh a hundred tons, he thought.

He drank deeply from the pool, imagining that the knot of hunger in his gut was loosening, and then returned to the sunlight. He looked around carefully. A few sticks and twigs had fallen from the opening above. He began to pick them up and stack them on the flat rock. He felt in his pockets and found three wooden matches. Had they drawn dampness? Would they light? He decided to wait until almost dark before trying to strike them. He couldn't bear the thought of spending another night without a fire to keep him company.

He circled around his spot of light looking for more wood, finding several large sticks and two small logs, probably thrown into the cave by curious explorers. One slick, gray piece of wood showed in the dirt on the cave's floor and he began to sweep it free with his hands. As he worked, he realized that it was a bone. He worked faster, uncovering a long thigh bone, obviously human in origin. He looked around quickly and soon located bits and pieces of skeleton and finally a skull with pale, long-whiskered cave crickets crawling in and out of the eye sockets. He shivered uncontrollably.

So, he wasn't the first man to be thrown into the cave. Whoever he was, had been here for a long time. There was no sign of clothing or other possessions.

Boyd walked back to his pile of wood. The sun spot had moved on leaving his camp in semidarkness. He used his pocket knife to make some shavings from the driest piece of wood, found on a rock where the sun hit for a few minutes each day.

Boyd walked again to the rim pool and drank. He wasn't really thirsty, but it was something to do. Time passed slowly, and the light began to fade. As dusk approached, the bats awoke and made a noisy exit through the opening. He stacked a pile of rocks at the point the light last struck the cave's floor to mark the time of dusk, and returned apprehensively to his meager pile of wood. A mockingbird sang cheerfully above, its music falling lightly through the opening.

Would his match light? Was it too damp? With shaking hands he struck the first match on a rock and sighed with relief as it flared into life. He held the precious flame to the shavings and watched a satisfying yellow flame eat into the wood. It smoked badly, but the flame caught and soon he had a tiny, cheerful fire throwing eerie shadows on the walls and ceiling above.

Boyd held his hands over the fire, rubbing them together, and felt the heat lift his spirits. He fed the fire, careful not to squander his hoard of wood. Feeling cheered by the flames, he danced around the fire, whooping like an Indian, making monsters and goblins of his shadows on the wall.

Panting with effort, he sat down suddenly, somber again. How was he going to get out of here? Could he climb back up on the stalagmite and toss the rope up to the opening? Even if he had a grappling hook, it wasn't possible. The rope was too short. He had fallen from its end, hadn't he? No, that wouldn't work. And, there was no way to climb up the wall and out. The opening was in the center of the cave's ceiling. There was no way out that he could see.

He sat quietly, a film of sweat generated from his dance cooling on his skin. A sudden sadness swept over him. Feeling sorry for himself, he curled around the tiny flame and tried to sleep. Maybe tomorrow, when the light returned, he could think better and find a way out. He drifted off to a fitful sleep and dreamed of a beautiful girl, dressed in her best party dress, laughing with her hands extended. The hands were white as ivory, but the face was dark and dusky: Nellie's face.

♪ ♪ ♪ ♪

Boyd awoke, shivering in the dampness and cold—his stomach cramped in hunger. Sunlight filtered down through the opening and struck the cave's floor in the morning position. He was stiff again after the night spent on the hard rock. The fire had burned out leaving a pile of dark ash and some unburned sticks. He looked toward the opening above. How was he to get out? Was this cave to become his tomb with his bones joining those already on the floor?

He walked to the stalagmite and grasped the rope that trailed down from above, testing its firmness. With great effort he climbed back up the rock, bracing his feet against the wet, slippery side of the abutment. He stared at the opening from his new vantage point and yelled tentatively. The bats twittered sleepily. No answer. He'd already spent almost three days in the cave. Soon his strength would begin to fade, so he must act quickly if he was to escape.

He coiled the rope in his hand and tossed the loose end upward toward the opening. It fell short. He was afraid to untie it from the rock stump for fear he'd drop it. If that happened, he would be stuck on the top of the stalagmite. No, he'd have to find another way out.

Suddenly, he remembered what Charlie had said about the caves. Most of them opened onto the river more than three miles away. Maybe he could walk out. He quickly slid down the rope and began to explore in widening circles around the edge of the cave. He could feel air moving against his cheek, and followed the flow to an opening in the wall of rock. It was just wide enough for him to squeeze through, but was pitch dark within. Perhaps he could make a torch out of his shirt. He moved into the opening, testing the floor carefully with his toe before stepping. Even with a faint light coming from the main grotto, he could see nothing before him. If he got halfway out of the cave and his torch went out, he'd never be able to find his way. If he only had some candles... He stood quietly trying to decide what to do. He could hear, far along the narrow tunnel before him, the faint roar of water. A subterranean waterfall. No, this wasn't the way out. The opening in the ceiling, although beyond his reach, was his only viable opportunity.

Boyd returned to his rock, now in full sunlight and sat with his arms around his knees. He thought suddenly of Lexus. What would she think? He had missed the party. Let's see now, he thought, it would have been last night. He remembered her quick smile and the way her hair fell around her face. Her face, not Nellie's! He remembered the dream vividly. What did it mean? In his dream he had seen Lexus, but with Nellie's face.

He dozed briefly, warmed by the sun and awoke only a few minutes later thinking of the men who had put him there. Who was the white haired man? The soldiers were involved in buying stolen goods from him, that was clear. But where was he from? Was anyone else involved? He had ordered the men to kill him without so much as a blink. And Hank! He was delighted to see Boyd suffer. He had even taunted him as he cut through the rope. He had surely thought he had killed Boyd. When he got out of this stony prison, he'd hunt them down and...and what? Did he want to kill again? He could still hear that guard picketed at the river scream when Boyd shot him. He remembered the carnage of the brief, vicious battle. He pressed his hands over his ears to block out the dreadful sounds.

The sun's rays struck the rock at an angle just short of perpendicular. It was about noon, he guessed. He moved over into direct sun and lay flat on his back, covering his face and eyes with the crook of his arm. He soon dozed again in the sun's warmth.

Without warning a rock struck beside him and shattered into fragments, striking the side of his face and arm. He rolled quickly out of the sunlight, trying to understand what was happening. His mind raced, seeking solutions. Had the rock fallen from the ceiling? Was the cave collapsing? Had the men returned and thrown it at him?

Laughter floated down from above, and a child's voice said something he couldn't understand. There was more laughter and the light falling from above flickered as shadows fell across the bright opening. Another rock fell, shattering the silence, followed by a large stick.

"Hey," Boyd yelled, "is anyone there?" The laughter stopped, replaced by whispering.

"Hey, help me. I'm trapped in here. Help," Boyd yelled.

The bats began to twitter and a few fell from the ceiling and began to circle in the gloom.

"Hello," Boyd yelled again, "Help!"

A tiny head appeared in outline at the opening's edge, then another at its side.

"Help," Boyd yelled as loudly as he could.

The two heads disappeared suddenly as if jerked away by an invisible hand. All was silent.

Boyd looked hopefully at the opening but no one appeared. He yelled sporadically until his voice was almost gone, but to no avail. Whoever it was had gone. He sat again on his rock and watched the disc of sunlight march steadily toward the pile of marker rocks.

With great sadness he watched as the light reached the marker and began to fade. No, he screamed silently, don't go. Don't leave me here alone in the darkness again.

But the light faded, and with heavy heart Boyd drew his last match from his pocket and lit his fire. With his tiny pile of sticks, he sat hunched over the fire, feeding them in one by one, as a great depression settled upon him.

He awoke in the night to the far away rumble of thunder. The opening above flickered with light as the storm approached. He watched in fascination as the light flashed, first bright and then dimmer, above him. It cast weird shadows around him.

A stream of rain fell silently through the opening as the storm raged above. The falling water struck his tiny fire and, as it flickered out, he grabbed a glowing stick in an attempt to save the precious flame, but it was too late. It smoldered damply and was gone.

He sat in a miserable huddle, looking up at the opening, so far out of reach. The storm moved away after dumping tons of water on the valley. Suddenly he heard a deep rumble coming from the bowels of the cave. The rock beneath him vibrated ominously. An earthquake? No, it wasn't likely. A sudden rush of air swept past him, and then he knew what it was: water rushing through the tunnels like a flash flood.

He sprang quickly to his feet and rushed toward the stalagmite. In the darkness he could only feel his way, illuminated by an occasional, feeble flash of lightning. He stumbled blindly over the rubble on the floor, found the rope, climbed with the strength born of sheer panic to the top of the rock, and perched like a pigeon on a flagpole.

The flood roared through hidden tunnels, hurting Boyd's ears, but it did not reach the main chamber of the grotto. Tons of water poured through a neighboring chamber, rushing toward the river. Boyd sat atop the stalagmite shivering, and looked up at the opening. Stars shone brightly now, after the storm.

Despair claimed him again as he suddenly began to think of his father. They had fished together, lived together and had enjoyed the bittersweet relationship of the young and old. His father's sudden death had left him with a void that couldn't be filled. He lived, again, that dark, stormy night on the tossing ocean when his father was lost. He closed his eyes tightly and said a silent prayer, as much for himself as for his dead father.

As dawn broke, after a miserable night on the stalagmite, Boyd slid down the rope and confirmed that the water had not reached his grotto. He sat on the rock in the sunlight trying to think of a way to save himself.

"Hey, anyone down there?" a woman's voice yelled from above.

"Here, I'm down here," Boyd yelled back excitedly. Thank God, they've found me, he thought.

"How'd you get yourself into this fix, mister?" she asked. Her voice sounded weak and strangely hollow.

"Yank soldiers," Boyd replied. "They dropped me in here on the end of a rope. But that's a long story. Please help me get out of here, I'm starving."

"I don't have no rope. How're we goin' to get you up out of there?"

Boyd stood on the cave's floor with his hands on his hips and craned his neck looking up at the opening. The woman leaned cautiously over the opening and peered down at him.

Boyd climbed back up the rope to the top of the stalagmite where he was closer to the opening.

"I've got a piece of rope here, but its not long enough to reach you." He shook the coiled rope at the woman.

"There's a short piece of rope tied to a tree here," she announced. "It must be part of the rope you have."

"How long is it?" Boyd asked hopefully. "Maybe we can tie the two pieces together and make it long enough to reach."

"Its about fifteen feet long, but how are we goin' to get the parts tied together?" the woman asked.

Boyd thought. Nothing came to mind. They had two pieces of rope, but neither of the two pieces were long enough alone to reach him.

"I know," she said, "there's some grape vines up here. Maybe I can use them." She quickly cut a long section of vine and tied the rope to its end. By dangling them into the hole, Boyd finally caught the end of the rope. He quickly tied on his end and she pulled the vine and rope back up. Boyd clung to his end. The rope just reached up and out of the opening.

"Now, tie your end onto a tree," Boyd yelled.

"I can't, mister, the tree's too far away. What'll we do now? I don't think I can hold on to it tight enough for you to climb out. What if I dropped you?"

"See if you can find a log or branch long enough to reach across the opening. Then, you can tie the rope to the log."

The woman left the opening and after some time returned. She dragged a large tree branch behind her. She quickly tied the rope to the branch and slid it across the opening.

"I've got it, mister. You think you can climb out?"

"I'm gonna try., I'm not going to spend another night in here," he replied firmly.

He yanked on the rope, testing its firmness, and then, taking a deep breath, began to climb. He swung back and forth like the pendulum of a clock as he climbed hand over hand using his feet to give extra purchase on the rope. He stopped frequently to rest, and forced himself not to look down. As he neared the opening, he could see the woman looking down at him. Her encouraging smile gave him added strength.

He finally reached the heavy branch and grasped it with one free hand, then slipped the crook of his other arm over it. He hung there that way, regaining his strength, with his body and legs dangling into the void below him. The bright sunlight made him squint, but he had never seen anything so beautiful as the green countryside around them. The woman had drawn back from the opening, and now she rushed forward to help him. With her assistance, he scrambled out of the opening and fell on his back in the sunshine. He gasped for breath, drawing in great rushes of warm summer air.

Two children, a boy and a girl, sat on a limestone outcrop nearby, their eyes large and curious. Boyd was covered with mud and grime and his beard had grown, leaving a dark stubble on his chin and cheeks. His hair was matted to his head with a gray slime.

"You look funny, mister," the boy said. "You look just like a 'coon with its mask an' all." The girl squinted her eyes and giggled.

"Hesh now children," the woman said. "Give the soldier some of the food we brought fer him." The boy unwrapped cornbread and sliced meat from a cloth bundle he held. Boyd accepted the food gratefully and ate slowly, forcing himself not gulp it down too quickly.

As he ate, he related the events that lead him to be imprisoned in the cave.

"You were real lucky, mister," the woman exclaimed. "If you hadn't fell on that...what did you call it...a stalagmite, you'd have been killed for sure. They say its over five hundred feet deep from what I hear."

"Yes, I'm very lucky to be alive," Boyd said thoughtfully. He ate slowly and drank warm spring water from a glass jar the children gave him. His strength began to return and he stood and rubbed his sore arms and shoulder. The wound ached and throbbed, but didn't feel like he had done much damage.

Together they walked across the fields and rolling hills toward the woman's farmhouse, pausing frequently to allow him to rest. Her name was Arbuckle, and Boyd thanked her sincerely for coming to his aid. She said that the children had told her about hearing someone down in the cave, but had not said anything to her until bedtime. They weren't allowed to be over at the cave because of the danger of falling in, and were afraid of being punished. But Sissy, the little girl, was afraid he'd die in there and had finally confessed. Mrs. Arbuckle had waited until morning because of the storm before going to see if the story was true.

Boyd grinned at the children, and reaching in his pocket, gave each of them a nickel. They laughed and ran into the house to put their newly acquired wealth in their piggy banks. Boyd sat tiredly on the steps of the porch and soaked up the wonderful sunshine.

✒ ✒ ✒ ✒

Lexus sat at the breakfast table and pouted. She idly stirred the bacon and eggs on her china plate. She thought about the party the night before. It was a very successful get-together. All of the important people from town had been there. The orchestra was very good and everyone had complimented her on her new gown, and the few young men who had attended had given her a lot of attention.

But that Boyd Houston hadn't shown up. He was the main reason that she had talked her parents into throwing the party in the first place. How could he? He hadn't even sent a note making excuses for not coming.

George, the house boy, entered the dining room and stood quietly by her side waiting to serve her. He was tall and his dark hair was shot with gray. He stood rigidly with staring eyes. He didn't interfere, but waited for her instructions as he had been taught.

Lexus slammed her fork onto the china dish, making a clatter, and then rushed from the room. George began to clear the table, frowning after her. What she needs, he thought, is her fanny paddled.

"Mother," Lexus pouted, "Boyd didn't come to the party last night. What makes men do that, anyway?"

Mrs. Saunders sat primly on a ladder-back chair and cut a huge piece of white cloth into strips for bandages. A great pile of rags was arrayed around her. She looked up at her daughter and smiled knowingly.

"I don't know, dear, your daddy was the same way. I didn't know what he would do from one moment to the next. It takes a few years to get them to do what's important."

"Yes, but I did look forward to seeing him. He's so handsome, and all of the girls want him to talk to them. He's a hero, you know."

"I wouldn't put too much stock in this hero business, dear. What do you know about him? Where's his family from? You don't know anything about him."

"He told me he and his father were fishermen in Charleston, South Carolina before the war," Lexus replied brightly.

"A fisherman? What would everyone say if you start seein' a fisherman?" Mrs. Saunders said in a shocked voice.

"Oh Mother," Lexus frowned, "He's a hero and that's all I care about. All the girls are dyin' to meet him," she retorted.

"Yes dear," Mrs. Saunders replied as she began to cut another long strip of cloth, "but what about a house and money? How could he support you? You don't want to end up in some awful log cabin like that Taylor woman. She comes from a fine old family and look what's become of her—stuck up there on that terrible mountain with a bunch of kids and no one around for miles."

"Mother!" Lexus exclaimed, "it wouldn't be like that! Boyd's a fine man and he'd find a way to support us. Maybe he could work with Father."

"Well, we'll see," Mrs. Saunders said, knowing how to handle her daughter. Too much pressure now could only make her set her heels deeper. Better to wait and see how this mismatched romance proceeded before being too forceful.

✿ ✿ ✿ ✿

"I don't care what you say, Sister, I'm agoin' to help any way I can. Everyone say Mr. Lincoln'll sign the 'mancipation, but we're not agoin' to wait. What ifin he change his mind?" Mazel asked.

Nellie and Mazel stood at the kitchen table stringing green beans. They broke off the ends and removed the long, fibrous strings before tossing the bean pods into a large pot. Later, they'd spread them out on newspapers to dry in the sun. The beans, dried in their husks, would keep all winter and after being soaked in water would be cooked into "leather breeches" just as fresh green beans were.

"But Mazel, ifin you're caught Sheriff Brown'll hang you for sure, an' that'll just make things worse," Nellie argued. She used a small paring knife to cut rust spots off of a long bean pod before snapping it into small pieces and tossing it onto the growing pile in the pot.

"He ain't agoin' to ketch us. We're agoin' to break free an' the masters better watch out. I don't want to kill 'em like some, but if they get in my way, well then..." her voice trailed off as she stood staring out of the window into the back lot, her hands idle before her.

"Mazel, you must be very careful. I don't want y'all gettin caught."

"Why don't you come with me, Sister? We're meetin' agin in a couple o' days, an' you'd be a big help with you bein' able to read an' all. Besides, ifin we get freedom, you'll get it too. You should be doin' your part," Mazel said, looking intently into her sister's eyes.

Oh, what was going to happen to Mazel, Nellie wondered? She had changed so, and she was always angry. Even Mr. James had noticed and had told Mazel if she didn't give him some respect, he'd take her out to the barn and teach her a lesson she'd never forget. And, she had killed that Reb soldier in the cellar and it was all Nellie could do to keep Mazel from killing Mr. Boyd as he lay on his sick bed.

"I don't know, Mazel. I'll have to think about it. I want to be free as much as you do, but I just don't know."

Nellie took the pan full of bean stems and leaves around the kitchen house and tossed them onto the waste heap. She listened carefully as a mourning dove called its sad call from the brush behind the barn. The dove and its mate had made a nest there in the spring and had raised a brood of young. Would she ever have a mate? If so, would she be able to choose for herself, or would she be bred like a broodmare by some darkie of Mr. James' choosing? She liked children and would like to have a house full of them but she couldn't stand the thought of having them sold to another owner and never seeing them again.

And what about Mr. Boyd? She really liked him and would be proud to mate with him, but he wouldn't even look at her, her being a slave and all. She pressed her eyes tightly together, and envisioned Boyd's kind face. Oh, why, she moaned, had she been born a slave? Better to never have been born at all. She stepped back into the kitchen and looked at her sister, so much like a stranger now.

"I'll do it," she said quietly. "I'll go with you."

❧ ❧ ❧ ❧

Boyd sat on the porch of the farmhouse with the children on either side of him. He told them about his life as a fisherman, or as Michael called him—a sailor. He tried to explain the difference, but the boy only grinned at him.

Mrs. Arbuckle, a short, stout woman with a pretty smile, stood to one side, smiling at them. Her husband, she had explained to Boyd, was fighting in Lee's army. She worried constantly about him. The news from obscure battle sites in northern Virginia was good for the South, but not so good for individual soldiers. The casualty rate was very high. The children missed having a man around, and the farm, like most in the valley, was not kept well.

Boyd had eaten ravenously and had spent the day playing with the attention-starved children. Now, as the sun began to set, he thought about the Taylors and how they would be worried about his disappearance. In addition, he fretted about the loss of Charlie's horse. How would he ever repay him? The loss had been his fault, and he vowed to do all he could to find and recover it.

Later in the afternoon Boyd rode Mrs. Arbuckle's mule up the winding trail to Muddy Creek Mountain. Its bony back worked painfully on Boyd's behind as it trotted stiff-legged along the trail. He winced as the mule moved up the mountain. Mrs. Arbuckle had instructed him to turn the mule loose when he arrived.

"That ole mule'll find his way back home. Just turn him loose and he'll be back home in no time," she had said.

Boyd worried about the soldiers stealing it, but the woman had said they had left for Meadow Bridge and wouldn't be back for several days.

As he rode, he thought about his stay here in the valley. The soft, green mountains were beautiful and he liked the people—at least most of them, but he also missed the ocean. He'd thought that all he wanted was to get away from there after his father had died, but now he wasn't so sure.

The mule's ears perked up and Boyd could tell that it smelled something up ahead. He drew up and looked intently up the narrow, tree shaded lane.

A doe with twin fawns trotted into the road. The fawns were half grown and still had faded spots on their flanks. The mule snorted and shook its head. The doe raised her white flag and leaped gracefully into the brush along the road, her fawns following.

Boyd's nerves were about shot. He'd had a narrow escape from the Yank soldiers and was lucky to have survived his drop into the cave. The Yanks had also taken his parole papers. That meant that if he were caught again by the Yanks, he'd be treated as an enemy, or worse yet, shot as a spy. He'd have to be very careful.

On impulse, he decided to stop by the Cooper's cabin to check on them. It was only a couple of miles out of the way, and Boyd thought that maybe he'd get there about supper time.

He kicked his heels into the mule's flanks, trying to break the stiff-legged trot into a canter, but succeeded only in causing it to buck and flatten its ears against it head. No use trying to hurry a stubborn mule, he decided.

An hour later Boyd sat on the mule looking down at the Cooper's cabin from the ridge above. Something was wrong. It was nearing supper time and there was no smoke rising from the chimney. All was quiet. No one was out and about. Cautiously, Boyd rode the mule down the dusty road toward the cabin.

6

Boyd rode cautiously into the yard of the farmhouse. He tied the mule to the gate and walked quietly up onto the front porch. Standing to one side, he pushed the door open and peered inside. The interior of the house was dark with only a soft yellow light, as from a kerosene lantern, filtering from the kitchen door at the back of the parlor. He could hear splashing water and someone sobbing softly.

Walking cautiously across the darkened parlor, he could see that all of the curtains had been drawn. As he stepped into the kitchen, the scene before him was one he would remember forever.

Pop Cooper, once so lively and full of good spirits, lay dead on his back on the kitchen floor. He was naked to the waist, his pale skin lying in cadaverous folds. His eyes were closed and his hands had been crossed upon his chest.

Mrs. Cooper knelt at his side with a dish pan full of red water and a rag, washing his body. She worked with her good hand, the other curled before her on her stomach. She cried quietly as she worked, hardly looking at Boyd as he entered.

"He kilt him, Mr. Boyd. Pop weren't hurtin' nobody, but he kilt him just the same," she said quietly as she worked. "That man came in the night an' tried to steal our meat from the smokehouse. The dogs got to barkin' an' Pop took up his shotgun to go see what was goin' on. Sometimes a fox or a weasel comes in the barnyard an' the dogs start to barkin'.

107

"He walked out the back door an' whoever was there just shot him. He fell in the doorway and crawled back in the kitchen. He died on the floor there an' there weren't nothing I could do about it. Why do you reckon someone would kill an old man like him fer a few smoked hams an' a couple o' gallons of corn whiskey? What kind of a man would do that?"

"I don't know, Mrs. Cooper, but we'll find whoever did it, you can be sure," Boyd said softly. "How many were there?"

"I can't rightly say. I didn't go outside until after they'd gone. I only seen one man briefly through the winder. I was afraid he'd come in here an' kill me too," she said shamefacedly.

"Did you get a good look at him?"

"Well, no, not so good, but he had on a big felt hat. He was a tall man—right skinny. I ain't never seen him before."

"You can be sure we'll find him, Mrs. Cooper. We'll find him and then he'll pay for what he did," Boyd said with more conviction than he felt. With all the movement of men through the valley, it would be hard to find out who had killed Pop.

"I don't much care what happens to him. Pop's gone an' nothin' that happens will fetch him back. Just see that he don't do it to no one else," she said with her eyes riveted on Pop's lifeless face.

She moved around her dead husband on the floor, washing his body as she went. She took a tortoiseshell comb from her apron pocket and carefully combed his sparse hair, patting his cheek tenderly.

Boyd threw the bloody water out of the back door and refilled the pan.

"Mr. Boyd, help me get his breeches off an' I'll finish washin' him."

Together they pulled off his bloody pants and Mrs. Cooper modestly covered his lower body with a towel. Boyd built a fire in the iron cook stove and soon had warm water ready, then stood quietly aside as she continued her loving ritual.

"I'll be back in a few minutes, Mrs. Cooper, I'm going to ride up to the Taylors' and let them know what happened. Will you be all right while I'm gone?" he asked.

"Yes, I'm all right. I have to get him washed all proper like, an' get him dressed fer burrin'," she replied sadly. "I'll be right here with Pop. I ain't goin' nowheres."

Boyd kicked the reluctant mule into a rough gallop, moving up the mountain valley toward Charlie Taylor's place. The trip was uneventful, except for the occasional snort and buck of the mule. He arrived just as dusk was settling over the valley.

"Someone killed Pop Cooper," Boyd announced without prelude as Charlie and Kate greeted him on the porch.

"Slow down, Sonny," Charlie said with a pained look on his face. "Tell us what happened."

Boyd told them what he had found when he arrived at the Cooper farm. Charlie's face took on a dark look and Kate cried quietly, blowing her nose on a handkerchief she had fished out of her apron pocket. Boyd could hear the children playing in the creek below the house.

Kate took charge, telling Charlie what she needed from the house—all the cooked food she had on hand and a ham from the smokehouse.

They quickly rounded up the children, loaded them into the wagon along with the food, and set off down the valley. Boyd noticed a pistol stuck into Charlie's belt and couldn't help but see the heavy rifle that Jacob had been instructed to put in the back of the wagon.

The ride to the Cooper farm was solemn, and neither Kate nor Charlie had asked Boyd about his absence, or the appearance of the mule in place of Charlie's fine horse. The wagon rattled along the dirt track with the sounds of jingling harness, the plod of horses' hooves and the quiet sniffing of the children in the back. Colleen clung to Kate, as if afraid that something would take her mother from her.

At last they pulled up in front of the house and Kate stepped down and quickly entered. When Boyd started to follow, Charlie raised his hand to stop him.

"No, Boyd, not now. This is woman stuff—burrin' an' all. Kate'll take care of it. We have other work to do. Jacob, you an' Matt take the team on down the draft to the Hinkle place an' tell 'em what happened. Tell 'em to spread the word and to keep a lookout for a tall man with a big hat. The burrin' will most likely be tomorrow afternoon at the church. You be careful now, an' come right back here, you hear?" Charlie instructed.

"We'll be careful, Dad, an' we'll be right back," Jacob promised.

"Come on, Boyd, we've got us a casket to build an' a grave to dig," Charlie said as he walked toward the run-down barn. "An' then we've got some more killin' to do. I'd hoped we'd put all that past us, but it looks like we've got one more battle to fight." His face was a frightful dark mask.

⸕ ⸕ ⸕ ⸕

Nellie lay on her hard pallet under the eaves of the kitchen house, listening to the night sounds outside the tiny, open window. The katydids sang noisily in the trees along with the screech and whirr of other night creatures. Fall's just around the corner, she thought. When the katydids began to sing and the nights became still and cold, summer would soon be over. She pulled the tattered blanket up under her chin and closed her eyes.

They'd be having the meeting soon and she was nervous about attending, but if there was any way, she'd be free. As Mazel had said, it'd be better to be hanged dead than to spend the rest of her life like this.

And Mr. Boyd! Maybe after all this was over....but, no, that couldn't be. She pressed her knees tightly together, feeling the warmth spreading from her thighs upward through her with a searing heat. Why did that happen when she thought about the tall white man? What was this attraction she felt? But then there was that nagging doubt: he was a white man and she...well, she wasn't like him. Would he really want to be with her, to raise the family she wanted so badly? How could that ever work out? Their family, and especially their children, wouldn't fit in with the whites, and they wouldn't fit in with the blacks, either. But, maybe they could work it out. Maybe...

Footsteps outside her window broke her concentration. Who was there, she wondered? Henry? No, Henry went to bed at dark and awoke at daylight. It must be someone else. She sat up on one elbow and squinted into the night.

The moon, only half full, cast a ghostly glow over the side yard, making a mottled pattern of light and dark under the maple trees.

A man, tall with light hair, stepped across the yard and slid silently down the steps and into the cellar. In a few minutes, Mr. James left the back of the house and he, too, entered the cellar. A light was soon struck and filtered out from around the door. One wider shaft extended out of the air hole in the foundation.

What in tarnation? Mr. James met often with other men, but they always came to the front door, and always during the day.

Her curiosity piqued, Nellie crept soundlessly from the kitchen house and flattened herself on the ground near the air hole. She couldn't see inside, but she could hear clearly what was being said.

"You did what?" Mr. James rasped in a hoarse whisper. "I told you there'd be no foul play and that's what I meant. Now you've done it. Everyone in the county will be looking for you."

"Just hold on, Mr. James," the other man hissed in reply. "No one saw me, and with all the soldiers roaming around here, everyone'll think they did it."

"I tell you I don't like it. When I started buying food and such from you, I didn't mean to get involved in a killing."

"Don't go soft on me now. I don't aim to get caught and I'll do whatever I have to do to stay clear of the law. You just remember that if you get to thinking about talking."

Nellie twisted around trying to see the two men in the cellar, but all she could manage to see was the floor sills and the top of the cellar wall beyond.

"Why did you have to kill an old man, for only a few hams and all?" Mr. James asked quietly.

"It was him or me. The dogs started barking and the first thing I knew he was coming out of the back door with a shotgun in his hands. Like I said, it was him or me—so it was him," the man said with a shrug. "How was I supposed to know but what that smokehouse was full? Besides I got a couple of gallons of good whiskey. That's worth more than food in any man's army."

Nellie could hear the two men shuffling around in the cellar and then the creak of a wooden crate as someone sat down.

"Well," Mr. James said with a sigh, "what's done is done, but I don't want anyone else hurt. It'll attract too much attention."

"Just what I thought you'd say," the other man sneered. "When it comes to money I always know what you'll do."

"You just mind your own damned business," Mr. James retorted angrily.

The mysterious man said, "I'm going up to Falling Springs next month and raid the McMillion farm. I'll be gone 'til then, but will be back by the end of September. I got me some business to do over near Lexington. I hear old Mac has a full smokehouse and he raises some of the best horses around. The Sergeant said he could get rid of all of them we could get," he whispered. "And you're going with me."

"Oh no, I'm not," Mr. James recoiled in horror. "I don't do that kind of thing. Buying stolen goods from you is bad enough, but stealing is worse."

"You think you're not going, do you? Well think again. You're in this as deep as I am, and you're going and that's that."

"No, I won't go."

Nellie heard the ominous cocking of a pistol's hammer.

"See here, now," Mr. James blustered, "you can't..."

"Just you watch. You've got one other choice. Either you go with me, or I'm going to kill you, too. I don't need you now that I can sell directly to the Sarge. Make up your mind," he said matter of factly.

"Okay, Okay! Just put down that gun. But this is the only time. After that I'm going to clear out. My God, man you're crazy."

"Suit yourself, but this is a two man job and you'd better be there. If you leave me hanging out there by myself, you'll join that old man in the grove. You hear me?" he said threateningly.

"Yeah, Yeah, I hear you," Mr. James said with a trembling voice. He'd do what he had to, then clear out. No telling how many this madman had killed.

"You be at the bridge at Spring Creek at about midnight on the first day of October. I'll be back from my trip about then and that'll give him time to get his butchering done if the weather's cold enough. We'll take a good haul."

"I'll be there, if you insist," Mr. James said reluctantly.

Nellie shifted her weight and pressed closer to the opening. Suddenly, Mr. James' dog trotted around the corner of the house, and frightened by the strange form lying along the house in the moonlight, yelped, jumped sideways, then began barking furiously.

"What's that," the tall man hissed.

They rushed out of the cellar in time to see the dog barking over near the kitchen house. Casually, Mazel stepped from the doorway and threw a shoe at the dog, striking it broadside. The dog yelped and ran around the house with its tail tucked between its legs.

"Dumb mutt," Mazel grumbled just loud enough for the men to hear. "You hesh up now." She shuffled back to her bed in the corner of the kitchen.

The two men stood in the shadow of the house.

"You think she heard anything?" Mr. James whispered to the tall man.

"Does it matter? She's your girl, isn't she? Take care of it."

The tall man silently left the yard and Mr. James entered the house, slamming the door behind him. Nellie nervously crept inside from her hiding place behind the house and climbed up to her loft. She was lucky that they hadn't checked her bed. A missing slave at night was serious business.

"Sister, ifin you're goin' to go galivantin' 'round at night, you'd better be a little more careful. Mr. James'll skin your hide," Mazel giggled.

♪ ♪ ♪ ♪

Charlie pushed the long wooden plane over the edge of an oak board, making a curl of wood shaving. The floor at his feet was littered with them. He bent down and sighted along the board, clamped in a wooden vise, checking to see if it was plumb and square.

"I like workin' with good wood, Boyd, but the thing I hate worse than anything is makin' coffins," Charlie said wearily. "Seems like there's no end to the fightin' an' sufferin'."

"I'm about finished with the lid, Charlie, except for that final board. Let's see if it'll fit now."

Together they fit the last board in place and nailed it down. Then, with each man on an end, they carried the coffin into the house, placing it on the floor of the kitchen. Kate and Mrs. Cooper stood silently by as the men carefully lifted Pop and put him in the raw, new box. Mrs. Cooper lifted Pop's head gently and placed it on a small silk pillow, then arranged his hands over the vest of his dark suit and nodded at the two men.

They carried the coffin, now heavy with its lifeless burden, into the parlor and set it carefully on a pair of old, well used sawhorses. The room was dark now in the hours before sunup. Even after it became light, the room would be kept dark by covering the windows with heavy cloth.

Mrs. Cooper took up her vigil beside her dead husband. Sitting there on a straight-backed chair, she looked small and somehow shrunken as if something vital inside her had been removed. She rocked gently from side to side with her hands folded in her lap and hummed an ancient hymn.

Boyd and Charlie stepped onto the porch and stood briefly in the darkness without speaking. Finally Charlie broke the stillness.

"We better get up on the knoll and see how Mr. Hinkle and the boys are gettin' on with the diggin.' I reckon they could use a mite of help 'bout now."

"It's good of him to come to help," Boyd commented.

"That's the way it is here," Charlie nodded toward the dark, unseen hills around them. "Folk herebouts have known each other all their lives. In times of need, they just naturally pitch in. Come daybreak they'll come from all over fer the funeral. Word'll spread fast. Too bad we can't have a proper wake an' all, but in this summer heat we best get him in the ground soon as possible. Folk'll understand. Light'll be here in 'bout two-three hours an' that's all the time we'll have fer a wake."

Together they walked across the valley and up on the knoll. A lantern hung from the limb of a giant red oak, casting an eerie circle of light. Beneath, Mr. Hinkle and Jacob took turns digging and shoveling soil from the narrow grave. It would be finished soon if they didn't hit rock. Shovelful after shovelful of orange-red clay was added to the pile alongside the opening. Matt lay curled up on a coat near the base of the tree, sound asleep. Charlie covered him with his jacket.

The three men stood silently by, watching as Jacob worked in the hole, now shoulder deep. A screech owl warbled in the still darkness.

"My grandma used to say that if you heard a screech owl in the night, it meant that someone was goin' to die," Mr. Hinkle commented. "I reckon it must be true."

Morning light had come when the men loaded the coffin onto the back of the wagon and a solemn group moved off down the valley toward the church. Neighbors from the surrounding hills and valleys had arrived throughout the morning.

Solemnly they moved down the valley, accompanied by the creak and groan of the wagons. The women, dressed in dark clothing, sat on the wagons talking quietly among themselves. The men rode silently, grim looks of anger and frustration on their faces. Boyd rode the mule beside the wagon carrying Pop's body.

Would the war ever end? Would this once peaceful mountain return to what it had been before? How would the mountain people react to this senseless murder? Boyd knew how he felt about it. He had only known Pop briefly, but he liked what he had seen. What would Mrs. Cooper do now that her husband was gone? Together they had lived a good life, but now that he was gone, how could she survive?

The grim procession stopped in front of the small mountain church that had been built just off the road, among the ancient oak and chestnut trees. The one-room building sat on a foundation of cut limestone blocks. The tin-covered roof rose sharply to a peak with a belfry perched on the front; the bell inside tolled mournfully.

Six men, dressed in their best dark clothing, carried the coffin into the church, and the congregation entered behind. The coffin was placed before the altar and the congregation walked slowly, in turn, to pay their last respects to Pop Cooper. Mom Cooper, last to step forward to say good-bye to Pop, patted his hand and looked sadly at his peaceful face. She stood aside as two men placed the lid on the coffin, then took her seat on the front bench, flanked by her friends.

The funeral service was plain and brief. A choir of six stern-looking women and men sang with accompaniment from a tinny piano, played by a teenaged girl:

"It is finished!" Man of Sorrows!
From Thy Cross our frailty borrows,
Strength to bear and conquer thus.
Still to Thee, whose love unbounded

Sorrow's depths for us has sounded,
Perfected by conflicts sore.

The preacher, a tall, thin man with a permanent scowl and slicked-down black hair, began the funeral sermon amid the sounds of sorrow from the congregation.

"Jesus said, 'I am the resurrection, and the life; he that believeth in Me, though he were dead, yet shall he live; and whosoever liveth and believeth in Me shall never die,'" the preacher quoted from the Methodist Order For The Burial Of The Dead. He stood beside the open coffin reading from the pages of the worn Hymnal held in his left hand, his wrinkled face reflecting his own personal sorrow. "The eternal God is thy refuge, and underneath are the everlasting arms."

The Preacher completed the passage and then asked the congregation to bow their heads in prayer. With his head canted downward, Boyd looked at Mrs. Cooper. She seemed to have shrunk even more since last night. Her shoulders shook as she cried quietly; a straight, dignified, elderly woman held Mom's shoulders in a firm embrace with one arm, frowning at the casket.

"Almighty God, Fount of all life, Thou art our refuge and strength," the preacher intoned, "Thou art our help in trouble. Enable us, we pray Thee, to put our trust in Thee, that we may obtain comfort, and find grace to help in this and every time of need; through Jesus Christ our Lord. Amen."

The congregation joined in prayer: "Our Father, who art in Heaven..."

Boyd sat rigidly on the uncomfortable church bench, slick from generations of use, and listened passively, his thoughts wandering to his father's funeral at sea, so different from this. The service continued with a long prayer by an elderly member of the congregation who told of Pop's life and implored the Lord to care for his soul.

Charlie sat stiffly, looking with unseeing eyes at the cross on the wall over the altar; Kate wept quietly by his side. Her slender hand gripped Charlie's arm. The children fidgeted and squirmed. Tears ran in a steady stream from Charlie's eyes, but no sound came from him. The tears fell from his dark cheeks and the lapel of his dark coat. Pat, pat, pat! This sound, the fall of compassionate tears upon a strong man's lapel, would follow Boyd forever. Never, even in raging battle, would the strength and bravery of any man be better demonstrated.

The preacher's message to Mrs. Cooper and the attentive congregation was brief and simple: Yes, Pop Cooper was a sinner. He liked the taste of corn whiskey and sometimes missed Sunday church, but all could be assured that he had gone to a better place. He then read again from the New Testament: "Let not your heart be troubled; ye who believe in God, believe also in Me. In My Father's house are many mansions: if it were not so, I would have told you. I go to prepare a place for you. And if I go and prepare a place for you, I will come again, and receive you unto Myself; that where I am, there ye may be also. I am the Way, the truth, and the life..."

The preacher, with head bowed, then returned to his chair behind the pulpit as the choir again rose to sing:

There's a land that is fairer than day,
And by faith we can see it afar,
For the Father waits over the way,
To prepare us for a dwelling place there.

In the sweet by and by,
We shall meet on that beautiful shore,
In the sweet by and by,
We shall meet on that beautiful shore.

Their voices affirmed, strong and true, their belief that God had made a place for them in the hereafter. The sound rose from the small frame church and echoed from the ancient, green mountains, a testimony to the faith of a caring people, for all to hear.

♪ ♪ ♪ ♪

That evening, as the 'poor wills called from the meadow, Pop Cooper was lowered into the open grave on the knoll behind the house and covered with the orange-red soil.

♪ ♪ ♪ ♪

Boyd and the Taylor family sat at the kitchen table after the funeral and talked in subdued tones.

"And that's how I finally got out of the cave," Boyd concluded. "If those kids hadn't gone to the cave to play, I'd still be down in there."

"Do you think the tall blond man is the same one who killed Pop?" Charlie asked.

"Most likely, don't you think so? He was selling supplies and such to the Yanks, so he's probably stealing them from the farms here and in the valley. Have you heard of other folks being robbed?"

"Well, yes, but you can't tell if its by the soldiers or civilians. Mr. Creigh down to town caught a Yank goin' through his house an' shot him dead. The Yanks have him in prison and aim to shoot 'im if the law can't get him off. They even stole Reverend McElhenney's horse! Time was when a man could leave his house and stock fer days an' they'd be just where he left them when he got back. It ain't like that no more. There ain't nothing I hate more than a damned thief!" Charlie said forcefully.

"Even if we'd talk to the sheriff about this feller, most likely he'd just tell us he can't do anything about it because we don't have any proof. Mrs. Cooper said she didn't get a good enough look at him to be sure," Boyd added with a troubled look on his face.

Kate set mug of hot coffee before the men, then turned to put the children down for the night.

"I'm sorry that they took your horse, Charlie. I'll repay you somehow. It may take me some time, but you'll be repaid."

"Now, don't you go worrin' about that, Sonny. It weren't your fault.

But that's not your biggest problem. You lost your parole papers, you know. If the Yanks find you without 'em, they'll either kill you, or put you in prison. You'll have to be mighty careful from here on out. If Crook returns to Lewisburg, we may be able to get him to give you new papers, especially since it must have been his men who stole them, but you can't depend on it"

Just as they were getting ready to turn in for the night, Charlie heard a horse approaching the cabin. He put his hand on Boyd's shoulder and whispered, "Get out the back and watch from the yard while I see who it is." He thrust a pistol into Boyd's hand as he went out the back door.

Charlie stepped onto the front porch with a pistol in his hand and greeted the rider. He was an older man with rumpled clothes and a grizzly beard. Dark circles under his eyes made him look even older than he was.

"Howdy. Looks like you folks are expectin' trouble," he said, still sitting on his horse.

"Man can't be too careful these days," Charlie answered. "What can we do for you?"

"Just aheadin' over the mountain on my way to Charleston. Plan to hit the Greenbrier and foller it on down to the New River. That'll take me on down to Charleston."

"Yeah, I know," Charlie replied without enthusiasm.

"I'm lookin' fer a man named Houston. You seen him?" the weary traveler asked.

"All depends on what you want him fer," Charlie said.

"I'm Boyd Houston," Boyd said stepping from the darkness. "What do you want with me?"

The traveller looked him up and down, a smirk making his face ugly.

"I don't hold none with white folk messin' with darkies, but it seems you made quite a mark on one of 'em. Nice lookin' nigra, she was. Asked me to give you this here note. Said you'd give me some money if I did." He held a bundle of paper in his dirty hand, resting his wrist on the saddle horn.

"How much?" Boyd asked.

"Well now, it ort to be worth five dollars. She said it was pretty important."

Boyd dug into his pants pocket and found five dollars—about all he had left. The traveller tossed him the bundle of brown paper. It was tied up with a piece of twine.

"You read this?" Boyd asked.

"Naw. I don't read so good. Besides, what could a darkie have to say that would interest me?" He turned his horse and rode off into the darkness. Charlie gave Boyd a strange look.

The note, written in childlike block letters, told him what Nellie had heard in Mr. James' cellar and about the raid set for the first day of October.

♪ ♪ ♪ ♪

"You be careful, now, Boyd. The Yanks'll probably be over at Meadow Bridge an' you shouldn't have no trouble. But, still..." Charlie said to Boyd a few days later. Boyd sat on the mule as he prepared to ride into town.

"I will, Charlie. I just want to ask a few questions to see if anyone knows who this man who killed Pop could be. Maybe I'll get to talk to the sheriff to see if he's made any progress on the murder, and I want to see Mrs. Arbuckle and return the mule. I know that it would go on home if I turned it loose, but what if the Yanks took it too? She needs the mule to work the farm."

"I reckon you're right. You goin' to tell the Sheriff about the raid on the McMillion farm?"

"No. I thought we'd take care of that little problem ourselves. We'll go up to Falling Spring and wait for those thieves. We'll take care of it," Boyd replied.

"Yeah, that's my way of thinkin' too. Besides if the sheriff found out about that darkie sending you that letter, she'd be in a lot of trouble," Charlie squinted at Boyd. "You best tread careful there, Sonny. Folk don't take kindly to a feller messin' with their nigras. Mr. James'll raise a hell of a stink if he thinks you're foolin' 'round with his property."

"You don't have to tell me, Charlie. I grew up in Charleston, South Carolina where almost everyone had slaves. I know how people feel about it."

"Just so's you know what you're doin'," Charlie said. "You're a growed man."

"Yeah, I guess I am."

Late that afternoon, Boyd rode across the covered bridge over Milligan Creek and on toward town. He waved at the miller where he worked the water flume as it flowed down the race. He remembered the man's face from Pop's funeral. The mule trotted briskly, knowing it was on the way home. Boyd was enjoying the ride. The leaves were just beginning to turn colors and the air was crisp and clear. Blue jays squawked in the trees along the road and tawny chipmunks with black stripes down their backs raced across the road in front of him, holding their tails up stiffly behind them.

He watched carefully for soldiers. He would be more careful this time and not let them get the upper hand, he resolved. If the Sergeant and his men caught him, he wouldn't get off as lucky as he had before. They'd shoot him on the spot. Boyd cursed under his breath. They'd taken him like a sheep to slaughter and only dumb luck had saved him.

The mule trotted faster as they neared town, twitching its ears back and forth. Suddenly, it stopped dead in its tracks and raised its nose to test the wind. A minnie ball whipped past Boyd's head and struck a tree beside the road. The roar of a musket followed. He sprang from the mule, slapped it on the rump, and dove into the brush along the road. The mule bolted and galloped toward home.

At least they wouldn't catch and take it like they had Charlie's horse, he thought. He didn't take time to look back or to try to locate the shooter. He ran like hell toward town; they couldn't very well shoot him in front of everyone if he could only make it that far.

He ran in a crouch with his head down, dodging trees and jumping over windfalls. He paused briefly on a rise and, looking back, could see blue-coated soldiers running through the trees toward him. It was the Yanks after all. If they caught him it would be all over. He ducked over the ridge as a volley of shots rang out behind him. Leaves and twigs, cut by the minnie balls, showered down on him as he ran. It was probably no more than a mile to town, but he wasn't sure of exactly where he was. He moved in an easterly direction and hoped for the best.

He could hear the men behind him yelling and shouting to each other although he couldn't understand what they were saying. They crashed noisily through the brush. Boyd ran. He had Charlie's pistol in his belt, but it was almost useless against soldiers with muskets. His only chance was to reach town and lose them among the buildings.

He leaped across a brook and ran up another small hill. A flock of quail exploded from the brush and grass around him, causing his heart to leap in his throat. His breath came in great, rasping gulps. He'd have to rest soon. Finally, he came to a huge boulder in a small valley. He dropped behind it, out of sight. Maybe they'd pass him in their rush. He remained as still and quiet as possible, trying to remember what Charlie had taught him. A bullet struck the rock beside his head throwing up shards of rock that struck him on the side of the face. He leapt to his feet and crashed through the brush, running as fast as he could.

Stumbling badly, his legs about gone, Boyd ran down a long hill and into town. It was almost dark and no one was in sight. A large dog barked viciously at him from the yard of a big brick house as he ran down the street. The soldiers broke from the woods behind him and ran in pursuit. Another bullet tugged at his shirt as he turned a corner. He dodged between two buildings that faced the main street and ran silently down the alley. He stepped around the back corner of the building and pressed himself against the wall. He tried futilely to control his breathing, fearful that they could hear him gulping for air.

The soldiers ran past the alley and continued down the street. He had lost them—at least for now. He needed somewhere to hide. He didn't want to kill them, even if he could. So he must find a place to hide until they left.

He crept cautiously along the alley and crossed the main, north-south highway, moving from house to house up a narrow, steep street.

Suddenly he saw a blue-coated soldier searching along the main street behind him. He frantically looked for a place to hide. A tall building loomed beside the street: a church. He ran down a set of stairs leading to the cellar and felt for the doorknob. It turned under his hand and he quickly pushed the door open and stepped inside, quietly closing the door behind him. There was a rustling of clothing in the pitch dark room and a whisper. Someone was in there with him.

"Who's there?" Boyd demanded.

"Take it easy Mister. Ain't nobody here but us darkies," an elderly voice said from the dark room.

"What are you doing in here," Boyd asked. He could smell candle smoke and unwashed bodies in the tightly closed space.

"We ain't hurtin' nothin," the voice said.

Boyd got the feeling that there were several people in the cellar as he stood quietly in the dark trying to decide what to do. He didn't want to go back outside—the Yanks would kill him for sure. They'd search the town from one end to the other to get him.

A familiar voice spoke from the darkness. "Is that you Mr. Boyd? What you doin' here? I thought you were up on the mountain with Mr. Taylor. We ain't doin' nothin' wrong," she said with a rough whisper. It was Nellie.

"Why don't you strike a light? I won't hurt you," Boyd replied.

There was guarded whispering and shuffling in the back of the room as someone fumbled for a light. Finally a match was struck and a single candle lit. As his eyes adjusted to the light, Boyd could see six nigras including Nellie and Mazel seated around a crude table. There were two rifles and several pistols on the table between them.

"What's going on here?" Boyd asked with a shocked voice. An old black man, sitting at the head of the table facing him, pointed a pistol at Boyd's chest. The sound of the hammer being cocked was frightening in the confined room. There was no chance that he could miss.

"Now see here," Boyd blustered, "you put down that gun. You're in bad enough trouble having weapons, let alone if you kill someone."

"I don't aim to kill you, mister, but we do have a problem, now don't we? We can't let you go, you seein' these guns an' all."

They sat around the table as if frozen in place. No one spoke. Nellie sat quietly, wringing her hands on the table before her. Boyd shuffled his feet.

" We goin' to have to kill him," Mazel said curtly. "We don't have no choice. Besides, he's a Reb."

"No!" Nellie said suddenly, more loudly than she had intended. "We're not goin' to kill anyone. You won't tell will you, Mr. Boyd?"

"I don't know what you're up to, but I can't let you butcher your masters in their sleep," Boyd said thoughtfully.

"We ain't goin' to do no such thing," Nellie said forcefully. "We ain't a bunch of animals!"

"All right, now," the old man said, "we'll tie him up 'til we can figer out what to do with him." Two of the other men were instructed to tie and gag him using strips of Nellie's and Mazel's skirts. They found the pistol in his belt and added it to those on the table.

"What are you going to do with those guns?" Boyd asked as he was being bound.

The old man looked at him and grinned. "Why, Mr. Boyd, that's 'bout as plain as mud on a hog's snout. We're goin' to take back our honor...and our freedom."

♪ ♪ ♪ ♪

Boyd sat propped up in the corner of the cellar room. His hands were bound tightly with brightly colored strips of cloth, and a gag covered his mouth. He looked at the group of black men and women sitting around the table as they leaned forward, with their heads together, whispering urgently to each other. Nellie cast a fearful look at Boyd. Smiling tentatively at him, she turned back to the conversation.

Mr. Joseph, as they called him, led the discussion. He was tall and terribly thin with swept-back, oiled hair. He was neat and clean-shaven with a pencil thin moustache. It was difficult for Boyd to guess his age, but he seemed quite old. Two of the other men were young, probably in their early twenties, and one was middle-aged. All three were dressed in rough, worn clothing, heavily patched. One of the three men wore work shoes. The other two were barefoot.

Boyd struggled with the bindings on his wrists and legs, but could not feel any give in them. He was uncomfortable and his limbs were beginning to go numb. The group talked on.

Finally, Mr. Joseph came over to Boyd and slid the gag down over his chin. He looked deeply into his eyes.

"Miss Nellie say that you're to be trusted. She say that if you give your word you'll keep it. Is that true?"

"Well, yes, if I give my word I'll keep it." He put heavy emphasis on the word "if."

"If we let you go free, what'll you do?"

"I don't know. Like I said before, I can't let you go killing folks. I sympathize with your cause, but I don't hold with killing."

Mr. Joseph searched Boyd's face carefully. "With all due respect,

Mr. Boyd, you don't know the first damn thing about our cause. You don't have no idee what it's like to be another man's slave, and if it don't happen to you firsthand, don't even try to understand. But that ain't the point. If we swear not to hurt nobody, lessin we're attacked, an' we let you go, will you give your word not to tell nobody?"

Boyd hesitated. A troubled look crossed his face.

"We just as well go on an' slit his throat. First thing we let him go, he'll be screaming at the top of his lungs like a stuck hog," Mazel said with emotion. "Ain't no other way to hannel it, that's what I say." The men noisily agreed.

Nellie sat very still, looking at Boyd. What should she do? She was sure she could trust her life to Boyd and she would do so without hesitation, but did she have the right to risk the lives of her friends? She wouldn't stand for his death, but what solution was there?

Mr. Joseph asked Boyd, "What harm do you think there is if you let us go? We'll swear that we won't hurt nobody. All we want to do is to go away from here. We don't plan to go 'round slittin' folk's throats. We just want to go free."

"What guarantee do I have that you'll do what you say? Mazel there, was quick to suggest just that remedy to my intrusion," Boyd questioned, pointing his chin at her.

"Mr. Boyd, I reckon I'm gettin' on to seventy-five year old. My folks were slaves, an' their folks before them were slaves. I was born a slave an' my children are slaves. All my life I been treated just like a ole work horse. I been worked from daylight to dark, bred like a stud-horse to women I didn't even know, taken from my momma when I was just a boy, an' ain't had no family but them I worked with. All I want is to spend the last o' my days a free man. To make my own decisions an' to stand up as tall as the next man. That's all I want.

"They say that we come from Aferka. We ain't 'lowed to have our own religion, an' we don't have no history or customs of our own.

The owners don't 'low us to meet together, more 'in three at a time. Tell me, Mr. Boyd. If you was a slave like me, what would you do?"

Boyd looked thoughtfully at the six intense people, crouched in the dark cellar of the church. He looked at Mr. Joseph who stood patiently, looking down at him. Nellie smiled at him, Mazel frowned, causing deep creases to line her forehead, and the three other men looked blankly at the scene before them. One of the men cleared his throat noisily and a horse and buggy rattled by on the street outside.

"I don't know how to answer your questions. You're right. I don't know anything much about your...situation," Boyd said carefully. "Mr. Joseph, I tend to believe you, but what about the others? What guarantee do I have that they'll do what you say?"

"I don't ast them to do what I say. I ast them to do what they say they'll do. If they give their word, Mr. Boyd, it's as good as yourn."

"All right. If you swear not to hurt anyone, I won't tell anyone about this meeting. But if you do other than what you say, I'll help the sheriff hunt you down," Boyd said with conviction.

"Thank you, Mr. Boyd, thank you. Everything will be all right. Just you wait an' see." Mr. Joseph laughed and bobbed his head as he reverted back to his role as the obedient servant, averting his eyes from Boyd's. The tension in the room melted like butter on a hot summer day.

Mr. Joseph untied Boyd and helped him up, held him gently by one arm, dusting off the seat of his pants and straightening his clothing. Boyd nodded at him and the others in the room and stepped outside. The hard- packed, dirt street was deserted. A whisper of sound told him that Nellie had followed him into the dark night. She touched his hand and smiled up at his face, as she pressed his pistol into his palm.

"Thank you Mr. Boyd." she whispered as her lips lightly brushed his neck, then turned and was gone.

Boyd looked up at the clear, starry sky and breathed deeply. He could still smell the clean, soapy smell of her. How could he feel this way? This relationship couldn't be; he could not allow it.

He traversed the steep street, darting from shadow to shadow. He had lost track of time, but he must have been in the church cellar for an hour or so. At this time of year, darkness fell at about eight o'clock, so it must be nine o'clock or later. Many of the houses along the street were dark, the residents having gone to bed. Here and there he saw a light in a window. Where should he go now?

Turning down a side street Boyd promptly arrived on the main pike. A large brick house sat to his left with a light in the front window. He could see someone in the front room and laughter drifted out through the open windows on the still air. It was Lexus. He walked closer. Maybe he could talk to her, and perhaps she could help him. He knocked on the front door, looking over his shoulder for Yankee soldiers.

Light footsteps approached in the foyer inside, and she opened the door. Her eyes became large and she took a step backward as she recognized him; as if he were a thief.

"Oh, what're you doing here? I thought maybe you'd left the country or something," she said with a pout forming on her red lips.

"I guess you haven't heard what happened." he began.

"No, I haven't heard anything about you," she said shortly.

"Well, I couldn't make your party. Maybe I could come the next time. But I need to talk to you now."

Lexus pushed him gently onto the porch and closed the door behind her.

"I need your help, Lexus. The soldiers are looking for me and I don't have anywhere to go."

"I'm real sorry you're having trouble, but there's nothing I can do to help. Everyone in town knows they're looking for you. The Yankees said that you'd violated your parole and they said you were a spy. Daddy said that I'm not to see you again."

She looked at Boyd, her feet figeting as she sneaked an occasional, nervous look down the pike toward the center of town.

"If they catch you here they'll burn our house like they did poor old Mrs. Welch's when that sniper shot one of their soldiers," she said fretfully.

As Lexus opened the door to re-enter the house, Boyd heard a young, male voice calling to her from inside. "Lexus, who's there," the voice said. "Come back inside. I have another story to tell you." Over her shoulder, Boyd caught a glimpse of a tall, handsome young man looking toward the doorway, trying to see who was on the dark porch.

"I have to go in now," Lexus said nervously. "I hope you don't get caught. You be careful, now, you hear?"

What more was there to say? Boyd excused himself awkwardly and walked away from the house. He again began to move cautiously through town. He'd head west and walk back up on Muddy Creek Mountain, he decided suddenly, but he couldn't stay with the Taylors. The soldiers would burn their cabin and revoke Charlie's parole if they found him there. It would be best, he decided, to leave the valley as soon as he could. Maybe he could find a place to stay on the mountain for a few days before moving on. But, he had a meeting with that tall blond man on the first day of October.

He was walking along, deep in thought, when a shout arose behind him. A Yankee soldier yelled to his companions.

"There he is. He's heading downtown. Come on."

✧   ✧   ✧   ✧

Nellie listened to the soldiers yelling to each other as they searched for Mr. Boyd in the center of town. She stood outside of the church and listened intently. What could she do to help him? If they caught him he would be shot for sure. She moved cautiously along the street toward the soldiers, crossing the pike and following the wagon road that led out of town to the north. Wounded animals always ran down hill, or so she had heard. Maybe he was hiding in the bottom of the huge sink that formed much of the town. She must not be caught. If she was, there would be hell to pay. Mr. James would beat her.

She reached the bottom of the sink and stood quietly listening to the sounds around her. Before her was the spring house. It was a small rectangular limestone shelter. It glowed dully in the moonlight. From it ran a stream of water that flowed across the bottom of the sink and disappeared into an opening two hundred yards away.

She listened intently and just as she had decided to move on, rustling leaves behind the spring house alerted her to someone's presence. Was it a soldier, waiting as she was, for Mr. Boyd? Or was it Mr. Boyd himself? She moved closer.

"Mr. Boyd. Is 'at you," Nelly chanced a whisper. No answer. She whispered again, louder this time, "Mr. Boyd. Is 'at you?"

"Nellie?" Boyd answered. "What in the world are you doing here? If the soldiers catch you they'll punish you badly."

"You got to get out of here, Mr. Boyd," Nellie whispered as she moved to his side. "They's soldiers everywhere. They's got all the roads blocked. You'll get caught if you try to get out of town this way."

"I don't know what to do, Nellie," Boyd confessed. "I'm really getting tired of running."

"I'll help you. Come on," she urged as she tugged at his sleeve.

"Where are you taking me?"

"Shush, now. You foller me and don't talk," she cautioned. They followed the small stream past the jailhouse set on the side of the sink above them, staying in the shadows as they moved. Within minutes, they had crossed the sink and stood at the crevice into which the water flowed.

"The water goes into this hole and into the cave," Nellie instructed quietly. "This whole valley has caves underneath. You can squeeze into the hole and then foller the cave 'til you come out down by the river. They's hunderts of miles of caves here."

"I'm not going in there, Nellie. I spent three of the worst days of my life in Grapevine cave. I'm not about to go in there."

"You ain't got no choice, Mr. Boyd. The soldiers are agoin' to ketch you if you don't. Come on now, get in there. They's candles on a ledge just inside. You can light one o' them and foller the markin's on the cave walls. I ain't never been in there, but Mazel has—all the way to the river. When we leave, that'll most likely be the way we'll go. You go on now."

"I'm telling you, I'm not going in there," Boyd hissed.

"Oh, yes you are. You get in there now," Nellie insisted. What was coming over her? She had never talked this forcefully to a white before.

A shout from the jailhouse just above the cave opening caused them to shrink into the shadows. Boyd crouched slightly as Nellie clung to him. He could smell her smell again.

"Okay, Nellie. I'll do it. You get on home before they catch you. Where will the cave come out?"

"Down 'bout the river where the pike crosses. You can circle 'round town 'an then go back up on the mountain. You'd better stay there, least while the Yanks are in town."

"Nellie," Boyd whispered. "I haven't had a chance to thank you. You know, the note and all. It'll help to catch the men responsible for Pop's death."

"Never mind 'bout that. Just you be careful an' don't get caught."

Nellie stood on her tiptoes and kissed Boyd lightly on the lips. She searched his face in the dim moonlight and touched his cheek with her rough, calloused fingers. Boyd embraced her lightly, feeling her soft body press urgently against his. With a sob, she broke away and melted silently into the night.

Boyd stood quietly, listening for her departing footsteps, but heard nothing. Another shout from a soldier arose from the pike and Boyd looked in dread at the dark hole before him. Water tinkled over the rim and into the darkness.

He moved into the funnel-shaped opening and let himself from rock to rock down into the earth's bowels, sliding his hand along the cave's wall feeling for the candles Nellie promised would be there. Panic gripped him and it took all of his will to keep from climbing back up to a friendlier, yet far more dangerous, world above.

At last in the narrow passage, he felt the candles. He fumbled in his pockets for a match and lit one of the long, slim tapers. Unlike Grapevine Cave, this cave was only a narrow, winding passage, littered with weirdly shaped formations left by the flowing water, and leading sharply down into the earth. It would be better to be caught by the Yanks than to be lost in the dark in this hole, he thought. But he resolved to move on. He stuffed three of the candles into his pocket, leaving the remainder for the next person who passed this way. Nellie had said "they" would use the cave when they left. Who? The slaves?

Sliding down on the seat of his pants, he continued into the passage, bumping his head on the low ceiling. Finally, the passageway leveled out, but in places he had to crawl on his belly like a snake to get through. The dirt floor was dry as powder, and as he paused occasionally to rest, he could not hear running water in the darkness as he had in Grapevine. He moved on. The passageway became broader and higher, and finally he could walk upright, but soon came to a fork, with another passageway leading to his right. He searched along the cave's wall for a sign, and discovered an "X" smoked with a candle on the wall of the left fork. He walked on, lighting his second candle from the stub of the first.

He found two more passageways leading away to his right, and at each one someone had marked the way with the soot from a candle. He became more confident. How far had he come? It was hard to judge. At times he had to climb over fallen rocks, and once he had to wade through a shallow pool.

Then, as he rounded a curve, the cave came to an abrupt end. He stood silently, looking dumbly at the solid rock wall before him.

He had taken all the right turns. He had followed the marks correctly, but now there was no way to go on. Again, panic swept through him. He was going to die here, he just knew it. He turned quickly to retrace his steps, and the sudden movement snuffed out his candle. The darkness rushed in upon him and in his uncontrollable panic, he began to run. He slammed into a stone wall and sat down abruptly.

He breathed deeply, clearing his head. Boyd, he said to himself, if you don't get control of yourself, you're a dead man. He forced himself, there in the darkness, to think about something pleasant. Nellie. Why did she pop into his head? He remembered her kiss, only a few minutes ago, in another world, and could still feel the softness of her as she pressed against him. A smile crossed his face.

He opened his eyes as widely as possible, until they hurt, but could see nothing. His panic faded away and he felt a strange calmness, as if an inner light had been lit. He felt in his pocket for a match and struck it on a nearby rock. Light flooded his stone prison as the candle glowed again.

He rose cautiously to his feet and returned to the stone wall. Holding the candle high above his head, he inspected the wall. There, streaked with bat droppings was a symbol, an arrow, faded and dim, pointing straight up. As he looked toward the cave's ceiling he could see a dark ledge and he scrambled up the wall to discover a narrow slit several feet wide, but little more than a foot high. The light of the candle revealed another symbol on the stone ceiling of the slit. Was he to crawl through this intimidating passageway? There was no other way, so he began to scoot and crawl on his belly, holding the candle before him. He scraped the top of his head and back repeatedly on the roof. He stopped occasionally to rest, and again lit a candle from the stub. As his strength began to fade, he had to stop to rest more frequently, and after what seemed like hours, he had to light his last candle. What if this candle burned out and he still wasn't out of the cave? Would he have to crawl on in the darkness? He put the thought out of his mind and crawled on, straining and grunting with the effort.

At last, the cave widened again and the ceiling rose enough for him to walk if he bent over. Suddenly, a flow of fresh, cool air reached him, causing his candle to flicker dangerously. Within a few more yards he stepped out of the cave and into the moonlit forest. Far below him he could see a sliver of silver river flowing peacefully. Night sounds rushed in on him. After the total silence of the cave, the night creatures that screeched and hooted from the trees around him sounded as loud as the roar of the surf on a deserted beach.

Boyd gathered sticks and branches and soon had a roaring fire to cheer him. He sat with his back against a huge tree and gazed thoughtfully into the flames, looking occasionally at the moonlight on the river in the valley below him, and waited for the dawn.

7

To Charlie's dismay, Boyd refused to stay with them in their snug mountain cabin. After describing his latest run-in with the Yankees, Boyd asked if there was a place he could stay without endangering Charlie and his family. He carefully avoided telling them about the meeting of the slaves, and also avoided telling them about Nellie's part in his escape. Charlie laughed as Boyd described crawling through the narrow slit in the cave.

"Fat man's misery, that's what they call it. I've never been in there myself, but every kid in town knows about that cave," Charlie chuckled. "You were lucky to get away. Yep, you're one lucky feller."

"Guess I'll have to stay out of town from now on. It took most of the day to walk back up here on the mountain and I expect that the Yanks will be here looking for me since they know that you and I are friends. That's why I'll have to find another place to stay until we go after that blond-headed man. Its only about two weeks until October."

"Well, if you insist, Sonny, but I ain't afraid of no Yanks. You could stay here with us an' slip away if they show up."

"No, I won't run the risk, Charlie. I've already lost one of your best horses and I don't want you to lose your parole papers. Kate and the kids need you here to help them," Boyd replied.

"They's a old cabin up on Blackbird Knob that some of the men here abouts use when they go ahuntin'. You can stay there. The Yanks don't know 'bout it, an' none of the men'll be usin' it this early in the season, so's you'll have it all to your own self. It's right cozy an' you

136

can shoot a squirrel or two to eat. Maybe Kate'll give you a sack of food to take with you, that is if you behave yourself and don't get her Irish temper riled up," he grinned, looking toward Kate to see her reaction.

⁊ ⁊ ⁊ ⁊

Boyd walked up the valley, following the stream and the faint trail that wound along its side. He paused beneath a shagbark hickory tree and looked again at the crude map Charlie had drawn on a scrap of brown wrapping paper. It was less than ten miles to the cabin, but as he traversed the narrow valley the land slanted sharply upward and the stream became a whitewater torrent tumbling over huge boulders. The leaves on the sugar maples, at this high elevation, were beginning to change from deep green into golden yellow, and here and there he could identify the burgundy color of the dogwoods. Up on the ridge tops, the scarlet foliage of red maples stood out vividly from the solid mass of the forest.. A man could get to like this country, he thought.

The forest was damp and close around him. Here, on the mountain, the timber had never been cut. The virgin forest rose in silent columns around him as he climbed. Why would anyone put a cabin up this high on the mountain? He leaned against a large, straight American chestnut tree to catch his breath. The ground was littered with the prickly burrs from the tree. The forest was still and he could hear thunder, far away like the rumble of a distant train, as the September air carried its burden of moisture eastward. He leaned the mountain rifle Charlie had loaned him against the ancient trunk and looked out through heavy foliage over the valley beneath him. The sun was bright and hot, and a red-tailed hawk soared on the thermals far below, but he could not see the thunderhead he knew was rising toward him from behind the mountain.

How different this land was from the ocean. There, the storms rose from over the horizon, usually with due warning. But here they popped over the ridges from nowhere, suddenly drenching everything before them. Such was the case now as the rain roared down on him, beating a heady rhythm on the leaves. Boyd crouched beneath a huge leaning maple, covering the rifle as best he could to keep it dry. In spite of the rain, he found the experience strangely pleasant, as lightning flashed and thunder roared and cracked over the steep ridge.

A red fox trotted down the trail toward him, testing the air with its black, pointed nose. Silver droplets of water glistened on its handsome coat. It stopped suddenly and looked intently at Boyd, trying to figure him out. With a whip of the tail, it disappeared into the underbrush.

The storm was short-lived and soon rumbled on toward the east, soaking the valley and town below. A brilliant shaft of sunlight soon pierced the gloom of the forest, setting the red maples and black gum aflame with vermillion brightness. A downy woodpecker backed rhythmically down the tree before him, searching for insects in the rough bark. And then a huge bird, fully eighteen inches in length, swept down through the forest to alight on the side of a dead snag. A pileated woodpecker. It canted its red crested head to the side, inspecting the tree intently. With startling loudness it began to peck huge slivers of wood out of the tree trunk, dropping them to the leaf-covered ground below in a steady patter. Finding nothing to eat, it swooped down the hillside, dodging trees as it went, cackling like a guinea fowl.

Boyd gathered his rifle and sack containing Kate's cornbread and sliced ham, and continued up the muddy trail. A bright blue salamander with red and yellow spots slithered across the trail before him. He hummed a tune he had heard Kate singing in her kitchen as he climbed upward and thought of Nellie. Oh, my, he thought, what am I to do about her? And what about Lexus? She was his own kind, but there was something about her manner that was not quite right. He shook off his thoughts and continued upward.

The cabin was just where Charlie had said it would be, perched on a steep hillside with the stream, flowing nearby. The silvery flash of speckled trout could be seen in the tumbling water. A sharp crag of cream-colored sandstone, strong and weathered, rose just behind, marking the summit of Blackbird Knob. Low and squat, made of hand-hewn chestnut logs, the weathered cabin seemed to have grown there like a huge forest mushroom. Lifting the wooden latch in the heavy plank door, Boyd stepped inside. The floor was swept clean; there were two sets of bunk beds attached to the far wall, and a fireplace, centered in the end wall, was crafted of the same stone as the crag outside. A simple table with a shelf above was stocked with battered pots and pans and a few pieces of chipped china.

He returned to the porch, dragging a much-repaired rocking chair behind him, and looked out through the brilliant leaves toward the smoky-blue valley that spread, wave after mountainous wave, as far as he could see. He sat in the chair, rocked slowly, and folded his hands in his lap. "Now," he said aloud for the hawk to hear, "I know why they built the cabin here."

♪ ♪ ♪ ♪

"I don't care what you want, darkie, you get your tail in the house and keep your yap closed," Mr. James snarled. He pushed Mazel toward the back door of the house. "Damned, hardheaded good for nothin'..." he muttered after she had left. Mazel had become harder to control than ever. There's something going on, he worried, that had made her so rebellious. Oh, well, he would be getting out as soon as he could. He'd sell his house and slaves and head for Richmond. Just as soon as he and Jones took care of the McMillion farm. He surely didn't want to put himself at that much risk, but there was little choice. He couldn't just up and leave—he'd lose a fortune on the house alone.

Nellie watched Mr. James from the kitchen house. He'd better walk easy with Mazel, or he'd find himself with a butcher knife in his neck. Mazel was getting harder and harder to keep in line. Mr. Joseph had better hurry up and make his move soon, or some of the slaves would do it for him.

She returned to her work. Her hands moved automatically over a big bucket of tallow as she cut the fat into large chunks and tossed them into the melting pot. She'd render down the fat and mix it with the lye Henry leached from wood ash, to make soap. This was one of her least favorite things to do, and her mind wandered.

What would she do if she won her freedom? Where would she go and how would she live? The whites would not give them land to live on, and they'd have no money to buy it. Maybe they could work and earn enough money. Wouldn't it be wonderful to be able to come and go as you pleased, and to go to bed and get up whenever you wanted? What would it be like to make your own decisions and be responsible for your actions? Being on your own was a frightening thing, yet it was the only thing that was important. Could she learn to support herself? Of course she could. She and Mazel had been taking care of themselves, and their masters, all their lives.

The next night, Mazel and Nellie slipped away after Mr. James had gone to bed. They waited until they heard his heavy snoring coming through the upstairs window. Sneaking across town, through the darkness, was very dangerous. If they were caught there would be hell to pay.

As they approached the church they could see a tiny shaft of light beneath the cellar door. All the others were already there, sitting around the table, talking quietly. Mr. Joseph looked up as they entered and smiled.

"'Bout time you got here," he said. "We's 'bout ready to vote."

"What you votin' on, old man," Mazel asked gruffly. "We waistin' our time talkin' and votin.' I say we do it now." Mazel glared at the men and stood with her fists on her full hips, a scowl furrowing her brow—a posture that had become very familiar to all of them.

"Just you settle down, sister," Nellie warned. "We ain't goin' to do nothin' 'til Mr. Joseph tell us to."

"Yes, well, I'm gettin' mighty tired o' takin' Mr. James' tormentin.' He don' do nothin' but ride my back, an' I'm agoin' to stick him like I did that..." she stopped speaking suddenly as she realized what she was saying.

"We's goin' to vote on when we make the break," Mr. Joseph said quickly. "I think we should go in 'bout two weeks. It'll be the dark of the moon 'bout then, an' if we're follered, it'll be harder fer them to find us. We'll crawl through the cave an' then walk up the river. We'll keep on goin' north 'til we get plum away. Johnny, you said you'd been through the cave, didn't you? What's it like in there an' how many candles will it take?"

"I was in there onct, an' it ain't so bad. You have to crawl part o' the way, but it ain't fur, an' it ain't wet or nothin.' But, we'll need more candles, there ain't but two or three left. It'll take 'bout four or five fer each of us. Where're we goin' to get that many candles?"

"Won't be no problem," Mazel spoke up. "Nellie and me can make candles out o' the taller fer the soap. They won't be so purty as Mr. James' but they'll work. Ain't that right, Nellie."

"An' everyone make up a sack full of food to carry with you," Mr. Joseph interrupted. "An' some matches and such. Take truck that won't spoil, 'cause it'll take us weeks to get far enough away."

Mr. Joseph called for the vote. They all solemnly raised their hands—except for Mazel. She stood, frowning at Mr. Joseph, then walked away into a corner.

Mr. Joseph gave some last instructions and they all slipped back through the dark to their masters' homes after agreeing to leave when Mr. Joseph gave the signal. Nellie and Mazel talked quietly as they prepared for bed. Where would they go, how would they live, what was it like in the north? They knew only what they had heard from word of mouth or what Nelly read occasionally in the papers. Their future was very uncertain, this they knew, yet it was bright and promising just the same. No matter what happened, it would be much better than spending the rest of their lives under Mr. James' thumb.

♪ ♪ ♪ ♪

The next two weeks slipped by quickly, with Boyd spending much of his time hunting for small game on the knob and sitting on the porch of the cabin, looking out over the valley. The leaves of the trees were turning steadily, and by the end of September were almost in full color. Boyd had never seen such color as now washed over the land. Nothing in his experience as a fisherman, except maybe the brilliant sunsets over the color-streaked ocean, had prepared him for this.

When, according to his count, the end of the month was near, he packed his few belongings and walked back down to Charlie's cabin. He approached carefully, keeping to the trees, and watched as Charlie walked toward the barn. When he was close by, Boyd spoke.

"Hot damn, Sonny, you like to scared me to death," Charlie rasped. "Looks like you finally learnt to move about in woods."

"I've had some practice. Up on the knob, it's either learn how to move in the woods, or starve. I reckon I've lost a pound or two, though."

"Well, come on in the house and Kate'll fattin' you up a mite."

"Charlie, did the Yanks come looking for me?"

"Yep. I reckon you were right 'bout them comin.' They were purty insistent that you were hid here somewhere, but after I let 'em search the barn an' smokehouse, they left. The sergeant wanted to burn the cabin, but the captain with 'em wouldn't let 'im. Just as well, I'd a had to kill him fer that."

Later that day, Charlie and Boyd rode off the mountain and up the valley toward the community of Falling Spring. They chatted quietly as they rode, and within a few hours had reached a hillside overlooking the quaint mountain valley. As darkness settled, they watched the dirt track that led into the village.

"Where do you think they'll strike, Charlie?" Boyd asked.

"Well, they'll pick one of the outlying farms for sure. They won't want to alert the men in the community. That wouldn't do. All of the men and most of the women are crack shots. Even with most of the able-bodied men off to war, they's enough folk left to make short work of anyone foolish enough to attack."

"How are we going to know which farm they'll hit."

"I reckon they'll be comin' up from the south, an' the easiest way to get here is to come up the road. We'll just wait here 'til we spot 'em on the road. The only other way would be along the river, it runs just on yon' side of the town. You can see the valley just there." He pointed to the east. "There ain't no road there, an' they's likely to have a wagon to carry the truck in. No, we'll spot them on the road if they're comin' at all. We'll just settle down here an' wait. Watch the horses. When they hear or see something, they'll perk up their ears."

They sat on the mountainside waiting patiently. Dusk rolled silently over the valley, turning the brilliantly colored leaves to a deep lavender and finally to darkness. Charlie sat on his heels looking out over the valley. He held his rifle cradled in the crook of his arm.

"My daddy come to this valley when he was just a tyke. His daddy was a young man then, an' he settled here with my grandma. They fought the Indians a time or two, and they was a major battle just over the mountain there at Fort Donnely. Several men were killed on both sides, an' the Indians went back down the Greenbrier an' through the New River valley past what is now Charleston. Their main camps were over 'cross the Ohio River. My grandaddy hated the Indians fer killin' the whites, but ever time I look out over this valley, I know why they fought fer their land so hard. I reckon I'd fight fer my land too. They was only doin' what any man would do, red or white.

"Ownin' land is important, Sonny. It's just like bein' an animal, an' havin' a territory to defend. Ain't no animal more ferocious than a man when it comes to defendin' his territory. I reckon that's what the war is all about, when you come to think about it—defendin' territory. It's been goin' on fer a right long spell, an' it'll go on after we're long gone and buried."

Charlie shifted his weight and squirted a stream of amber tobacco juice toward an unlucky beetle. The darkness settled about them like a friendly blanket. The temperature dropped sharply with nightfall, and another early frost was likely. Boyd drew his shirt closely around his throat. Charlie watched the valley intently, occasionally glancing at the horses. A blanket of brilliant stars swept in an impressive array across the mountain sky. As Boyd watched, a shooting star streaked briefly and then was gone.

"My grandma set great stock in sign an' such. She'd o' said that seein' a shootin' star was good luck. Maybe we'll have luck in ketchin' the feller that killed Pop," Charlie said quietly.

The two men talking quietly as they waited and watched. A heavy wagon appeared on the road, rumbling along toward the village. Charlie looked intently into the darkness, lit only by dim starlight.

"I reckon that'd be ole Mr. Carpenter. He lives in that log shack alongside the road there."

"How can you see in this darkness, Charlie? I can't see anything."

"Turn your head to one side instead of lookin' directly at the wagon. At night you can see better out o' the side o' your eye than lookin' straight on."

Turning his head slightly to one side, Boyd still couldn't see enough to tell anything about the wagon, much less identify who was driving it. An owl hooted on the ridge above them, and another, perhaps its mate, answered from the woods below. Their deep calls echoed across the dark valley.

The night crept on, and finally they heard the faint rumble of another wagon. Charlie spoke sharply to the horses to keep them from nickering at the wagon team. The wagon turned off the road and began to circle around the sleeping village.

"That's them I reckon. They's two o' them. They wouldn't be sneakin' around the town ifin they weren't up to no good," Charlie whispered. "Come on. We'll just tag along to see what they're up to."

They led their horses down through the woods and onto the road just north of town. They could hear the creak and rattle of the wagon on the road ahead.

"They're headin' to the McMillion farm, I reckon," Charlie whispered. "Down by the river."

As they approached the farm, the dogs began to bark. "We'd best hurry, Sonny. Ifin ole Mr. McMillion comes runnin' out to see what the dogs are barkin' at, they'll shoot him fer sure."

They rushed up the lane to the house just as someone shouted from the porch. "Hit the deck, Mac," Charlie yelled as a shot rang out from the darkness. A stab of flame lit the scene like a bolt of lighting. Two men, one tall and thin and the other short and stout stood by the smokehouse door. A shot from the porch let them know that Mac wasn't hit. Charlie rushed the two men, with Boyd close behind. There was a cry of terror from one of the men, and an angry oath from the other as both men bolted toward the river.

"Who's out there?" Mac demanded from the porch.

"It's me, Mac, Charlie Taylor from up on the mountain. We've been followin' these two thieves."

"Come on up here where I can see. Fer all I know you're one of them."

Charlie and Boyd approached the house with their rifles held over their heads. Mac looked them over carefully in the dim starlight, then struck a light in a lantern just inside the door. The yellow light flooded the porch and yard.

"Oh, yeah, I recognize you now, Taylor. What's this all about?"

Charlie told him quickly about the raid and their suspicions about who was behind it.

"They're going to get away," Boyd said.

"Naw, They ain't goin' anywhere without their horses," Mac said.

"Wouldn't be so sure, Mac. Are they any boats on the river? It'd be an easy float down to the bridge. They could be back down in town before anyone knew it, an' they'd deny they'd ever been here. We best get after 'em," Charlie said.

"I didn't think about that, Taylor. There're two canoes down there that my boys use for fishing. If they find them they'll have quite a start on you."

Charlie and Boyd left their horses with Mac and ran through the brush down to the river. From the darkness they could hear the splash of water and the knock of paddles against the side of the canoe. A voice swore as the raiders tried to make their escape.

Charlie searched upstream and Boyd down for the other canoe until Boyd saw it floating near the bank where it had hung on a rock. He waded out in the shallow water and pulled it to shore.

"Listen, Boyd, they ain't goin' to get far without a light. The river is low, an' there's rocks stickin' up in the rapids everywhere. They'll probably stove up the canoe unless they're lucky. We'll carry the canoe down the bank a ways and wait fer daylight. Judgin' from the stars, it can't be more 'in an hour til light."

They lifted the canoe to their shoulders and made their way down the river bank. The trail was narrow and the brush dragged on the sides of the canoe. They traveled slowly, struggling on the slippery bank. Finally the walls of the valley squeezed down until they could no longer make their way along the river. They put down the canoe and waited for the dawn.

They had only to wait a few minutes until the morning sounds of the forest began to reach them. They watched carefully until a canoe, low in the water, passed down the river, visible briefly through the willows and water birch at the river's edge.

"Damn, Sonny, they're gettin' away. Come on an' let's get after them," Charlie rasped.

They clambered into the canoe and pushed off from the bank.

"Charlie, do you know anything about paddling a canoe?" Boyd yelled as they made their way awkwardly toward the middle of the swiftly moving river.

"Well, now that you ask, Sonny, I ain't never been in a canoe before. You're the sailor. You should know how to make this thing go."

"Unless it has oars or sails, I'm afraid I don't know anything more about it than you," Boyd panted as he paddled frantically.

Suddenly, the canoe struck a partially submerged rock and threw them both forward onto the floor. Boyd's paddle slipped overboard as he clutched the sides of the canoe to steady it. Reaching as far as he could, he caught the paddle with the tips of his fingers. Cautiously they regained their seats and began to paddle rhythmically.

"Hot damn, Sonny. We're both going to drown ifin we hit a rock in one of them rapids."

"Don't worry, Charlie, its only a hundred yards to shore."

"Might as well be a hundert miles if you can't swim," Charlie complained.

Slowly they gained control of the craft. Boyd, in the back, quickly learned how to paddle and control the canoe's direction. They came to a section of rapids, and clumsily dodged rocks and boulders before entering the quiet pool below and paddling strongly forward.

Occasionally, far down the river, they could see the other canoe with two tiny figures paddling rapidly. Plumes of silvery-white water shot into the air behind them from their paddles as the two men awkwardly made their way down the river.

"I don't reckon we're makin' any headway catchin' 'em, Boyd. They ain't any better at this than we are, but they're good enough to keep ahead of us. We've got to catch them before they leave the river," Charlie said.

"We have their wagon. They can't deny it was them," Boyd replied.

"No, they'll just deny everything. They'll say it was stole."

"I guess that's so," Boyd admitted. "Who do you suppose it was with the white headed man, Charlie?"

"You know as well as me. Just like Nellie said in her letter, it was Mr. James from down in town. You stayed in his house when you was wounded. I've always knowed that he was tighter with money than bark on a birch tree, but I'd o' never figgered him for a thief and a murderer."

"No, I wouldn't have either, but he wasn't any too nice to me when I was there. He must have been paid for keeping the wounded."

"Well, he'll have to do some explainin' now. Folk in the valley are right mad about all the stealin' an' all. He'll be lucky to get out o' this with his hide. An' they both have to answer to me fer killin' Pop. You know what the Good Book says: a eye fer a eye."

☙ ☙ ☙ ☙

Ping! Something struck the tiny window in the kitchen house up under the eave. Nellie opened her eyes and listened. What was it? Maybe she had been dreaming. She drifted off to sleep again, burrowing comfortably into the thin covers on her bed. She could hear Mazel's snores drifting up reassuringly from the floor below.

Ping! There it was again. This time she was sure it was not a dream. She rose up on one elbow and listened intently. She could hear a faint rustle in the leaves outside. Cautiously, she left her bed and crept to the window, peering outside. The sky was clear, but there was no moon. The stars twinkled dully, shedding only a faint light on the scene below.

Someone spoke. "Psst! Nelly. You there?" the voice asked. It was Mr. Joseph. "Nelly, kin you hear me? It's time. We's goin' to go now. Come on."

"Mr. Joseph you just 'bout scared me to death. We're ready. Just let me get Mazel and we'll be there." She quickly gathered the sack hidden beneath her bed and went downstairs to wake Mazel. She shook her shoulder gently whispering her name. "Mazel. Mazel. Mr. Joseph's here. Time to go. Wake up, now."

"Wha... What you want Nellie. I'm tryin' to sleep. I got to get up early an' start the wash. Mr. James'll be after me again ifin I don't."

"No, you don't. We're done with all that, now. We's goin' to leave this place an' go up north where we'll be free," Nellie whispered, a lump rising in her throat. "Come on, now, sister. We're goin' to be free."

Mazel groped under the bed for her sack of stolen food, and rose to dress quickly.

She looked around at the only home she had known throughout her adult life. Although she hated being a slave, she still had fond memories of her life here in the kitchen house. Tears rose up in her eyes.

"You fool girl, what you snifflin' about. I cain't wait to get out o' here. I ain't never goin' to be another man's slave. I'm goin' to be free. Come on now," Mazel said gruffly.

They slipped quietly out of the kitchen house and followed Mr. Joseph between the houses, down toward the center of town and the cave's opening in the bottom of the huge sinkhole. The houses were dark and quiet. Mr. Joseph was right, Nellie thought, it was best to leave on the dark of the moon. She could hardly see where she was going. No one would see them.

They reached the spring house where Boyd had hidden from the Yanks only a few weeks before. The other men stepped from behind the silvery, stone building. Starlight glinted off of the barrels of muskets and pistols in their hands.

"Here, gimmy one o' them guns. Ain't no one goin' to ketch an' whip me again," Mazel growled. "I'll shoot his eyes out ifin he try."

"Shush! You're goin' to wake the dead. If we's caught now, we're gonners," Mr. Joseph warned. "Give her one o' the guns before she wake the whole town." Mazel ran her hands over the barrel of the weapon, smiling into the night, hefting its comforting weight.

The motley group of slaves huddled together, whispering their plans as they prepared to move down the tiny stream to the mouth of the cave. A dog barked across town, and was answered by another farther away. Nellie shivered under her thin sweater. She had taken a heavier coat from Mr. James' closet, but didn't want to take the time to remove it from her bag and put it on.

Finally, Mr. Joseph gave the signal to move out. They splashed along the wet bank of the stream skirting the jail perched on the side of the sink. Cautiously they began to cross the road that ran north to Falling Spring.

Suddenly, the door of the jail was thrown open. A man stood in the doorway, a lantern's light from inside outlining him. "Who's out there?" he yelled with a loud, gruff voice. "Whoever it is better speak up."

The slaves froze in their tracks. Easily seen against the pale dust of the road, there was no place to hide. Nellie heard Mazel cock her musket. The gun roared and threw a spear of fire toward the doorway. The man in the jail grunted and crashed backward into the building. The violent crash of the musket broke the slaves' trance and they scrambled down the creek toward the cave.

"Oh, you've done it now, sister," Nellie wailed. "They'll kill us all now fer sure."

"Just you shet up, Nellie. I didn't have no choice. He'd o' woked the town anyhow. At least now we have some time 'til the townsfolk figger out what happen."

Dogs began to bark furiously near the houses around the rim of the sink. Lights were struck in the houses and men began to yell in question and make their way toward the jail. The slaves ran toward the cave's mouth.

♪　♪　♪　♪

Late morning found Boyd and Charlie wearily paddling down the river, dodging rocks and logs. They had not gained on the two men ahead of them. Indeed, they seldom saw them ahead, as the river twisted and turned through the narrow valley. The dazzling mountains rose steeply from the water's edge and towered hundreds of feet above them.

The water of the river was crystal clear, and he could see the rocky bottom below. Fish swam below them, and occasionally a huge carp splashed noisily on the surface. They shot down numerous rapids and paddled across each quiet pool below. Kingfishers sat on limbs that reached out over the river and dived deftly into the swift-moving current for minnows. As they rounded one bend in the river, a huge blue-grey bird rose into the air. It dangled its skinny legs behind as it flew, and stretched out its long, thin neck. A great blue heron. Boyd had seen them many times along the coast, but what was it doing here in the mountains? Maybe it was migrating. The morning wore on.

"I've got a idea, Boyd. It can't be much farther 'til we get to the horseshoe bend. The river has cut a big curve in the mountain. They's one place where it's almost cut across the bend. Can't be more 'in a few hundert feet across. Ifin I could climb over the top, I might be able to ketch them before they passed."

"How much farther," Boyd asked.

"Well, it's hard to tell. Most of this gorge looks the same, but it can't be more 'in a mile or so. I think we'll be able to tell if we watch close."

"Charlie, do you think you can manage, with your wound and all? That climb may tear something open inside."

"I'll be just fine, Sonny. I been exercising some while you were sittin' up there on the mountain. I'll be all right."

They paddled in silence for some time until, finally, Charlie pointed to the curve of the river before them.

"That's it. You can see where the mountain is lower alongside the river there. That's the neck of the bend. Here, paddle over to the side there."

They paddled the canoe over toward the bank, and Charlie nimbly jumped out, pulling his musket behind him. He began to scramble up the steep, shale covered slope.

"You go on and paddle around the horseshoe. Keep your eye out. Ifin I see them, I'll try to get them to stop. If I can't, then I'll have to pull down on them with my musket." Charlie quickly disappeared into the brush covering the mountain, pulling himself from one scrubby tree to the next.

Boyd moved back into the current. The canoe was harder to control, now that Charlie's weight was gone from the front, but with the craft riding higher in the water, it moved faster. He paddled steadily, watching ahead. What would happen if Charlie did manage to get ahead of the fleeing men? Would they stop, or would he have to shoot them? Maybe Mr. James would give up, but that blond-headed man wouldn't. He had nothing to lose. Sheriff Brown would hang him for sure, especially if Boyd told the sheriff about his trying to kill him by dropping him in the cave.

The late morning sun was hot. A pale blue dragonfly hovered over the boat, eyeing him, before skimming away over the water. A smallmouth bass leaped into the air in an attempt to catch it. Boyd was sweating profusely as he paddled. Occasionally he scooped up handfuls of water and drank, splashing some across his face. The water was cool on his hot skin. The roar of a musket reached him from around the next bend in the river.

He rounded the bend suddenly, shot through an especially steep rapid, and sailed into smoother water below. He could see, some distance down the river, the other canoe hung up on a rock. Charlie stood hip deep in the river, holding his musket on someone in the bottom of the craft. Charlie paddled quickly toward them.

As he approached he yelled to Charlie.

"Who've you got there Charlie? Where's the other fellow?"

"It's Mr. James, Sonny. Just like we knew it was. I plugged him plum through the shoulder. That other feller took to the woods when the shootin' started. I yelled at 'em to stop, but they started to paddle on by as quick as a cat, so I cracked down on 'em with the musket. That's when the other feller lit out. I'd a got him too, but my musket was empty."

Boyd approached and they dragged both canoes to the shallow water at the river's edge. Mr. James lay in the bottom of the canoe groaning lightly, rolling his head from one side to the other. He held a dirty rag against his bloody shoulder.

"Oh, hesh up, Mr. James. You ain't agoin' to die. Now you know what it's like to feel the hot lead tearin' into you. I ort to go 'head an' finish you off, but I'll wait an' let the sheriff take care o' you. You'll hang fer sure."

"No, oh, no, you can't," Mr. James moaned. "I didn't have nothing to do with killing that man up on the mountain. Jones did it. He told me he did. I was really mad at him for doing that. He was stealing food and plunder from the farms here abouts and selling it to the Yankees. I'll admit that I bought some of the stuff, but I didn't kill anybody."

"Maybe not," Charlie admitted, "but it's goin' to be right difficult to get the farmers in the valley to believe it. You were with Jones when he hit the McMillion farm last night, and who knows what else you've been up to."

"I tell you I didn't kill anyone. Go on, take me to the sheriff. You can't prove I killed anyone, because I didn't!" Mr. James blustered. He'd much rather face the sheriff and a judge than face this fierce man from up on the mountain.

Boyd got into the canoe with Mr. James and pushed off from the river bottom with his paddle. Charlie followed in the other canoe. With Boyd in the lead they began to shoot the rapids again. Charlie paddled uncertainly, zigzagging down the river as he paddled first on one side of the canoe and then the other. He laughed as he struggled to keep up with Boyd. Water sprayed from his paddle tips, splashing noisily behind.

Within an hour they reached the charred remains of the bridge over the river. This is where it all started, Boyd thought. They dragged the canoes well above the water line and helped Mr. James up the slippery bank to the pike where he dropped heavily onto the dusty road. His face was gray and drawn and his shoulders slumped sadly. He sat in the dust with his head down and held the crude bandage on his wounded shoulder.

Boyd stood in the middle of the pike and looked across the river, over the burned timbers, at the other side where, months ago, he had killed a man—a boy really. That terrible night came rushing back, flooding him with emotion.

"Ain't nothin' you can do 'bout it now, Sonny," Charlie said over his shoulder, reading his mind. "What's done is done. They's been many a good man killed in this war, an they's goin' to be more, an' they's nothin' we can do 'bout it." Charlie gently patted him on the shoulder as they turned away from the river.

They sat beside the pike, resting in the shade of huge sycamore trees, as they waited for a wagon to come by. Neither Boyd nor Charlie had the strength to climb up the mountain road to town, and Mr. James was in no shape to walk. Charlie, in a better mood now that he had solved Pop's murder, laughed and joked with Boyd.

"Charlie, what about Jones?" Boyd asked. "How will we ever catch him. He'll be out of the county before we know it."

"No, Sonny. We'll get him all right. Once we put out the word, the folk in the valley'll keep a lookout for him, an' nothin' happens in this valley that folk don't know about. We'll find him." Charlie concluded.

The men rested along the road. Charlie snored lightly as he sat against a tree with his chin on his chest. He twitched and jerked in his sleep, reliving battles that were better forgotten. A beaver swam slowly up the still water of a back slough just above the remains of the bridge. It slapped its tail on the water as it dove below the surface.

At dusk a wagon made its way across the river, fording near the bridge. The team pulled it up the sloping bank and Charlie walked over to the driver.

"Hey, Clyde, how about a ride up the mountain to town," Charlie asked. "We've got a load fer you to haul."

"Hey, Charlie," Clyde answered. "I heard you were back from the war, but I ain't seen you around."

"I been up on the mountain recuperatin," Charlie grinned. "Kate's been fattin' me up some. Winter's comin' you know. Got to lay on a layer o' fat to keep me warm."

"Who you got over there?"

"Why, that's Mr. James. He got a mite careless with a musket an' took a ball in the shoulder. We figger to take him up to the sheriff and let him explain why there's so much truck bein' stole in the valley here, and why Pop Cooper's dead an' buried."

"You don't say, now!" Clyde exclaimed, raising his eyebrows.

They loaded Mr. James onto the wagon and Charlie and Boyd climbed onto the driver's seat beside Clyde. He cracked the reins on the horses' rumps, and the wagon lurched forward toward town.

♪ ♪ ♪ ♪

The slaves, dirty and frightened, huddled in the dark passages of the cave. They were trapped. The men in town had soon realized that the slaves had attempted an escape through the cave. They had sent a detachment of men on horses over the mountain to guard the cave's opening on the river. When Johnny had tried to get out of the cave after crawling all the way through, he had been captured, but not before he had warned the others. They had fled back through the cave, and now with all of their candles gone, they sat in a miserable heap just inside the cave on the town side.

Nellie could hear the men outside talking and yelling noisily. Tiny shafts of light danced on the cave's walls from the bonfire someone had built near the cave's opening. Daylight had come. The men outside were afraid to enter, since they were well aware that the slaves were armed. They had yelled into the cave, telling them to come on out, but Mr. Joseph had not let anyone answer.

"What we goin' to do now, Mr. Joseph?" Nellie asked hopefully.

"I don't know, child. They say that man at the jail is dead, shot in the chest. They'll kill us if we go out, an' we'll die in here if we stay. I don't reckon that they's much of anything that we can do."

"Hit's all your fault, Mr. Joseph," Mazel shouted. "Ifin we had left when I say, none of this would o' happen. It's all your fault."

"Now, that's not fair, Mazel. You're the one that shot that man. Maybe ifin you hadn't o' shot him we'd o' got away," Nellie argued.

"Shush, now girls. It ain't no use to say what we shoulda done. We're trapped in here an' we gotta figger a way out."

They sat on the dirt floor and listened to the crowd of men outside. Occasionally they could hear a feminine voice mingling with the others. It wouldn't be much longer. The crowd would become impatient and then they would make a run at the cave, or worse yet, they'd try to smoke them out. Nellie rocked back and forth as she sat on the dirt floor. Her body shook with the cold. How close they had come. If only that man hadn't opened the jailhouse door when he had. They'd have gotten clean away. Why had this happened? She had been so sure that they would be able to escape. Now she would never know what freedom was like, and they were fighting among themselves like a pack of feral dogs.

"Hey, you darkies in there. Come on out and we won't hurt you." Sheriff Brown yelled.

"Just you come on in here, Mr. Brown, an' I'll shoot your eyes out," Mazel yelled back.

"Now settle down, Mazel," the sheriff replied. "Y'all come on out of there and no one'll be hurt."

"You ain't foolin' no one, Sheriff. I know that man I shot is dead. I heard y'all out there talkin' about him. I'd rather die in here of starvation than come out there an' allow you to put a rope 'round my neck," Mazel screamed. "I 'member what happened to Uncle Reuben!"

The sheriff retreated and the slaves were silent again. Mazel sat by herself, muttering under her breath. Finally, Mr. Joseph stood up and looked toward the cave's opening.

"I'm goin' on out there. Ain't no use in sittin' in here. Maybe I can talk to them an' they'll let us go back to our work," he said hopefully.

"Don't you go out, Mr. Joseph. They gotta kill us. They can't let slaves have guns and go 'round killin' folk, an' do nothin' about it," Mazel shouted. "Just you sit down."

"No, girl. It ain't no use," he said sadly. "You can stay in here ifin you want to, but I'm too old fer this. My bones are achin' somethin' fierce with this damp an' all. Maybe I can do some good out there."

He stood up and began to feel his way along the wall toward the opening. The two other men also stood and began to follow him out.

"Mazel, what's we goin' to do?" Nellie whispered. "We're done fer."

"This is all my fault, sister. Ifin I hadn't talked you into comin' you'd be at home in bed right now," Mazel whispered miserably. The girls could hear shouting outside as Mr. Joseph and the other two men appeared.

"Mazel, I'm sorry, too. I know how much freedom meant to you. Just when it seemed like we'd make it, the world fell in. They'll beat us to death ifin we go out there." Nellie hugged her sister and cried softly on her shoulder.

"Don't you worry, now, sister. I got myself an idee. Do you reckon them men outside know how many of us there were in here?" Mazel asked.

"Well, now that you mention it I reckon they don't have no way of knowin,' but what good will that do us?"

"You could hide in the cave fer a day or two an' come out after they take all of us away. Then you could creep out one night an' go on up north an' be free, just like we planned. They'll prob'ly search the cave, but ifin you hide in one o' the side tunnels, they'll never find you. Here, I got a little bit o' candle left." She thrust a stub of candle in Nellie's hand, along with two matches.

"No! Mazel, I won't do it! If you go out there, I'm goin' too."

"No, you ain't, neither."

With a swift movement, Mazel struck Nellie on the head with the barrel of her musket. She slumped to the dirty floor with a sigh and Mazel picked up her sister's limp body and carried her back in the cave, gently laying her on a ledge in a shallow branch tunnel. She placed Nellie's hands on her chest and patted her cheek. Then, with a deep sigh, she returned to the mouth of the cave and stepped outside.

❧ ❧ ❧ ❧

The wagon groaned and creaked as the team pulled it up the pike toward town. Charlie cheerfully told Clyde about the chase down the river in the canoes. He elaborated somewhat on their prowess in handling a canoe, and gave Boyd much more credit than he felt he deserved. Clyde laughed and slapped his thigh when Charlie told him about climbing over the neck of the horseshoe bend and jumping Mr. James and Jones. He frowned when Charlie told him about Jones getting away.

Mr. James groaned and cursed in the back of the wagon as it bounced over the rough road. Finally they reached the top of the mountain and began the descent into town. Boyd decided to walk behind the wagon in case the Yanks were back in town. He dropped to the ground and Charlie and Clyde rode on into town.

Boyd walked slowly down the pike, enjoying the cool evening air, and felt good even if he had little sleep the night before. The few hours of rest at the bridge had helped. The evening was cool and quiet. There were no night sounds, since the early frost had killed the night insects, and the birds had stopped singing now that the days were growing shorter.

"Mr. Boyd, is that you," a voice asked incredulously from the side of the road. It was Nellie.

"Is that really you, Nellie? Are you all right?"

"No, I ain't so good, Mr. Boyd, but it's good to see you again," she said sadly.

They stood at the side of the pike in the darkness, with only a house light here and there to provide illumination. Quietly, Nellie stepped into his arms. The scent of soap and cleanness was gone. In its place was the odor of sweat and dirt. But, still the warm softness of her body stirred him.

"Nellie, something's wrong, isn't it," he asked softly, enjoying her breath on his cheek. She began sobbing quietly in his arms.

"Oh, Mr. Boyd, they got us. We tried to escape last night an' they caught us an we were trapped in the cave all day. They took Mr. Joseph an' Mazel an' the others to jail. Mazel knocked me on the head so's I wouldn't go out with her. Mr. Boyd, she kept them from findin' me. I snuck out of the cave just minutes ago, an come back up here to Mr. James' house. I don't know what to do. I've got to get them out o' the jail. Do you think they'll hurt 'em?" she asked fearfully.

"Well, yes they'll probably punish them severely. Did they see you? Do they know you were with them?"

"No, I don't think so, but I got to get them out o' jail. They'll kill Mazel 'cause she shot that man at the jail."

"What!" Boyd asked, shocked at what he was hearing. "Did you say Mazel killed someone?"

"Yes, a man at the jail caught us tryin' to escape, and Mazel shot him. I reckon she just sorta panicked."

"Oh, Nellie, this is much more serious than I had thought. I'm afraid that Mazel and your friends are in deep trouble. There's not much that we can do."

"I got to see 'em. Ifin I go to the jail, will they let me in to see 'em?" she asked, still clinging to him. "I'll go an' get cleaned up an' they'll never know I was with 'em."

Boyd waited outside the kitchen house, pacing back and forth. What was he getting himself into? If they thought he was helping slaves escape, he'd be strung up along side them. But Nellie had helped him. He couldn't let her down now that she needed him. The light in the kitchen was snuffed out, and Nellie stepped out to him. The smell of soap and woman was back.

As they walked toward the jail, Boyd told Nellie about catching Mr. James and the blond-headed man in the act of robbing a farm house. She listened intently and then asked, "Ifin they hang 'im or put 'im in jail, who'll own me? I mean, what'll happen then?"

"Well, Nellie, I guess that his family, his children that is, will inherit all of his property," he said, realizing, finally, what it meant to be owned like a plow horse. "But, I won't let that happen." There he'd said it. What would he do? How would this work?

"After you see Mazel and the others, we'll decide what we're goin' to do. Maybe I can arrange to buy your freedom or something."

"Oh, I can't leave without my sister, Mr. Boyd. Just soon as I get 'em out, we'll see then." She slid her arm through his and he could feel the warm swell of her breast against his arm.

As they approached, Nellie fell back a step behind Boyd—they could see torch lights in the street in front of the jail. It looked like half of the people in town had turned out to see the runaway slaves. There were small groups of men standing, talking quietly. Something was wrong. The men were no longer angry—they talked in subdued tones, their eyes cast down. As Boyd and Nellie stepped into the light of the torches, it was all very clear.

On a long, newly cut and skinned locust pole, supported on each end in the crotch of a tree branch, hung the bodies of Mazel, Mr. Joseph and the other men.

"Noooooooo," wailed Nellie, the anguish of the horrid sight transforming her voice into something unrecognizable. "Nooooo, Mazel, what have they done to you?" she crooned as she sank to the street.

She sat there, rocking, staring up at the corpses as they rotated gently in the evening air. Their necks and heads were twisted grotesquely to one side by the rough rope, and Mazel's eyes, bulging and sightless, stared out of her purple-black face. Their bound arms were twisted behind their backs and their legs extended stiffly below them. A strong odor of body waste reached Boyd's nostrils. The town's men turned at the sound and looked at Nellie and Boyd.

Charlie appeared at his side. "You best get her out of here, Sonny. These folk think they've got all o' 'em, but you never can tell what they'll do, now that they've let some blood. Was she with 'em?"

"What'll I do with her, Charlie? Mr. James is in jail, isn't he?" he asked, avoiding the question.

"Yep, he is fer now, but there's some talk that the slaves have been doin' the stealin.' He may be able to lie his way out of this yet. Why don't you take her back to Mr. James' house an' tell her to stay there. You'd best not get yourself involved in this mess, or you'll find yourself up there on that pole with those poor souls."

Gently, in spite of the glares of the men in the street, Boyd lifted Nellie to her feet and led her away. He walked her back up the street, holding her firmly by the arm, as she sobbed quietly. What kind of men would do this? If they only realized what they had done.

He helped her up the steps of Mr. James' house and turned the knob of the front door. It swung open.

"No. I can't go in there," Nellie protested. "I won't. It's his house. I won't go in there."

"Okay, Okay. Do you want to sleep in the kitchen house?"

"Yes, of course, there in the kitchen house. That's where I live," she repeated mechanically.

Leading her around the house, they entered the brick building that had been Nellie's home for so many years. Her sobbing had stopped, but she still shook with grief. He led her to the bed in the corner and tried to get her to lie down.

"No, Mr. Boyd, that's her bed. I can't. My bed's upstairs."

"You go on up to sleep now, Nellie. We'll decide what to do in the morning."

She stood in the center of the room as if rooted to the spot. Tears streaked her lovely, brown face, and her lower lip quivered.

"Mr. Boyd, Mr. Boyd, why, oh, why did they have to die? All they wanted was to be free. To live like the deers and foxes, free and on their own. Is that so bad that they had to kill them? Why are you whites so mean to us?" she wailed. "Oh, I didn't mean that. Not you, Mr. Boyd. You ain't like the whites. You ain't."

She stepped again into his arms. He felt her trembling body press against him, her breasts burning into the front of his shirt.

"I don't know the answer to that question, Nellie," he whispered in her ear, "I don't know. If I could, I would change the way things are." He stroked her hair and held her tight. Slowly, she began to relax and her trembling stopped. And the feel of her burned into his brain.

8

Damn that Charlie Taylor, Troy Jones thought. He'd kill him the first chance he got. And that Houston feller; he thought the Yankee soldiers had done him in when they dropped him in the cave. Next time he'd do it himself and be sure that it was done proper. He was wet and miserable, sitting in the brush on the hillside overlooking the river. The two men had taken Mr. James down the river in the canoes and he watched as they rounded a bend out of sight. His face was dark with anger as he shivered in the cool October air. What would he do now? The men would report this to the sheriff and he would no longer be able to move about the valley unnoticed. He's have to get out while he could.

He walked back to the river's edge. He had no idea how far it was down the river to the bridge, but he knew for sure that it was a long way back up to Falling Spring. That would probably be the safest route, but he decided to head downstream anyway. He was in no mood to walk all that way back up the river. He stumbled along the bank, sometimes forced into the water by the encroaching mountain, at other times walking easily along the wooded edge. He began to warm up a bit with the exertion and was soon surprised to round a bend and see the burned bridge in the distance. He crept along the river bank watching carefully for Taylor and Houston. As he approached he saw them just as they climbed into the back of a wagon with Mr. James riding on his back in the bed. The wagon rumbled off toward town.

Hungry and wet, Jones walked onto the road and looked across the river toward the big brick house sitting comfortably on the opposite bank. He had a few dollars in his pocket, but he had lost his weapons. He needed a gun to defend himself. Making up his mind quickly, he walked down to the river ford and began to wade across. The water was warmer than the cool air and felt good against his wet legs. He sloshed up the muddy bank and stopped under the silver maples that lined the river and shook the sand and water out of his boots. Combing his rumpled hair with his fingers, he straightened his clothing as best he could and moved toward the house.

"Yes ma'am," Jones said humbly to the stout, gray haired woman at the door, "I've had me quite a time. I got jumped by a couple of men on the pike and they took everything I had. If you could just spare me some bread and cheese or something."

"Well, I guess I could spare a little mite for you to eat. Come on along to the back door and I'll give you something."

Jones walked around the corner of the house as the front door was closed quickly behind him. Just like a common field darkie, Jones thought. Well, she'll wish she'd let me in the front door. He looked around carefully. The house and vegetable garden lay in a perfectly flat field between two sharply rising mountains on each side of the mouth of Howard's Creek. The river flowed quietly along the side of the field where the creek joined it. The lawn surrounding the house was well kept, and he could see four slaves splitting and stacking firewood over toward the creek. They looked up curiously as he approached the rear of the house and leaned casually on their axes.

The back door opened a crack and the woman looked out at him distrustfully. "Here," she said as she thrust a small sack toward him, "this is all we can spare with the war and all. Those soldiers have just about wiped us out."

"Thank you, ma'am. I'll take anything you have available," he said as he stepped toward the door with outstretched hand. With a swift movement he thrust his arm and shoulder through the door opening and pushed his way inside.

"But, I'll just help myself, if you don't mind," Jones grinned viciously. "I'm not going to settle for a handout."

"What do you mean by this?" the woman sputtered. "My husband's upstairs and he'll kill you for this."

"I don't think so, ma'am, I think you're bluffing. No self respecting man would be upstairs in bed at this time of day."

Jones began to search the house for money and weapons. He shoved the woman ahead of him roughly as he moved from room to room opening drawers and cupboards. There was no money, but he found a room used as a library, and on the walls there were several rifles. He quickly picked the newest one, some powder and shot and herded the woman back toward the kitchen room. She stood quietly along the wall and watched him as he packed more food into the sack.

"You're that man who killed old mister Cooper up on the mountain, aren't you?" she asked quietly. "What are you going to do with me, now?"

"Well, I'm not admitting to anything, lady. And I don't plan to do anything with you. I'm not crazy. If I were to kill a woman, the whole county, including the Yankee army, would be after me. Hell, lady, even those yellow Rebs might come back and join in the hunt. No, I'll not hurt you." He jammed the food quickly into the sack and slipped quietly out the back door. A big dog sitting on the porch watched him as he trotted back toward the river. The slaves returned to their work.

✒ ✒ ✒ ✒

"Naw, Sheriff, I'm tellin' you that Mr. James and that Jones feller was all set to rob poor ole Mr. McMillion. Why, one of 'em took a shot at him as he stood there on the porch of his own house."

The sheriff sat behind the battered desk in his office and picked at the buttons on the front of his shirt. He leaned to one side and spat a thick stream of dark tobacco juice into a spittoon in the corner of the small, stuffy room. Boyd and Charlie sat uncomfortably on straight-backed chairs facing him.

"Mr. James has denied everything. He said that he didn't know anything about robbin' or nothing. He said that you an' this crazy Reb shot him down at the bridge. He said he didn't do anything to you two. I'll tell you what's a fact, I just don't know who to believe." Charlie stiffened in his chair. "Now you see here, Sheriff, I ain't lyin' to you and you know it. Ifin I say that he was robbin' folks you can bet that's just what he was doin." Boyd tugged at Charlie's coat sleeve, attempting to quiet him. All they needed now was to have Charlie and the sheriff get into a ruckus.

"Okay, calm down now, Taylor. All I'm sayin' is that Mr. James is denying everything. As a matter of fact, he wanted to press charges against you and Houston here fer shootin' him. I said I'd have to think some about that," the sheriff said, dropping his eyes to the top of his desk.

Charlie glared at the sheriff and Boyd could hear someone back in the jail cells coughing and noisily clearing in his throat. The sheriff shifted his weight to spit again, with marginal success, into the spittoon.

"Sheriff," Boyd spoke up, "Mr. James' slave girl, Nellie, told me that she heard him and Jones planning to rob the McMillion farm. That's why Charlie and I were up there waiting for them. And, we're pretty sure now that Jones killed Mr. Cooper up on the mountain."

"Who's goin' to listen to some ole darkie girl? You think folk'll take her word over Mr. James, him ownin' her an' all? You'd better just drop that thought, feller," the sheriff said sternly. "And besides that I heard some of the town's men talkin' about you and that nigra. If they think you're messin' with her, you're goin' to be in deep trouble. They'll skin all the hide off your back. One of them said he thought she'd been with the bunch what killed my deputy and they ought to string her up too. If I find out she was with them, I'll string her up myself. Anyway, you're lucky the Yanks have moved back to Meadow Bridge. They're lookin' for you for breakin' your parole."

"I didn't break my parole, Sheriff. I told you what happened. They tried to kill me," Boyd said hotly. "Besides, it's none of your damned business what I do." Charlie looked sharply at him, silently warning him to stop that line of talk.

"Well, I'm just tellin' you what I know," the sheriff concluded. "I'm goin' to keep Mr. James in jail until he gets himself a lawyer. God knows there's enough of them hangin' around Lewisburg. Then he'll be out quick enough."

Boyd and Charlie left the sheriff's office and walked around the corner to Main Street. "What about those men who hung Mazel and the others? What will the sheriff do about them, Charlie?"

"Why Boyd, he ain't goin' to do nothin.' Those darkies were the property of the men who hung them. You know as well as I do, they can do whatever they want to with 'em."

"I guess, down deep, I know that's what the law says, but it isn't right. I don't know what Nellie will do now. Mr. James'll kill her if he gets out of jail. By the way, I wonder where that other fellow, Henry, went."

"He's still around. From what I hear, he weren't with those others. He's probably lying low back at Mr. James' place."

The two men walked down the quiet street. An occasional wagon rattled by and Charlie waved to the drivers. He seemed to know them all. Only a few horses were tied at the rings set in the flagstone sidewalks—the hangings had cast a pall across the town.

"Well, Mr. Houston, I see you've come creeping back into town," Lexus said to him curtly from the market doorway. Her blond hair was piled up on her head and a shiny tendril lay on her slender neck. Her blue eyes snapped as she stepped onto the street facing him. Boyd's mouth dropped as he turned toward her. Charlie stood to one side, grinning his silly grin.

"Hello, Lexus," Boyd stammered. "Yes, I'm back. The Yanks are over at Meadow Bridge."

Lexus got straight to the point, "Everybody in town's talking about you and that darkie. They say that she was with the ones who revolted and killed the deputy. Next thing I know, you'll be wanting to buy her for yourself."

"Now, Lexus I'm not going to do any such thing. Besides, I don't have a cent to my name, being robbed and all."

"Some people are saying that you helped them get guns and all. What do you have to say for yourself?" she asked sharply.

"I don't believe that I have to say anything to you! I'm not in the habit of answering to some upstart woman," Boyd blustered. Charlie shuffled his feet, embarrassed to witness this conversation.

"Uh, Boyd," Charlie whispered over his shoulder," I reckon I'd better get on along to home. You come on up an' visit me when you ken. We need to talk 'bout what we're goin' to do next."

"Yeh, okay, Charlie," Boyd said absently, his eyes still on Lexus before him. "I'll be along in a day or so. I have some business to take care of here in town." Charlie departed swiftly, shaking his shaggy brown head, his grin replaced by a frown.

As Charlie disappeared around the corner, Lexus looked up at Boyd, her eyes bright with anger. "I'm not 'some upstart woman,' Boyd Houston," she snapped.

"All right, all right," Boyd conceded, holding his hands up before him. A slight grin crept across his face. "All I was saying was that I didn't have anything to do with the slave revolt. And, I certainly didn't do anything to help them get weapons." That was the truth, but just barely.

"That's all I wanted to hear, Boyd," Lexus said, cooling a bit. "I didn't really believe that you were doing what they said you were. You were a soldier fighting for the South, honorably fighting, I might add."

"Yes, well, that's all behind me now. Even though some of the

Yanks took my papers, I'm still on parole, as far as I'm concerned. I gave my word and swore on the Bible. But, that's not what's important now. Troy Jones is still out there somewhere and he'll be more desperate than ever. He killed Pop Cooper and he'll probably kill some one else if he isn't stopped."

"The sheriff'll take care of him. You need to recover from your wounds and maybe get back to your unit. The war's far from over and you could still serve the South well. Anyway, the Yanks took your parole papers. That leaves you free to go back and fight," Lexus said, a bright light now in her eyes. She looked at Boyd appraisingly, "Mamma and Daddy are having a dinner party Saturday night. Could you come? I know you stood me up the last time, but I'll give you one more chance."

The woman has only two things on her mind, Boyd thought; the War and parties. But she surely was a pretty thing, standing there on the sidewalk. She smiled up at him, all anger now gone from her comely face.

"What about your gentleman friend? You know, the one who was sitting in your parlor the night the Yanks were after me," Boyd asked.

"Oh, him. He's just a friend from school over at Lexington. He was on leave from the war, an' the Yanks would have captured him too, had they caught him here. I told him not to come back 'til after the war's over."

"I don't know, Lexus. I'll come if I can, but with this thing about Mr. James and Jones, Charlie and I will have to think some about how to handle that. Besides, you never know when the Yanks will be back," he grinned.

Lexus smiled sweetly at him and touched his cheek with her soft fingers. "You just be careful, now Boyd, and stay away from those darkies. You know the ones I'm talking about."

She turned and walked down the sidewalk toward the center of town. Boyd watched her go, a tantalizing swing to her hips. She looked back over her shoulder and laughed.

Boyd stood for a few minutes on the sidewalk, soaking up the October sun. Now what? he asked himself. He really was attracted to her, but somewhere in the back of his mind was the nagging fear that she wasn't sincere, only playing with him. But, he could still see her youthful form before him. He closed his eyes and rubbed his wounded shoulder. It still ached when he used his arm too much. Suddenly, another vision crept into his consciousness. A dark, slender figure, with large liquid eyes, burned into the backs of his eyelids. Nellie! He shook his head and rubbed his eyes with the backs of his hands. No! He'd help her if he could, but after that he'd be on his way. Lexus was his kind and he sure liked the looks of her. He walked down the street, deep in thought.

♪ ♪ ♪ ♪

Mr. James lay in the huge bed amid a pile of comforters and pillows. His shoulder was wrapped in bandages and the blood seeped through them where the bullet wound was bleeding again. He had thrown the blankets back and his huge stomach bulged through the thin nightshirt that was his only clothing. Nellie stepped quietly into the room and placed a tray of food on the nightstand beside his bed.

"Damn you girl," he snarled, "I'm about starved to death. They don't feed a man enough in that jail to keep a jay bird alive."

"Yes, suh," Nellie mumbled as she averted her eyes from the man. She'd have to step lightly or this man would kill her. But then, she didn't really care. Mazel was gone. How would she survive now that her sister was dead and buried? She was alone.

"It's all your fault that I got shot. You just wait until I get well. I'm going to skin your hide good. And besides, you cost me a perfectly good slave. Mazel wasn't worth much, but I could have sold her for something. Oh, don't worry. I'll not harm you too much; you're worth too much money. Some rich master would like to own you. Here, help me sit up so I can eat. What's in here," he asked, looking toward the covered tray of food. "It had better be better than that last slop you tried to feed me. Too bad Mazel was the cook. I'll probably have to get myself another one," he muttered to himself.

Nellie left the food with the wounded man as she left the room. Mr. James ate slowly and worried about his situation. Things were falling apart on him. His lawyer had gotten him out of jail quickly enough, but he'd probably have to stand trial for attempted robbery. Whatever happened, his reputation in the valley was shot. He'd have to leave, and soon. The problem was that he'd lose his house and all his property, including two valuable darkies. That Jones had caused all this by insisting that he go with him. He'd probably leave the valley and Mr. James would be left holding the bag. If the sheriff thought that he was involved in the Cooper killing, he'd get blamed for that too.

He couldn't run and lose everything. His best bet was to stay on and fight in court. If he was acquitted, he could sell everything and move to Richmond like he'd planned. Yes, he decided, that's what he'd do. If he had to, he'd testify against Jones and place the blame where it belonged. Now that he'd decided what to do, he felt better.

Later that day, Nellie carried Mr. James' chamber pot out to the wooden outhouse along the path to the barn. It smelled something terrible, and the outhouse didn't smell much better. She scooped some lime from the bucket beside the door and tossed it down the hole. As she returned to the house, she could hear blue jays squawking in the trees. A black-striped chipmunk sat on the wood pile and gnawed on a nut. October was her favorite time of year, except for spring. The brilliant-colored leaves and the warm afternoon sun usually picked up her spirits, but everywhere she looked, she was reminded of Mazel. Mazel who loved to gather and crack hickory nuts to use in the pound bread she always baked.

Nellie stepped back into the kitchen house and looked mournfully at the empty bed in the corner. She would never forget the sight of her sister hanging from that locust pole like a side of beef to be skinned and cut up for sale. Every night she woke crying and trembling from the bad dreams that haunted her sleep. Would she ever find peace? They hadn't allowed her to go to Mazel's burial. There had been no funeral. They just cut them down and carried them away in a wagon and buried them in a hole in the ground. Nellie didn't even know where. A sob escaped her trembling lips and she leaned against the table and cried, dabbing at her eyes with the corner of her apron.

"Don't cry, Missy," a deep voice said from the doorway behind her. She jumped and whirled around to face the intruder.

"Easy, now. It's jus' me, Henry. I seen you come out of the house an' I thought I'd see how you doin."

"Oh, I'm all right, Henry. Where have you been? I haven't seen you for a week."

"Oh, I've been hidin' in the barn. I don' know what was happenin' so's I jus' lay low in the barn. Me an' Jake. When I heared the shoutin' an stuff down at the jail the other night, I knew somethin' mighty bad was happenin.' So's I jus' hid in the barn."

"Henry, they killed Mazel an' Mr. Joseph an' the rest. Mazel didn't mean to hurt no one. All she wanted was to be free. That's all any of us wanted. It was so dark and awful in the cave. I thought we'd all die in there."

"You mean you was in the cave too? How'd you get out without gettin' hunged?" Henry asked in surprise.

Nellie told him about the attempted escape and the death of the deputy. He listened intently as she described what it was like to be trapped in the cave, and how Mazel had saved her by hitting her on the head. She rubbed the bruise on the side of her head as she spoke.

"What you goin' to do now, Missy?" Henry asked softly.

"I don't reckon I have much choice. Mr. James's back an' nothin' has changed. I reckon I'll be here the rest of my life," she said slowly, feeling sorry for herself.

"Where's Mr. James been?" Henry asked in surprise. Nellie told him about the attempted robbery and Mr. James being put in jail. Nellie had to explain what bail was and how Mr. James had gotten out.

Henry shook his head. "Has Mr. James been askin' fer me?"

"Why no, Henry, he ain't. I reckon he figgers you're still here, just like you sposed to be."

"Nellie, don' tell 'em that I hid in the barn. I ain't done a lick o' work since that night," he said, referring to the night of the hangings.

"I won't tell, Henry. You go on out an' start your chores now like you 'spose to."

Henry left the kitchen, carefully closing the door behind him.

Henry was almost like a child sometimes, Nellie thought. He'd been around for as long as she could remember, and she'd never thought much about him, except that he was, well, he was just Henry. Mazel had been her sister, but who was Henry? The thought struck her like a thunderbolt. Was Henry her brother? No, Henry was probably too old for that. Why, he was way up in his forties. Maybe he was an uncle. Or maybe he wasn't any kin. If she could get Mr. James in a better mood maybe he'd tell her.

A scratch at the kitchen door brought her back from her thoughts. She opened the door and Mr. James' dog came inside and sat down before her. Looking up at her hopefully, he whined and thumped his tail on the worn wooden floor.

"Here, boy, where you been? Hidin' out in the barn with Henry? I don't reckon you've had much to eat, have you now?"

The dog stared at her as its tail thumped again on the floor. "Mr. James'd skin me if he find out, but here," she said as she tossed the hungry dog a piece of meat from a platter on the table. The dog deftly caught the meat and trotted back out the door.

What now, Nellie? she asked herself. What you goin' to do now? Tiredly, she began to clear the table. She put a pot of water on the fire to heat for washing the dishes. Now that Mazel was gone she'd have to do all the work, but that didn't bother her. What mattered was that Mazel and Mr. Joseph were dead and gone, and so was all hope.

She had heard somewhere that you should never take away a man's hope. It may be all that he has. Slowly, she poured the hot water in a large metal pan and began to wash the dishes.

♪ ♪ ♪ ♪

Boyd stepped onto the Saunders' front porch and knocked lightly. He straightened his worn jacket and shirt, and rubbed the tops of his boot toes on the backs of his legs. Footsteps approached in the hall and the door was opened by a tall, gray-haired man in a tweed jacket and a tie. He looked Boyd up and down without speaking.

"Uh, I'm Boyd Houston. Lexus asked me to dinner tonight?" he stuttered. Why was it that he always stammered and stuttered when he was around these people?

"Yes, she said you'd be coming. I have to tell you Mr. Houston, I'm not sure that I approve of you seeing her, or being in this house for that matter, with your reputation and all."

Boyd was taken aback. He had expected to be treated coolly by her parents, but had not expected such a blunt confrontation. The man, Lexus' father, he assumed, frowned at him from beneath bushy eyebrows. He withdrew a blackened pipe from his jacket pocket and stuck it in the corner of his teeth.

Boyd found his tongue. "Well, Mr. Saunders, if you don't want me here, I guess I'll be on my way, but maybe next time you should tell your daughter who to invite, and save us all some trouble." Boyd turned to leave.

"Now wait up, young man. If I run you off now, I'll never hear the last of it. You know how women are, don't you," he smiled grudgingly. "Come in. We're about ready to eat."

Lexus greeted Boyd in the dining room. She was wearing a pretty green dress, low cut at the throat, that showed off her shiny hair and fair skin. She smiled broadly, took his arm, and introduced him to the other dinner guests. Two other couples, her parent's ages, shook his hand grimly. His reputation in town had definitely taken a turn for the worse. Mrs. Saunders smiled tentatively at him.

They sat at the long dining table and a house servant appeared silently and began to serve them. The china and silver were better than Boyd had ever seen before. He wondered vaguely where they hid it when the soldiers were in town. Probably buried it in the back yard, like everyone else.

Lexus sat beside him, chattering with the guests and smiling happily at her father. Another battle won. She prompted Boyd discreetly as he tried to make his way through all the silverware. He had never seen so many forks and spoons at one setting before, and he could soon feel the sweat running down his sides. After the initial nervousness, he began to relax and enjoy the food. It was excellent; he had never eaten such delicious dishes before.

He talked easily with the guests and soon found that the Williams' lived on a small farm outside of town, and before the war had raised short-horned cattle. The soldiers had wiped them out, stealing every last head. The other couple, the Carpenters, lived in town and owned the general store. As they talked, they began to warm to him. The talk at the table soon turned to the war and Boyd was called upon to tell about his part in the battle in Lewisburg. He got through it without telling too much about his fear, or making himself look like a hero. He gave Charlie all the credit for their survival.

"He's just bein' modest," Lexus interrupted. "He's a real war hero," she said as she squeezed his hand. "Those other soldiers ran like dogs, but Boyd here didn't. He stood and fought." The guests laughed at Lexus' enthusiasm, but Mr. Saunders only chuckled politely.

Later, after they had left the dinner table and moved into the comfortable library, Boyd found himself telling them about his experiences as a fisherman. They were fascinated by his account of seeing pods of whales and dolphins, and everyone was properly frightened when he told them about the sharks that sometimes followed their boats. Mr. Saunders, who fancied himself an amateur fisherman, plied Boyd with question after question, and related his own experiences from many fishing trips to the Atlantic coast and the Chesapeake Bay. Soon Mr. Saunders and Boyd were talking excitedly about ships and captains they had seen and known.

The evening passed quickly with Lexus sitting on the floor at her father's knee, looking up at him worshipfully. She also looked in pride at Boyd as if he were her discovery, pleased that he was such a hit.

Soon the other guests left for home and Boyd shook hands with Mr. Saunders, who smiled and slapped him on the back.

"Come back again, son. I've surely enjoyed talking to you. I hope you catch that Troy Jones and maybe after this war's over you'll decide to settle in the valley," he said.

Boyd thanked them for the wonderful dinner. As he stepped out onto the front porch, Lexus followed him to say good night. She smiled up at Boyd prettily and placed her hand on his arm, a now familiar gesture.

"Oh, Boyd", she said breathlessly, "Mother and Daddy really do like you. I've never seen Daddy so excited when y'all talking about that fishing stuff. Now, didn't you enjoy yourself?"

"Yes I did," he admitted. He had to confess that the evening had been something of a success, even if it did get off to a rough start. "I really appreciate you giving me another chance, after not getting to come last time."

She rose to her tiptoes and kissed him lightly on the lips. He could hear her sharp intake of breath and feel the warmth of her in the cool evening air. He took her in his arms and kissed her again. She giggled and gently squirmed free.

"You will come again, won't you Boyd? When will you be back?"

"Oh, I can't say for sure. I have to go up on the mountain to see Charlie. We still have to find Jones."

"Oh rats," she pouted, "Why don't you forget about him. You could come back for Sunday dinner." Boyd was tempted, but decided against it. He quickly said good night and left.

⸙ ⸙ ⸙ ⸙

Boyd walked down Main Street toward the center of town. He had found a place to stay at a boardinghouse, but was reluctant to go in. A sliver of moon hung over the town, and he heard, high in the sky, geese honking to each other as they flew southward. He remembered autumn days on the inlet when the water was covered with them—Canadas and snows—some mallards and black ducks among them. A sudden homesickness swept over him. Maybe after this was all over he'd go back to Charleston. He liked the sea, and the conversation tonight had awakened old memories, good memories, of his life there. Being a fisherman hadn't been as bad as his youthful viewpoint had made it seem. Perhaps it was the loss of his father that had soured that life for him.

He sat on the bench in front of the hardware store and pulled his thin jacket up around his neck. He was surprised at the cold air this early in the fall, but then he had been used to the warmer southern weather.

He thought about Lexus and felt, again, the press of her body against his as they had said good night. What did he feel for her? He was definitely interested, but would he fit into her world? He liked her father and mother, and the evening had been very pleasant; but despite her father's interest in him, he sensed something amiss. However she surely was a pretty thing.

⸙ ⸙ ⸙ ⸙

Troy Jones threw the coffee cup across the filthy shack. Shards flew away from the wall and a dark stain spread downward toward the floor. He frowned at the mess and sat wearily on a broken chair. Damn, damn, damn! he swore. Everything he had worked for was falling apart. Rising suddenly, he strode toward the room's corner and knelt on the dirty floor. Drawing a knife from under his jacket, he pried a board from the floor and drew out a cloth sack. It contained a money belt and a leather pouch full of coins. At least he had the money. Even if he couldn't work in the valley again, he could easily move on to another town and set up the same kind of operation. The two fighting armies did not have enough men to occupy the mountains, so they rushed back and forth like a dog trying to protect two bones. It was an ideal opportunity to rob the citizens and sell to the starving armies.

On a sudden impulse, he decided to leave immediately. He packed his meager belongings in a sack, tucked his stolen rifle under his arm and left the shack. As he strode down the mountain, he made his plans. He would sneak into town after dark and steal all he needed to travel—a horse and some food. He smiled to himself, pleased with his plan. He'd go north over Droop Mountain and on to Elkins. It was over a hundred miles, but he could make that in a couple of days on a good horse.

Within an hour he was at the edge of town. He sat just off the pike on a rock and waited for dark. He searched his pockets for tobacco and papers and built a cigarette. The smoke drifted over his head as he watched the town. A few people wandered the street, and he could hear the clear ring of the blacksmith's hammer. One by one lights came on in house windows and he saw smoke climb from chimneys in straight columns as darkness closed in. Troy Jones was devoid of appreciation for the still beauty around him. He concentrated only on planning his next selfish move.

He waited until darkness had closed completely over the town. Crouching behind the rock, he watched an elderly couple in a buggy pass on the pike heading west out of town. At last the town was quiet and lights went out, one by one.

He rose stiffly from his seat, checked the load in his rifle, and walked toward town, keeping to the darker shadows.

He decided to try the blacksmiths' shop first; he would find a horse there, and then he'd head north, stealing food on the way. He walked along the deserted sidewalk cautiously, straining to see ahead of him. Only a shred of new moon hung in the sky to light his way. He turned the corner and suddenly saw a man slouched on a bench with his feet stretched before him. His head was down and he appeared to be asleep. A quick victim for a stolen wallet? He was leaving town anyway. He approached silently, drawing his knife.

The rustle of his clothing alerted the man on the bench and his head swung up and around at the sound. Jones was within a few feet of him and he froze at the man's quick movement.

"Jones! It's you," Boyd spoke quietly.

"Yeah, it's me, Reb," Jones replied, surprised at the identity of his intended victim, "And I'm going to snuff out your light for what you've done to me!"

"It wasn't anything I did, Jones. You did it to yourself," Boyd answered. He grasped the back of the bench with his outstretched hand, and drew his feet back under himself, preparing for Jones' attack.

Boyd was unarmed. He could see the faint glint of moonlight on Jones' knife. Jones held his rifle in his left hand, the knife in his right. The rush would come suddenly—and soon.

"Why did you have to kill him?" Boyd asked, stalling for time. "He wasn't going to hurt you."

"You talking about that old man up on the mountain? I killed him because he caught me in his hen house, so to speak," he chuckled. "Came running out on his porch and would have shot me with that old shotgun of his. I didn't have a choice."

"Not the way I see it! You made your choice long before you arrived at his farm."

"I'm getting tired of your meddling, Houston, and I'm going to take care of that right now." He made a sudden lunge at Boyd, slashing at his neck with the knife. Boyd pushed himself backward off of the side of the bench, away from the attack, rolling into a crouch. He heard the knife strike the back of the bench where his head had been. Jones dropped the rifle and stepped quickly around the bench, swinging the knife before him. He feinted suddenly and Boyd scrambled backward, tripping and falling to the ground.

He heard a grunt of pleasure from Jones, and prepared for another attack. Jones was quick for such a large man, and there was strength in those arms and hands. Boyd scrambled backward trying to rise to his feet. He saw an arc of light glint from the knife as Jones struck with a roundhouse sweep. Boyd caught his wrist with both hands, the tip of the blade only inches from his face. The two men struggled, grunting and swearing, locked in a deadly dance. Jones thrust with all his strength, but Boyd pushed him back.

"Damn you, Houston," Jones grated between his teeth as they struggled. "I'll kill you."

Boyd twisted his body suddenly, and whirled Jones away. The two men circled each other warily. Jones thrust and feinted. Suddenly he rushed Boyd and slashed viciously at his stomach. The knife ripped at Boyd's jacket sending a button flying to rattle on a nearby flagstone.

Jones rushed him again, gouging at Boyd with the knife. Boyd struck his wrist, but Jones came on clutching the knife before him. They scuffled back and forth, each trying to gain an advantage. From somewhere in the houses behind them, a dog barked, startled by the commotion, and a light came on in the rooms over the print shop.

Jones thrust the point of the knife at Boyd's chest, but Boyd caught his wrist again, twisting it painfully. Beneath his hands, Boyd could feel a bone snap. Jones yelped with pain and dropped the knife. "Damn you to hell, Houston. You've broken it," he whined. Boyd tackled him around the knees, dragging him to the dirt. The two men rolled on the ground, grunting and scratching. Boyd caught the distinct scent of horse manure. Grappling in the dirt, Jones found a rock with his good hand and struck Boyd on the side of the head. Suddenly, Jones rolled free, and clutching his injured wrist against his stomach, hobbled up the street. Boyd lay dazed in the dirt, a halo of dust rising slowly around him, illuminated like a shroud by the weak moonlight.

An old man, dressed only in his long underwear, approached Boyd cautiously from the print shop. He held a flickering candle high above his head as it threw a weak circle of light over Boyd. He rolled onto his back and sat up. The candlelight threw a ghostly cast over the old man's face, and his scraggly gray hair stood on end. He worked his toothless mouth as he stared at Boyd.

"Here now, what you doin' out here? Who was you fightin' with?" Boyd rubbed the side of his head where a huge knot had risen. "It was Troy Jones. He tried to kill me. He hit me on the head and got away."

"Well now, Sonny, I don't 'preciate bein' woken up in the middle of the night with folk fightin' in the streets." He squinted at Boyd, thrusting the smoking candle in his face. "You're that Houston feller, ain't you? There ain't been nothin' but trouble since you got to town. An' I heard you was messin' with them nigras. Folk should ride you out o' town on a rail," the old man mumbled. He turned abruptly and shuffled back to the print shop. The door slammed behind him.

Boyd stumbled back to the bench and sat wearily on its edge. He leaned forward and held his head in his hands. It throbbed with pain, and he could feel a cut and dampness on the crest of the knot. His shoulder ached from the strain on the old injury. He rose wearily and recovered Jones' knife and rifle, but returned to the bench as a wave of nausea swept over him. He leaned back and looked up at the moon. He could see the entire circle of the moon, lightly outlined, and the bright sliver illuminated along one edge. A dim halo encircled it. It would rain within one day, he thought to himself, if the old sailor's prediction was true. He wrinkled his nose at the acrid odor of horse manure. His pants leg was wet and sticky and he really didn't want to know what it was.

He chuckled to himself, in spite of his aches and pains. What else could happen to him? He'd fought a battle, was wounded, had been involved in a murder, was tossed into a cave, was witness to a mass hanging, Jones had tried to kill him, and he had fallen in love. Now all he had to do was to find out what all this meant...and who it was he loved.

He threw back his head and laughed aloud, then began to gather up the rifle and knife when the window over the print shop was thrown open with a bang.

"Go on home and go to bed, you damned fool," the old man yelled.

✔ ✔ ✔ ✔

Troy Jones sat in the shack and held his broken wrist in his left hand, squeezing it as hard as he could stand. It hurt...bad. He gritted his teeth and looked around for something to use as a splint. He settled on some dirty rags and a piece of splintered wood. He sat on the broken chair and used his good hand and his teeth to wrap the splint in place. When he was finished, he began searching through the empty whiskey bottles on the floor for a little something to drink. He turned up a bottle that he had found in a corner and swallowed the single mouthful of amber liquid that was left in its bottom; it burned pleasantly as it slid down his throat. A search of the cupboard yielded a half bottle of rye. He smiled an evil smile as he sat down on the chair and began to drink.

While his mind began to dull, he made himself a promise. Soon, he would hunt that Boyd Houston down and kill him. Not quickly, but slowly and painfully. He would shoot him in the belly and make him hurt, but before he let him die he would break his wrists. Jones smiled as the last swallow burned into his stomach and his eyes drooped. He crawled onto the dirty bunk and covered himself with a rumpled blanket and drifted off to sleep.

♪ ♪ ♪ ♪

Charlie Taylor sat on the front porch of his home on Muddy Creek Mountain and looked out over the fields. Colleen sat on his lap, curled up like a squirrel in a knothole, her hands clasped tightly to her chest, eyes closed. She twitched slightly, like a sleeping pup on a hearth. Kate occupied another rocking chair with her right leg curled up under her. She read silently from a leather-bound book. The brassy afternoon sun spread a pleasant warmth over them.

Charlie was troubled. His brow was furrowed with concentration as he tried to sort through the events of the last few days. He was surprised that he hadn't heard from any of the farmers in the valley concerning the whereabouts of Jones. Could he have left the valley without being seen? Charlie doubted it. It was strange that no one had seen him. He must have gone to hole like a rabbit before a storm.

Charlie shifted his weight and Colleen mumbled in her sleep. He was worried about Boyd. The youngster was always getting into trouble. He seemed to have a knack for being at the wrong place at the wrong time. Jones would kill him if he had a chance, and Boyd plunged into things without much thought about his own safety. And, the folks in town were on the verge of turning on him. Particularly if they decided that Nellie was with the runaways. They had seen him with her on the night of the hangings, and several of the townsfolk had grumbled to Charlie about him.

No, Boyd didn't understand how these folk thought about such things. The people in town were good folk, for the most part. Only a few of them owned slaves and were overly protective of their property. Not that the majority wouldn't support their right to own slaves; they would. They didn't like to have outsiders meddling in their business.

He hadn't heard from Boyd in several days, and that worried him. Having Boyd in town by himself was just asking for trouble. No, he'd better slip down the mountain and see what was going on. Maybe check with the sheriff to see what was happening.

"Kate," he said suddenly, "how'd you and the youngin's like to go into town? Maybe pick up some supplies. Weather'll be settin' in soon and we need some things."

"Charlie, you can't fool me. You're going to go and check on Boyd. But that's all right. We'll ride in with you. The kids and I haven't been in town for months and it'll be fun," she laughed.

"Darlin' I never could fool you, could I?"

"Not for a minute, Charlie Taylor. Not for a minute."

Early the next morning they loaded the children in the wagon and set off for town. Kate sat straight as an arrow on the wagon seat as Charlie clucked the horses into motion. As they started down the valley, he looked at his wife out of the corner of his eye. The sharp morning sunshine sparkled on her red hair. No matter how long they were married, he decided, he would always love this woman. She turned suddenly toward him, her green eyes sparkling. "What?" she questioned. "What are you looking at?"

"Why, I'm lookin' at you darlin.' I don't ever get my fill of that."

Kate rolled her eyes toward the heavens and grinned at him. The children in the back of the wagon giggled at their parents' subtle courting.

The wagon rattled and banged down the high valley. The children exclaimed at each brightly colored tree they saw. Colleen decided that she liked the scarlet black gum trees best. Matt and Jacob chose the maroon color of the dogwood. They discussed the warm October weather and laughed at the jerky movement of the chipmunks that rushed back and forth across the road ahead of them.

Finally they topped the high ridge that overlooked the Greenbrier valley. The sight was breathtaking. Rolling far to the horizon was hill after hill covered with the brilliant colors of fall. Charlie stopped the wagon and the five of them sat in silence and took in the wondrous sight. The morning light played on the land as on the bright plumage of a jungle bird. A low cloud crossed the sun and they could see its shadow, like a sailing ship, scud across the valley to rise over the far mountain rim and disappear. Kate placed her hand contentedly on her husband's knee.

♪ ♪ ♪ ♪

The Taylor family rolled into town about mid-morning. The quiet mountain town had returned to normal since the Yankee army had moved out. A brightly colored stage coach rolled in town from the east, causing a cloud of yellow dust to hang in the air. It pulled up before the tavern near the hospital and its occupants began to get down, stretching and slapping the dust from their clothes. Charlie, from long years of habit, looked the travelers over carefully. Two men, dressed in business suits stomped the kinks out of their legs, picked up their satchels, and trooped into the tavern.

A young woman was met by an elderly man and his wife. They embraced and the woman led them down the street, all talking excitedly at once. Last to disembark from the stage was a small, spindly man with sharp blue eyes and the bushiest moustache Charlie had ever seen. Dark eyebrows swept back from his eyes giving his face a hard, hawk-like appearance and a full head of gray hair hung over his ears like a wet cap. He looked at Charlie and his family as if they were bugs, dragged his battered suitcase from the back of the stage and headed purposefully toward the tavern.

"Who was that little man, Daddy?" Colleen asked. "He looked like he didn't like us much."

"I don't rightly know, child," Charlie replied absently with a troubled look on his face.

Kate and the children walked toward the general store, stopping to visit and gossip with friends on the street. Everyone smiled and teased Colleen as Matt and Jacob stood by grinning. Charlie turned from the scene and walked down Court Street to the courthouse to find the sheriff. He was sitting behind his desk as usual, frowning at a pile of papers arranged in an untidy pile. He held a stub of a pencil in his left hand as he thumbed through the paperwork.

"Sheriff," Charlie nodded in greeting.

"Oh, it's you, Taylor," Sheriff Brown acknowledged, leaning back in his chair. "I wondered when you'd come into town again."

"What's happening, Sheriff? When will Mr. James stand trial?"

"Waal," the sheriff drawled, "that's hard to say. That all depends on when the judge gets to town. Should be any day now."

"What's he look like, Sheriff?" Charlie asked.

"Little bit of a feller with a big bush of a moustache an' gray hair. He'll come in on the stage and hold court for a couple o' days. Won't take him long to decide what to do 'bout ole Mr. James. I reckon you haven't ever seen him, what with you being away at the war an' all."

"I reckon he came in on today's stage." Charlie described the traveler he had seen arrive only minutes before. "Looked like he made a beeline for the tavern."

"Yep, that's him all right. Judge Bright likes his liquor. Like as not he'll be 'bout half tanked when he sits at the bench, but even then, he'll render a good decision. He ain't hardly ever overturned by the higher courts."

"What do you hear from Mr. James' lawyer?"

"Well, that news ain't so good. He wants to charge you an' Houston with attempted murder. Claims you two jumped Mr. James and tried to rob him. I reckon it all depends on how Mr. James' trial turns out. Good thing you came into town, or I'd of had to send someone up on the mountain with a summons. You saved me a might o' trouble."

"Sheriff, have you seen Boyd around anywhere? Last I heard he was staying over at the boardinghouse."

"Yep, I seen him in town yesterday. He's been around town for a couple o' days. Folks say he's courtin' that Saunders girl. I can't figger how her daddy would let him near her, him bein' broke an' all."

"That's good to hear, Sheriff. To tell you the truth, I was beginnin' to worry 'bout him gettin' messed up with that girl of Mr. James'."

"I'm not sure there ain't something to that. Folks like to gossip, an' I been hearin' some pretty rough talk about that, too. Oh, by the way, I don't suppose that you've heard that he had a run-in with Troy Jones. Old Mr. Arbogast over at the print shop told me he saw them fightin' in the street one night. Seems no one was hurt bad, but Jones left town kinda quick like."

Charlie and the sheriff talked about the trial. The sheriff warned him not to leave town, and to find Boyd and tell him to stick around too. The sheriff would let them know when to appear before the judge.

Charlie left the courthouse and rounded the corner onto Main Street. He spotted Kate and the children talking to Boyd in front of the store. Boyd grinned at Kate and answered the children's questions. He held his hat in his hands before him.

Boyd greeted Charlie cheerfully, glancing occasionally at Kate. Matt pulled at his sleeve, intent on asking questions.

"Boyd, won't you join us for some lunch?" Kate asked. "We brought some extra food in case we ran in to you." The children chorused their approval and the noisy group moved toward the wagon and team.

"May as well unhitch the team, Jacob, we're going to be here for a while. Take them around to the blacksmith's shop an' he'll put them up for us." Charlie explained quickly about the judge's arrival and the impending trial.

They sat under a big maple along the street and ate their lunch. They were interrupted frequently by passersby as friends stopped to talk to Charlie and Kate. Occasionally a dirty look was cast toward Boyd.

"What's this I hear 'bout you seein' that Saunders girl?" Charlie asked, grinning at Boyd. "I hear y'all are gettin' kinda thick. You must be some kind o' miracle worker after what I heard from her last time I was in town."

Boyd blushed, "How do you do it? You haven't been in town for more than an hour and you have already caught up on all of the gossip. Is there anything that you haven't heard?"

"As a matter of fact there is. What's this about you runnin' into Jones here in town?"

Boyd looked at him with his mouth open. "How'd you hear about that? I haven't told anyone about our run-in."

"Mr. Arbogast over at the print shop told the sheriff. It's all over town by now. He's the biggest gossip in town. It's a wonder it hasn't showed up in the paper."

Boyd told them quickly about the fight. Matt and Jacob sat close by, hanging on every word. Matt asked a dozen questions before Boyd could answer, but Charlie stopped him, saying this was grown-up talk. Kate sat in the shade and looked at Boyd with a worried expression.

"Now, Kate," Charlie grumbled, "a man has to defend hisself."

After they had eaten, Kate and Colleen walked down the street again to the store. Charlie and Boyd, followed by the two boys, walked up the pike toward the church. They stopped beside the gray stone building and looked reverently at the red mound of dirt that was the resting place of so many soldiers. Someone had placed a bunch of late summer asters on the unmarked grave. Charlie and Boyd doffed their hats and stood in silence, each remembering the battle and violence of that warm May morning, not so long ago. The boys stood beside their father, hats in hand, mirroring him.

Their quiet contemplation was shattered as a young man shouted excitedly to them from half a block away. "Hey, you fellers. The sheriff wants to see you. The judge's in town an' there's goin' to be a trial."

9

The judge pounded the court to order as he sat behind the bench with only his shoulders and head showing over the top of the scarred oak balustrade. He frowned down at the packed courtroom and nodded toward the sheriff who moved to a side door and opened it briskly. Mr. James entered slowly with his lawyer at his side and sat behind a narrow wooden table facing the judge. His wounded shoulder was done up in a huge white bandage. He folded his hands carefully on his lap and glowered at the prosecuting attorney, Howard Clayton, who sat at a matching table, also facing the bench, fiddling with a stack of papers. The prosecuting attorney didn't look up at the judge.

Howard was none too anxious to face this miniature whirlwind who glared down at him. During the last session of court, a fancy lawyer from Lexington had defeated him soundly in a suit over a property boundary dispute. Folks had whispered that Howard had shown up in court drunk. Judge Bright was overheard telling the sheriff after the trial that amateur drunks made a bad name for serious drinkers.

"You ready, Mr. Clayton?" the judge asked gruffly.

Howard stood up shakily and replied, "Yes, your honor."

"How 'bout you, counselor," the judged nodded toward Garnett Russell, the attorney for the defense. He was a red-faced man with a large protruding stomach. Short and squat, he carried himself with much self-importance and his florid faced was creased with a per-

189

petual frown and boasted a prominent, bulbous nose. He had arrived in town only a few months back and was working hard to make a name for himself. Howard was no match for this man, and everyone in the courtroom knew it.

"Ready yer honor," the lawyer replied.

"Now, I wanna tell you fellers, I don't plan to set here all day and listen to you shoot the breeze at me. I want the facts of this case in a hurry, an' I want you to get on with it now. You, there, Mr. Clayton," he sneered, "what charges do you have 'gainst this man?"

Mr. Clayton stood facing the bench. "Your Honor," he began tentatively, "the State charges Mr. James with attemptin' to steal stock and food stuffs from Mr. McMillion up at Falling Spring. I got a couple o' witnesses here; Charlie Taylor from up on the mountain an' the Reb here, Boyd Houston. They saw him an' another man, a Mr. Troy Jones," he consulted his notes, "sneakin' up on Mac's house in the middle of the night." He sat down abruptly.

"Is that it?" the judge frowned down at him. " You tellin' me that all you got is two fellers claimin' that two other fellers were creepin' up on a house in the middle of the night? What do you have to say about the charges, Mr. James?" he asked as he swung his head around toward the defendant's table.

Garrett Russell cut off Mr. James before he could answer and stood quickly. "Your Honor," he laughed comfortably, "this is about the most ridiculous charge I've ever heard. I can't see how the sheriff had the gall to hold this honorable, upstanding man on charges so stupid. It's right curious how a man like this could be charged with this 'crime' by a driftin' Reb an' a man like Taylor there. Why, they aren't even town folk."

Charlie stiffened on the hard wooden bench and snorted his contempt for the lawyer. Kate cautioned him while keeping her eyes locked on the judge.

A murmur of affirmation rumbled through the courtroom. The judge glared at the spectators and pounded his gavel on the bench.

He drew his attention back to the lawyer. "You just keep comments like that to yourself, counselor."

"Sorry, Your Honor. But, the charges are so hideous that they'd be laughable if the reputation of such an outstanding citizen as Mr. James wasn't at stake." His face had begun to take on a crimson color as a result of his strenuous efforts. Howard sat passively at his table and fiddled with his stack of papers.

"Okay, okay, counselor, simmer down. You'll get your chance to question everyone and to prove your point."

The judge quickly outlined the court procedure. As was the custom of the court for such a minor charge, a jury would not be called. The judge would listen to the evidence and render a decision.

Howard called Boyd to the stand. He ran through Boyd's testimony, roughly sketching the facts. Boyd looked at him curiously, wondering why he wasn't being led more carefully through the events of Mr. James' part in the raid. Howard sat down abruptly and began to stack and restack his hoard of papers.

"Your witness, counselor," the judge smiled at Russell.

"Mr. Houston. That's your name, is it?" Russell asked.

"Yes sir."

"Mr. Houston, just what were you doin' up at Falling Spring on the night that the alleged attack on the McMillion farm took place?"

"Well," Boyd began, "Charlie and I were there to catch a couple of thieves..."

"Just what made you think there'd be an attempted robbery?" Russell interrupted.

"Well, ah, I'd heard that someone was going to rob him." Boyd answered obliquely. His response brightened Russell's eyes. Something was being hidden here.

"And, just who might that have been, Mr. Houston. An' I'll remind you that you're under oath," the counselor frowned, his lower lip sticking out at Boyd. He rocked back and forth on his heels and wrinkled his red forehead.

Boyd squirmed on the witness chair. In only a few minutes Russell had successfully put him on the hot seat. He didn't want to tell them that Nellie had informed them about the raid, but he didn't want to lie on the stand either. This bandy rooster of a judge would slap him in jail for the next decade if he was caught lying.

"Do I have to answer that, Judge?" Boyd asked hopefully.

"No, Mr. Houston, you don't," the judge mimicked him. "Course you'll spend the best part of your young life in my jail here if you choose not to. It's your choice,"

The crowd in the courtroom chuckled at the judge's humor. Boyd wasn't laughing.

"Mr. Houston," Russell prompted him loudly, "who told you that there'd be a raid on the McMillion farm?" He waited with a smirk on his face.

"Ah, uh, well, Mr. James' nigra girl, Nellie, told me that she overheard Mr. John and Troy Jones planning the raid." He warmed to the subject, now that the news was out. "She gave us the time and place, so Charlie and I were waiting on them at the farm. They showed up just like she said they would."

Boyd glanced at Mr. James. He sat behind the table with his head down and played with a pencil. The veins on the sides of his neck stood out. Nellie would have a hard time of it tonight.

"Are you telling me, Mr. Houston, that you put faith in what a darkie told you? What made you think that she was tellin' the truth?"

"I know her. She helped Mr. James nurse me back to health after the battle last spring."

The counselor jumped on his response like a quail on a hapless dung beetle. He made a big deal of Boyd spending time in the same house with Nellie, and the crowd began to murmur again.

"I don't have any more questions for this man," Russell said contemptuously.

"Cross-examine?" the judge asked Howard.

"No, Your Honor," Howard replied as he stood awkwardly. His

hands shook noticably and he placed them palms down on the table.

"Didn't reckon you would," the judge said tiredly.

Charlie was called to testify next. He climbed up on the stand and was sworn in. He sat stiffly in the witness stand and grinned foolishly at the crowd. Kate smiled proudly at him and the children looked at him with some apprehension.

Charlie responded patiently as Howard took him briefly through the events of the night of the raid. No new details were uncovered. Russell wasted no time beginning his attack on Charlie as soon as Howard sat down.

"Mr. Taylor, you live up on Muddy Creek Mountain' don't you?"

"Yep." Charlie was a man of few words for a change. The less said the better, he figured.

Russell paced before the bench, stopping with his back to Charlie. He smiled at the crowd. Without turning back to the witness he asked, "Did you shoot Mr. James?"

"Yep." Russell whirled back toward the witness and with his nose no more than six inches from Charlie asked loudly, "You mean to tell me and all these good folk in this courtroom that you shot an innocent man down in cold blood?"

"Nope."

"Well now, Mr. Taylor, make up your mind. Either you shot him or you didn't. Which is it?"

"I shot ole Mr. James, but he ain't hardly innocent." The crowd tittered at Charlie's response.

"Why did you shoot him?"

"Counselor, I've shot a lot of men in the last couple 'o years, bein' in the army an' all, but I ain't shot nobody that needed it any more than this ole' fart. He's a thief an' I don't have any problem shootin' thieves. Besides, he was probably with Jones when he kilt Pop Cooper from up on the mountain."

"Objection, Your Honor!" Russell shouted. "Mr. James isn't being charged with that killing."

"Simmer down, Counselor, an' you don't have to yell at me. I'm right here in the same room with you. Objection sustained. Keep your testimony to the case before the bench, Mr. Taylor."

Russell suddenly changed his line of questioning as he returned to the witness. "Is it your testimony that you and the Reb here rode all the way up to Falling Spring in the middle of the night to catch a thief that was identified by a darkie? Her owner at that?" Russell asked in mock amazement.

"Well now, counselor, since you asked," Charlie grinned, "that's exactly what happened. I'd trust a darkie any time over the likes of you. My daddy used to say that they was goin' to use big city lawyers like you fer mules to pull the wagons and such. Fer one thing they's a lot more lawyers in town than they is mules. An' besides that, they's just some things a mule won't do."

The courtroom erupted in laughter as the judge pounded furiously on his bench. Russell, redder in the face than usual, shouted insults over the din at Charlie, who sat calmly on the stand and smiled at him. Russell sat down quickly, slouching in his chair, and drummed his pencil on the table. Charlie climbed down from the stand grinning broadly at the crowd.

With no more witnesses, both sides rested. The judge left the bench for his chambers to deliberate his decision, slamming the door behind him.

Charlie leaned toward Boyd and whispered quietly to him. "This don't look too good, Sonny, even if I did score one on Russell. Ole Howard there aint' 'zackly on the good side of the judge. Like as not Mr. James'll get off scott free."

True to Charlie's prediction, the judge returned to his seat above the interested crowd, pounded the bench noisily with his gavel, and glowered down at Howard. The verdict of not guilty held little surprise to anyone in the courtroom since it was obvious that the judge didn't like the prosecutor, and unless he had a watertight case he'd have a hard time getting a conviction in this court. His presentation of the case was far from watertight.

The crowd drifted away, noisily discussing the merits of the case as they looked askance at Charlie and Boyd. Kate stood beside her husband with the children pressed around her. Howard pushed wordlessly by them and made his way quickly across the street to his office in a two story house made of cut limestone.

Mr. James and Russell shoved their way roughly through the crowd; Russell, still flushed and angry, glared at Charlie and Boyd. Mr. James shook his finger in Boyd's face and yelled at him, sending a shower of spittle into the narrow space between them.

"I'll get you, damn your hide," he blustered. He held his wounded arm tenderly before him. "You and that darkie will pay for this. I'll beat the hide off of her, and there isn't one damned thing that you can do about it. I'll get you yet. You mark my word."

Regaining his composure somewhat Mr. James was drawn aside by Russell who whispered advice urgently in his ear. The two moved quickly down the street toward the pike. Mr. James glared back over his shoulder at Boyd as they turned the corner.

"Ain't nothin' that turns my stomach like a poor winner," Charlie laughed. "You'da thought he'd lost the case."

↗ ↗ ↗ ↗

Henry forked hay from the loft down to the floor of the small barn behind Mr. James' fine brick home. He climbed down the rickety ladder and moved the pile of hay to the manger before Bessy. She munched on the hay, watching Henry from the corner of her eye. Henry was worried. Word of the trial had swept through the town like wildfire. All of the slaves were whispering among themselves about it, especially the part that Nellie had played. Mr. James had returned home from the trial to fall exhausted in his bed. Nellie remained in the kitchen house as he slept. What would he do to her when he awoke? Henry leaned on the pitch fork and frowned at Jake as he crawled from under the manger, expecting to be fed. Whatever happened, it wouldn't be good. Nellie would be lucky to get out of this alive.

Henry's problem was complicated. More than anything, he wanted to stay out of the ruckus. He would be content to stay in the barn with the cow and cat and mind his own business. But he also wanted to protect Nellie. She had always been good to him; better than that sourpuss Mazel. He remembered when she was born. Her mother was right proud of her and had let Henry hold her once. He remembered how she had grasped his finger with her tiny hand and kicked her feet at him when he tickled her. He didn't know who Nellie's father was. It could be him, but Mr. James had made several of the slaves bed with her mother, trying to make sure she would have a child. Henry had been one of those men, but it was unlikely that he, out of several men, was her father. In any event, he felt protective of her and knew that if the situation got too bad, he'd have to take action. He couldn't just stand aside and let Mr. James kill her; there'd been enough killing as it was.

Morning sunlight streamed through the barn door. The air was cold and there had been another hard frost the night before. Henry began to move about the barn, doing his morning chores. He wished that everything was like it had been only a few months before. It seemed as if all the trouble had started with the battle in town back in May. Why hadn't the Yanks found another town to occupy? That way the Confederate forces wouldn't have shown up here and started all the trouble.

Suddenly, Henry heard angry voices coming from the kitchen house. What was going on now? He looked out of the barn door to see Mr. James dragging Nellie along behind him toward the barn. He was snarling angrily at her as he pulled her along by her wrist. His bandaged shoulder seeped blood where he had reopened his wound.

"Henry! Where are you, you no good nigra! Come out here and help me," Mr. James yelled toward the barn. Henry didn't know what to do. Should he run and hide like he had during the battle? Too late.

"I see you there, Henry. You get your ass out here an' help me."

Henry stepped warily out of the barn and stood waiting for the approaching man and his struggling victim.

"I'm going to teach this darkie a lesson once and for all. Here, help me tie her up to that beam there. You remember, the one I used when I caught you eating my food." Nellie jerked her wrist violently, but could not break Mr. James' grasp. Her eyes were wide in terror.

"Get that rope over there and do what I tell you, or I'll haul you up beside her." Henry stood frozen to the spot. Mr. James glared at Henry and grated through clenched teeth, "You do what you're told. Now!"

The spell broke, and Henry scrambled to get the rope. He tossed one end over the ceiling beam and stood aside. Mr. James quickly tied Nellie's wrists together with the dangling end and then, grasping the other end, hauled down violently. The force of the act jerked her from her feet as the rope bit into her flesh. She clenched her teeth as her arms stretched above her; her toes barely brushed the straw-covered barn floor. No sound came from her except her labored breathing.

"Now I've got you where I want you, wench. I'll take care of you. Oh, I'm not going to kill you—you're much too valuable for that. All I'm going to do is take about half of the hide off of your back. I'll teach you to listen in on my private conversations and go telling that Reb boyfriend of yours," Mr. James screamed. He sat down on a feed barrel and rubbed his shoulder. "Look what you've done now. I'm bleeding again."

He stood up suddenly, strode to the barn wall, and took down a buggy whip. It had a long, wooden handle and a short narrow braided leather whip attached. He turned toward Nellie and looked into her eyes. "Let's see how long you can go without screaming your lungs out."

Henry watched in horror from the corner of the barn. He wrung his hands before him and shifted his weight from foot to foot. His face was contorted in terror. Mr. James stepped around behind Nellie. He braced his feet and swung with all his might. The tip of the leather whip whined through the air and struck her back. It cut through her thin dress, ripping a slanted gash through the fabric. Blood splattered on the straw. A low moan escaped her lips. Mr. James uttered a throaty laugh, causing his belly to shake obscenely. He drew back again, but at the top of his back swing, something hard and forceful clutched his wrist. He turned to face Henry who held his arm in midair as if it were that of a child.

"No, suh. You ain't agoin' to do this to her," Henry said. He stood nose to nose with Mr. James and looked him squarely in the eyes. He had never looked a white man in the eyes before. He always averted his eyes around them.

"Now you listen to me, you black bastard. You let go of my arm now or I'll take this whip to you again. Just like I did before."

"No, suh, I don' think so. You just let go o' that whip an' I'll let go of you."

Nellie struggled to turn herself to see what was going on behind her. "No, Henry. It's all right. Don't do this. Let him go, now."

The two men stared at each other with the tip of the whip making circles in the air above them. "You better listen to her, Henry. You better let me go right now." Mr. James' voice shook as a frightened look crossed his face. He had never seen such a terrifying look on a human face before.

Mr. James suddenly jerked his wrist free and struck Henry with the wooden stock of the whip. An angry welt rose on his cheek. The two men grappled with each other and Henry wrenched the whip from his hands. Mr. James gasped with pain as his shoulder was twisted and bruised. Henry grasped Mr. James' shirt-front with both hands and violently shoved him back toward the manger. Mr. James stumbled backward windmilling the air with his arms to keep his balance, but he fell heavily on his back. Henry stepped toward him threateningly and Mr. James covered his head with his heads.

"No! Henry, no!" Nelly screamed. Henry stopped. He turned slowly and approached her, loosened the rope, and allowed her to drop her hands. He quickly untied her and she rubbed her wrists. Mr. James watched them from the corner.

"Oh, Henry. I really got you in trouble. What're we goin' to do now?" Nellie wailed. Henry didn't know. He had always depended upon someone else to tell him what to do. Now he was in deep trouble with no inkling of what to do.

Suddenly, Mr. James rushed toward them with a pitch fork in his hands: Its sharp tines glistened in the dim light. Henry deftly brushed the fork aside and Mr. James crashed against the barn wall, splintering the handle. A flash of pain shot through his shoulder and an uncontrollable anger gripped him. He threw aside the broken half of the fork and, with a sharp stub of handle left attached, rushed Henry again. Henry easily caught the fork and pushed Mr. James violently back toward the wall. The tines rose sharply toward Henry as Mr. James held the broken fork in front of his chest with Henry's powerful hands crushing over his. Mr. James' back struck the wall again with a crash and the sharp splinter of the handle pierced his chest. A gush of hot blood drenched Henry's hands as Mr. James slid down the wall and sat heavily on the floor. His eyes bulged and his mouth worked up and down soundlessly.

Henry gasped in horror at the sight before him. Mr. James slumped forward then rolled onto his side. The splintered end of the fork handle protruded grotesquely from his back. Henry backed away and stared at his bloody hands.

"Oh, God Almighty, I done kilt him," he whispered. "I didn't mean to. I didn't mean to. All I ever wanted was to be left alone. Oh, what'll happen to us now?" Henry stood in the center of the shabby barn, staring at his shaking hands.

♪ ♪ ♪ ♪

Boyd stood across the street from Mr. James' house and shivered in the morning air. After the trial, Charlie and Kate took their family home, and Boyd followed Mr. James back to his house. He was afraid for Nellie. He didn't know exactly what he was going to do if Nellie was threatened. Mr. James had wearily entered the front door of his house and had not left. As darkness approached a single lamp was lit in the parlor and Boyd could see that Mr. James had settled in for the night. Boyd moved around the house to the kitchen house looking for Nellie. It was dark and quiet. He left quietly, planning to return the next morning.

Now, he stood under a huge sugar maple and watched the elegant brick house. There was no movement. A wagon loaded with barrels rolled from the center of town up the pike in front of the house. The driver, a man Boyd recognized from the trial, glared at him as he passed. The horses grunted and snorted up the grade as they headed east toward the crest above the river.

Boyd leaned against the tree and remembered the battle. He stood almost on the spot where his regiment had formed a skirmish line before the fight. He remembered the scene—blood and smoke...

A commotion behind the house interrupted his musings. He heard excited voices; a man and a woman. He walked across the pike and around the house. Just in front of the kitchen house, Nellie and Henry were talking excitedly. Nellie looked up suddenly to see Boyd striding toward them. She shushed Henry and gripped his arm. Henry looked sheepishly at Boyd and dropped his eyes to the ground.

"Mr. Boyd!" Nellie exclaimed. "We didn't 'spect to see you here."

"Hello, Nellie. I just wanted to make sure that you were okay. I guess you heard what happened at the trial yesterday," Boyd smiled at her. Henry stood to one side shuffling his feet.

"Yeah, Henry tole me. He heard from Mr. Pennington's boy. I reckon you jus' did what you had to," Nellie replied with her head down.

They stood in the yard awkwardly, wondering what to say next. Finally Boyd broke the silence. "I was worried that Mr. James would hurt you. I've been watching from across the street. I don't know what to do to help you. I'm afraid..."

Nellie interrupted, "You don't have to worry about me, Mr. Boyd, I'll be okay. Mr. James ain't goin' to hurt no one."

Boyd was baffled by her words. Mr. James had been very angry yesterday after the trial and Boyd was sure that he would take it out on someone. Nellie would be the logical choice since she would not be able to defend herself.

"If you're sure you're all right, I'll go. It would probably be worse if Mr. James found me here talking to you." Boyd began to move away and stopped. Something was definitely wrong here. Henry had a scared look and Nellie wouldn't look him in the eye. As he started again, Nellie caught him gently by the elbow. She came lightly into his arms for a brief embrace. Henry shuffled around the corner of the kitchen house out of their sight, embarrassed.

Boyd's arms went around her by reflex. Nellie winced as his fingers found the bloody tear in the back of her dress. He drew his hand away quickly and looked at his fingers.

"Nelly, you're bleeding! What happened? Here, let me look." He took her by the shoulders and turned her around. He drew his breath in sharply. Her dress gaped open where the whip had ripped it. A nasty gash, over a foot long showed on her back, trickling blood.

"Oh, Nellie, what happened? Did Mr. James do this? Where is he?" Boyd asked harshly. She only stood and stared at him with eyes that were pools of anguish. He took her again tenderly by the shoulders and looked intensely at her. "Talk to me, Nellie. What has happened? Did Mr. James do this to you?" he asked again.

Sudden tears welled up in her eyes and her shoulders shook as she sobbed. "It's all my fault. They kilt Mazel and Mr. Joseph an' it was my fault. An' now I done kilt Henry. He's a dead man jus' like them others as sure as the world."

"What are you talking about? Henry's back at the barn by now. He's okey, Nellie. I'll talk to Mr. James and make sure he doesn't hurt you and Henry. If necessary I'll try to buy your freedom."

"You don' understand, Mr. Boyd. Henry an' me done kilt Mr. James. He's layin' back there in the barn with a pitch fork through his belly."

Boyd's face took on a look of horror. Mr. James...dead? Boyd dropped his hands to his sides. Nellie stood before him with stooped shoulders, her head down. Her body shook with silent sobs.

Finally he found words. "What happened, Nellie? Why did you kill Mr. James? Did it have somethin' to do with the whip mark on your back?

The sobbing stopped as she raised her chin toward him. A look of defiance came into her eyes and she set her jaw. "Course it did. Mr. James he had me tied to a beam in the barn an' was jus' startin' to whip me. Henry tried to stop him. It was a accident. Henry didn't want nothin' but fer him to let me alone, but Mr. James jus' kept on. They fought over the fork an' Mr. James, he ended up with it stuck in his belly. I ain't cryin' over Mr. James, but the town folk here'll hang Henry fer' sure an' probably me with him. You know how they're talkin' 'bout the attempted escape an' all anyway. They're jus' waitin' fer an excuse."

Boyd knew she was right. Neither of them stood a chance in this town. Even if there was a trial, they wouldn't be found anything but guilty. If the sheriff didn't hang them, the people in town would. What would they do? He needed time to think. One thing for sure; they couldn't stay here. They'd have to slip away and get as far from this place as possible.

Boyd took Nellie's hand, lead her into the kitchen house and had her sit on a stool before the work table. She winced whenever the skin on her back was twisted and was in considerable pain. He found a shallow bowl, filled it with warm water from a pot over the fire, added a pinch of salt, and stirred the water with a clean cloth. Nellie dropped her dress from her shoulders and clutched the front over her breasts. Boyd began to gently bathe her bare back and clean the wound. The cut wasn't deep, but some of the flesh had been torn away; a scar would surely form. Boyd could only guess what her back would have looked like if Henry hadn't stopped Mr. James.

Nellie gasped as the warm salty water touched the wound. Boyd worked silently with a frown creasing his brow. What would he do now? There was nowhere for runaway slaves to go, except maybe to run for the north, but Boyd knew nothing about the northern states. He suspected that little would be different for them there. He had heard that the war had little effect on people out west, but that was thousands of miles away, and Nellie and Henry had no way to get there.

A sharp intake of Nellie's breath brought him back. She sat stoically allowing him to dress the wound. After cleansing with water, he gently spread some salve that Nellie had taken from the cupboard on the wound. When he finished, Nellie modestly pulled the torn dress back over her shapely shoulders.

Henry appeared at the door. He stood quietly waiting for Boyd to acknowledge him as he twisted his old felt hat in his gnarled hands. When Boyd looked his way, he asked, "What we goin' to do with Mr. James? You want me to bury him in the barn?"

Neither Boyd nor Nellie had an answer to the question. They stood mutely looking at each other. Nellie finally replied, "Come in an' close the door, Henry. We'll think o' somethin.'"

They sat around the fireplace talking quietly. Henry put another log on the fire to cut the cold. As they talked, the firelight flickered on their stern faces casting ghostly shadows in the hollows under their eyes.

Boyd said, "I guess we should leave Mr. James' body in the barn where it lays. The important thing is for you two to get out of the valley and away from all of this."

The three of them sat in the semidarkness and looked into the flames. What could be done? How did they find themselves here in this situation? What would happen to them?

◦ ◦ ◦ ◦

Mary McConnell looked out of her parlor window again. What was going on over at Mr. James' house now? She snorted at the thought. Ever since Mr. James' wife had died and the children had moved away, there had been strange goings-on at that house. Mary was a sixty-year old widow; her husband, Martin, had died twenty years ago in a farming accident. She lived alone in the huge house with four cats and a dog, wasn't really a gossip, but just naturally kept track of everything that went on in her part of town.

She had watched the battle back in the spring from the attic window with great interest. She hadn't been afraid of the shooting, although the cannon-fire had concerned her, but she decided that it was as safe in the attic as anywhere in the house. Besides she could see better from up there; not back toward Mr. James' house, but up and down the Pike.

Now something really strange was happening. After all the yelling by Mr. James earlier in the morning, everything was totally quiet. She had seen Henry and Nellie leave the barn together just about the time that she had finished breakfast, but had not seen Mr. James. As far as she could tell, he was still out in the barn. Then, that Reb soldier had come along. She had seen him standing across the pike watching the house a time or two, but he had come along after the yelling. She just knew that something really bad had happened.

And then, the unthinkable happened. That Reb soldier had put his arms around the nigra woman right there in the back yard. She was crying and sobbing and he had actually taken her into his arms.

She couldn't hear what was being said, but it was obvious that the rumors were true. He was fooling around with her. Well, she'd have to tell someone about this. It wasn't right. Besides something else was wrong there. Where was Mr. James?

Mary fed her cats and the dog and washed the breakfast dishes in a chipped porcelain bowl. She stepped to the back door and tossed the dishwater out into the yard. From the stoop she had a better look at Mr. James' backyard and kitchen house, where she could see Henry standing out back wringing his hands and pacing back and forth. After a few minutes he returned to the door and asked someone inside if they wanted him to bury Mr. James in the barn. She couldn't hear all that was said, but she had heard enough. Mr. James was dead. She went back into the house and put on her hat and coat.

With a frown on her wrinkled face, Mary walked purposefully down the pike and into the center of town. Her friends on the street spoke to her but she ignored them and continued up the street to the courthouse at a determined pace. They stared after her.

"Sheriff, that nigra girl an' that boy Henry have killed Mr. James and that Houston feller is in on it," she exclaimed upon entering the sheriff's office.

"Now calm down, Mrs. McConnell. Here set down an' collect yourself." He indicated a seat against the wall. After she was settled comfortably the sheriff asked, "Now what's this you're telling me about Mr. James?"

"I'm telling you, Sheriff, they've done killed him. I heard Henry ask where they wanted him to bury the body. That Houston feller was in on it, I tell you! I saw him and that nigra hugging each other right there in Mr. James' backyard. It's disgusting. He stayed there in the house while he was wounded, you know."

"Yes, yes, I know all of that, but are you sure that Mr. James was killed? I mean, I don't want to go charging up to his house and find him sitting in his parlor sipping corn whiskey."

"I'm sure, Sheriff. I may be getting old, but I can still hear perfectly well, and I know what I hear. You better get up there and catch them before they decide to take off."

Sheriff Brown rose heavily to his feet. This was all he needed. There had been enough trouble in this town in the last few months to last a lifetime. He would have been more than happy if Boyd Houston had never shown his face in the valley.

"All right. All right." the sheriff said holding his palms out toward his persistent guest.

He thanked Mrs. McConnell and asked her to stay in town until he returned. She smiled broadly and agreed, her mission accomplished.

She left his office and marched down the street toward the general store.

Sheriff Brown took a deep breath and hitched up his pants, attempting to get his belly under his belt, but with little success. He took his hat from the coat rack on the wall and placed it carefully on his shaggy head, then opened his desk drawer and removed his pistol. He checked the loads carefully and stuck it under his belt. He left the courthouse with a serious look on his face and began walking east along the pike toward Mr. James' house.

❧ ❧ ❧ ❧

Nellie was upstairs in her loft room. She had a cloth sack in her hand, into which she stuffed her meager belongings. She had only one spare dress and a few personal items. These she stuffed into the sack and returned to the main room below. Henry sat in front of the fireplace on a low stool. His body leaned forward, his elbows rested on his knees, and he clasped his hands before him with his grizzly head bowed.

Boyd stood near the front window and looked out toward the barn. The barn door was closed, but Mr. James' dog sat in the path and looked at the closed door. Oh God, Boyd thought, what have I gotten myself into? What will these poor people do now?

Nellie spoke to Boyd from across the room. He jumped at the sound of her voice. "I'm ready now," she said. "I'm sorry I got you into this mess."

"It couldn't be helped, Nellie. Henry couldn't just let that evil man beat you to death. It's likely that's what he would have done, as angry as he was."

Their plan was simple. Boyd would drive the buggy out of town and Nellie and Henry would ride along as if they were doing some errand for Mr. James. By the time someone figured out what had happened they'd be gone. The horse and buggy would be a dead giveaway once they were out of town, so they planned to tie the horse along the road and walk up the mountain to the cabin on Blackbird Knob.

⚘ ⚘ ⚘ ⚘

Henry hurried back to the barn and took the horse out of the box stall and began to hitch it to Mr. James' buggy. He tried not to look at the bloody body lying on the straw covered floor just inside the door. But, he couldn't help himself. The horse snorted and stomped its feet when it smelled blood. Henry looped his arm over the mare's head and stroked her nose. She quieted immediately and began to nose Henry's pockets for sugar. If Mr. James had known that Henry snatched sugar for the horse, he'd have whipped him good. Henry grinned at the thought.

He looked at the body again from the corner of his eye, stroked the mare's nose, and pressed his forehead against her neck. As long as he could remember he had lived right here in this mountain town. He had never been out of the valley and had only been as far north as Marlinton, forty miles away, and south to Hinton, along the Greenbrier River. He had begged Mr. James once to allow him to go with him on a business trip to Lexington, but he had been told to get back to work and stop worrying about what was over the mountain.

Henry deftly harnessed the horse and hitched it to the light buggy. He was sorry that Mr. James was dead, yet, he was excited about gaining his freedom, however brief it might be. He thought about Mazel's and Nellie's attempt to flee earlier, but knew that he would have been too frightened to go along. Now that it was here before him, the prospect of freedom thrilled him.

⚘ ⚘ ⚘ ⚘

Boyd and Nellie stood quietly beside the kitchen house. Nellie's cloth sack, containing all of her worldly possessions, lay at her feet. For the second time in only a few weeks, she was attempting an escape from slavery. She was even more nervous than before. This time, she would be hanged if she were caught, along with Henry and Mr. Boyd. She picked absently at a button on the front of her dress and looked nervously at Boyd.

"Here comes Henry with the buggy," Boyd said. "Now just act like you're going with me on a buggy ride. For God's sake, act natural."

The last thing Nellie felt like was acting naturally, and Henry was even more nervous than she was. If anyone looked guilty Boyd thought, these two did. He'd be lucky to get them out of town before one of them bolted.

Boyd was nervous too. He fully realized that if he were caught, he would likely be jailed and hanged for helping slaves escape and for the murder of Mr. James. Suddenly another thought grasped him with a steel hand: Lexus. What would she and her family think? Once Mr. James' body was discovered, it wouldn't take long for the sheriff to put the pieces together. Word would spread rapidly in the town and Lexus would be shamed for having let him court her. He would be a fugitive. A sudden thought entered his mind; he could turn Nellie and Henry in to the sheriff and be off scott free. His face flushed at the shameful thought. Nellie had been a good friend to him—maybe even more than a friend.

He looked at her standing nervously beside him and was again ashamed of even thinking about turning them in, but what would he do with them? What about his relationship with Nellie? He remembered the times he had held her in his arms. His pulse quickened at the thought. After they made their way to the cabin at Blackbird Knob, then what? Where would they go, what would they do?

His thoughts were interrupted as Henry brought the buggy around and they climbed in. Boyd slapped the mare with the reins and the light buggy bumped down the lane beside the house. Boyd pulled the mare to a stop before entering the pike.

Sheriff Brown stood before them in the road with his pistol drawn. A frightful scowl twisted his brown face.

⚹ ⚹ ⚹ ⚹

"Dang, Sonny. I don't reckon you coulda got into any more trouble if you'da tried," Charlie said shaking his head. Boyd sat on a stool behind the broad flat bars in the county jail and Charlie looked in at him with total exasperation stamped across his grim face. Boyd looked about as pitiful as a man could look, sitting there with his head down.

"I don't reckon you know how much trouble you're in. If a man ever deserved killin' that Mr. James did, but that ain't ezackly the way it shoulda been done. What happened, anyway?"

Boyd related the events that had lead to Mr. James' death, Nellie's beating, and Henry's attempt to help her.

"Don't make no difference if it was a accident," Charlie claimed. "Folks here have got their backs up over them slaves attemptin' to escape an' now with Henry killin' his master, they're goin' to be lookin' to make a example of someone. Henry'll do just fine an' they'll probably hang Nelly too. You, on the other hand, present a different problem. If Henry an' Nellie tells how ever' thing happened, you may not get hung, but I 'spect that they'll want to put you in jail fer a spell."

"Where's Nellie? I haven't seen her since they put us in here," Boyd asked.

"I reckon they got them down in the cellar. They won't put darkies in with whites, even ifin they is in jail. The sheriff said that he'd separate y'all an' see ifin your stories match 'bout what happened. You'd best forget 'bout that girl. Won't do nothin' but get you in more trouble."

Charlie and Boyd sat on their stools talking quietly. They could hear other prisoners coughing and talking in the cells down the narrow hallway. Somewhere over toward the center of town Boyd could hear the familiar hammering of the blacksmith. The front door of the jail banged as a man entered and the deputy on duty began laughing and joking with him.

As Charlie rose to leave he dug a package out of his sack and handed it to Boyd.

"Kate sent this here chicken and such to you. I had a hell of a time convincing the sheriff it didn't have saw blades in it," Charlie joked.

Boyd took the package through the bars. It was wrapped in paper, but inside several pieces of chicken and a couple of biscuits were wrapped in a checkered napkin. As Charlie's back disappeared down the hallway, Boyd sat back and began to eat.

Later in the afternoon the sheriff looked through the bars at the neat pile of chicken bones on the edge of the bunk. Boyd lay on his back with his hands clasped behind his head staring at the cobwebs suspended from the oak beams supporting the ceiling.

"Son, I reckon you're in a sight of trouble. You wanna tell me what ever possessed you to take up with a couple o' nigras like you did an' get involved in Mr. James' killin'?"

Boyd swiveled his hips and legs around and sat on the edge of the bunk. His head almost brushed the low ceiling beams.

"You know, Sheriff, I've been knocked around quite a bit in this town of yours and I've about had all I'm going to take. I think I'll get myself a lawyer and see if I can't get out of here. What was Mr. James' counselor's name? Russell wasn't it?"

"Now just take it easy. All I want you to do is tell me exactly what happened at Mr. James' place that he ended up dead. Before you begin, I'll tell you that both Nellie and Henry have told me their versions of what happened. Now it's your turn." The sheriff stood in the narrow hallway with his arms crossed over his massive chest.

"Sheriff, I don't have to tell you that Mr. James was a bit put out at Charlie and me when he ended up shot and all. I know that he and Jones were responsible for all the thievery in the valley and the death of Pop Cooper. Why, Mr. James probably stole my money belt and my twelve hundred dollars. After the trial he threatened me; said he'd get even. But, Sheriff, I didn't kill him. All I tried to do was to help a couple of people who were in a jam." Boyd looked at the sheriff through the narrow slits between the bars.

"What were you doing at Mr. James' house at that time of the morning?

"After the trial I knew that Mr. James would beat Nellie for her part in identifying him as a thief, so I followed him up the pike to his house and kinda stood around outside until he turned out the lights in his house and went to bed. First thing this morning I was there again to make sure he didn't do something foolish. I guess I got there too late. Nellie and Henry had already returned to the kitchen house from the barn. I was right about Nellie being beaten. You saw the mean slash she had across her back. He would have killed her if Henry hadn't stepped in."

The sheriff looked at him grimly. "I reckoned you fer a damned fool when I first saw you, and I ain't been disappointed. That story's so dumb that it's probably true. So, I ain't goin' to charge you with murder like I am those darkies, but we've still got this problem of you tryin' to help slaves escape. What do you say about that?"

"You know, Sheriff, I've had a couple of hours to think about that. When Mr. Russell gets here, you'll have to let me go, you know."

The sheriff looked at Boyd in surprise. "Oh, an' just how do you figger that?"

"Actually, it's pretty simple. Just think back to where you first stopped us this morning. Do you remember where that was?"

Sheriff Brown frowned at Boyd from under the brim of his hat. "Of course I do. What kind of a damned fool do you think I am?" he asked indignantly.

Boyd smiled, "I'd rather not answer that, Sheriff." He continued, "If you recall, we were in the alley beside Mr. James' house. Right?"

"Yeah," the sheriff replied cautiously. Something was going on here that he didn't understand, and he didn't like it.

"Sheriff, neither those 'darkies' as you call them, nor I had left Mr. James' place. How could I have been helping slaves escape if we were still on the owner's property?"

Finally, the sheriff caught on. "You can't get away with that. The folks in town will have your hide. They know what you planned to do, and they'll be yelling for you to hang right up there alongside your friends."

"That's probably true, but I'm sure Mr. Russell will be happy to defend me, if the price is right. He's good and the judge seems to like him. You know the law as well as I do; slaves that haven't left their owner's property can hardly be called runaways. No, Sheriff, you don't have a case against me," Boyd argued. He wasn't sure what the law said about slaves and was gambling that the sheriff didn't either. "Besides, I'll claim that I was just bringing the darkies to you to hang. Mr. Russell will be happy to use that argument at my trial. And, do you really think that Howard will be able to prosecute any case successfully before this judge?"

"Well..." the sheriff hedged, "I hate to admit it, but you're probably right. But, one thing is for sure. Those darkies are doomed. There ain't no way that the townsfolk will ever let them go. As a matter of fact, I reckon I'll be lucky to keep folks from lynchin' 'em."

"Come on, Sheriff, you might as well let me out of here. I'll be out sooner or later," Boyd continued the bluff. He put on his hat and began to gather his possessions together.

Sheriff Brown frowned and studied the dirt-rimmed nail on one crooked finger. Boyd waited patiently while the sheriff deliberated. Outside, Boyd could hear two men arguing. Their voices rose and fell through the bars of the window.

Taking the ring of keys from a hook on his belt, the sheriff opened the heavy steel door. "You know this is again' my better judgement, but I don't reckon that there's much of a case again' you with Henry confessin' an' all." He stepped aside as Boyd quickly left the cell. "Mr. Houston. If I was you, I'd find somethin' real pressin' up on the mountain to do for the next year or two."

"Right, Sheriff. I've had about as much of this town as I can take. I plan on doin' that very thing."

Boyd caught Charlie before he had left town. Charlie frowned at him and asked, "How in tarnation did you get out of jail?"

"I talked my way out. Sheriff Brown didn't want to face a trial with Mr. Russell as my counsel. Besides, I figure that he didn't know what to do with me. If the townsfolk took a notion to string me up, he'd be right in the middle, and he'd have to do something. Either decision he made, he'd be between a rock and a hard place. No, Sheriff Brown may be a bit slow physically, but there's nothing wrong with his brain," Boyd smiled. "All I did was give him a way out."

"What do you plan to do now?"

"I'm going to leave town for a while. I guess I've got a lot of thinking to do.

Charlie left for the mountain and Boyd walked down the pike toward the boardinghouse. He rounded a corner and ran headlong into Lexus, who dropped the packages she was carrying. Boyd bent to pick them up as she stood back and glared at him. Their eyes met and he knew instantly that she was angry at him beyond all reason. He handed the packages to her silently.

"Boyd Houston I hope you're satisfied! You've finally done it. Everyone in town is talking about you and that nigra woman and Mr. James' boy. Everyone knows that you helped kill him and here you are walking around in town as free as can be. I hope they hang you right up there beside them," Lexus screamed at him.

"Lexus, I can explain..."

"There's nothing to explain. Your reputation in this town is finally ruined, and my reputation with it." She was so angry that tears streamed down her pink cheeks. She whirled and stomped up the street, swishing her skirts. Boyd watched her as she flounced away. She didn't look back.

Suddenly it was clear to him: Lexus wasn't interested in hearing the truth. All she cared about was her reputation and what everyone thought about her. Now, for the first time, he could see that there wasn't much depth to her. She was pretty on the outside, but shallow inside. Why was it that it took him so long to realize that? A young man's fancy was often just that—what he fancied it to be. He knew now that there was no future here for him. Lexus was not for him and his future in the valley was not promising.

Boyd leaned against the wall of the store and listened for the rhythm of the blacksmith. The town was quiet. What would he do now? He's have to leave town quickly. Maybe he's make his way over Muddy Creek Mountain and down the river to Charleston. One thing was sure; he couldn't stay here.

Boyd picked up the rest of his belongings at the boardinghouse and began walking out of town. Occasionally a townsman looked at him sharply, but made no move to stop him. He walked wearily along the rutted road to the north of town. What would he do now? He couldn't leave Nellie in jail to be hanged even though he was confused about how he felt about her. Did he really care for her, or did he merely feel sorry for her? He frowned under the burden of his possessions as he shambled out of town.

10

Darkness had crept over the valley. Boyd sat beside a small camp fire and absently poked the glowing embers with a stick. He looked into the red flames and drew his eyebrows into a frown. Scarlet and gold leaves littered the ground around him, and more fell like silent rain from the dark trees. He had pulled the tinder-dry forest litter away from the fire in a broad circle to prevent it from escaping. The forest was dangerously dry and the leaves crunched loudly as he walked. The air was still and heavy, yet leaves drifted down in testimony to the approaching winter season. The branches would be completely bare in only a few weeks—less if it rained.

What now? He couldn't leave Nellie and Henry in the jail to be hanged by an angry mob. They hadn't done anything to deserve that. He shifted his weight and moved his back on the rough bark of the chestnut tree against which he sat. But what could he do to help her...them? Sheriff Brown wouldn't give him a second chance if he caught him trying to help them escape. He'd find himself swinging from a locust pole behind the jail if he wasn't careful.

Boyd searched his pack for a scrap of food, found a piece of bread and some greenish cheese, and began to eat. The night was cold, and Boyd shivered under his light jacket. If only he hadn't lost his money he could buy some decent food and clothing. He couldn't continue to depend on Charlie to help him, and soon he'd have to find a job. Maybe something would turn up in Charleston. Boyd wrapped himself with his thin blanket and curled up close to the fire. Quickly the cold began to creep through the blanket, into his back, making his shoulder wound ache. It would be a long, cold night.

♪ ♪ ♪ ♪

Nellie sat on the hard wooden pallet in the cellar of the jail, rocking back and forth, and wrapped her arms around herself to keep warm. The welt on her back burned, especially when she moved and stretched. Cold air drifted through the small window set in the limestone wall of the jail foundation. As she looked out through the flat, steel bars, she could see, just over the trees, a few stars in the cold October sky. Oh, how she longed to be back in her attic room over the kitchen house with a fire in the fireplace and Mazel snoring on her rickety bed in the corner. It was a meager existence she had lived, but it was all she knew.

Why did all of this have to happen to her? All she had wanted was to be left alone. And what about Mr. Boyd? What was this feeling she had for him? He had done his best to help her, yet he was a white man. Did she want to take up with a man so obviously different from her? Did she love this man, or was this feeling the result of not having anyone with whom to compare him? What would their life together be like? How could she fit into his world? What would their children look like? She felt her face grow warm in the darkness as she thought about having his children. Their children would be neither white nor black. What would their lives be like?

She knew that her doubts were even deeper than all of these thoughts. She wanted the opportunity to explore the world, to feel freedom in its fullest, to be on her own, to make her own decisions.

But when he smiled at her…

"Psst! Nellie!" Henry called from the cell at the other end of the cellar. "You there, Nellie?"

"Yeah, Henry, I'm here," Nellie replied in a mournful voice. "What you want?"

"Nellie, I think I can get outin here. This here bar in the window is loose an' I think I can jimmy it looser and pry it out. Ifin I can, I'll squeeze out an try to get you out too." A screeching sound reached Nellie's ears and then the sound of a rock falling to the floor.

"God Almighty! The whole side of the wall fell out!" Henry exclaimed. Nellie froze as she listened for the deputy in the office above to rush to their cells. No such response came. She let her breath out slowly, suddenly conscious, that she had been holding her breath.

She looked out of the tiny window again, trying to see the path that led from the office above to the cellar. Suddenly a dark face appeared on the other side of the opening. She stumbled backward violently, recoiling from the unexpected appearance. A chuckle floated through the window.

"It's me, Henry! I clumb through the wall an' now I'm goin' to get you outin here," he said proudly. Nellie returned to the window.

"Henry, you done scared me to death. Why didn't you let me know what you were goin' to do, you fool you!" Nellie hissed.

Henry used the bar from the window he had just torn apart to begin work on Nellie's window. He dug around the metal bars set in soft, weathered cement as quietly as he could. The sound reverberated in the shallow sinkhole below them. Henry, frightened that the deputy would hear the racket, crept around the jail and peered into the office window where the deputy reclined in a battered captain's chair with his hands clasped behind his head. He snored softly. Quietly Henry withdrew and returned to the cellar window. It took two hours of careful work before he was able to pry a single bar loose.

Nellie dragged the bed over to the window and climbed up to the window's level. With considerable effort, she was able to squeeze her head through the tiny opening, then her shoulders, and finally her hips. Henry caught her as she dropped heavily to the ground.

"Where we go now, Nellie?" Henry asked in a hoarse whisper. "We goin' in the cave?" Nellie could see his round, frightened eyes in the dim starlight.

"No, we ain't goin' in that place," Nellie replied with conviction. "Come on, we'll just hike out of town and hide in the woods 'til we can figger what to do."

Quietly, Nellie and Henry crept out of town, following the rutted wagon track north toward Falling Spring. North! It was the only place that they knew to go. North! Where nigras lived without being kept as slaves—at least that's what they had heard.

♪ ♪ ♪ ♪

Boyd scrambled up from his bed on the damp forest floor and fumbled for his musket. The sound, just down the hill from his camp, came again through the heavy underbrush. Someone was moving through the dry leaves toward him. His fire had burned down to only a few red embers and gave no warning of his presence.

He stepped behind a tree and waited with his rifle cocked, peering into the murky darkness. The sound was definitely that of at least two people walking in the leaves. They came closer.

"Nellie," Henry whispered, "I can't see nothin. Where we goin'?"

Boyd was shocked.

"Nellie," Boyd whispered in the darkness, "Is that you?"

The footsteps stopped. Nellie and Henry stood silently, trying to decide who had called to them.

"Nellie?" Boyd asked, louder, his voice shaking with incredulity.

"Mr. Boyd is that you? What you doin' out here in the woods like this?" Nellie asked with obvious relief as she and Henry crunched toward him through the dry leaves.

Boyd stoked the fire and soon had a small blaze going. The cheerful light flickered on Nellie's smiling face, highlighting her dark eyes. They sat together around the fire as Henry told Boyd excitedly about their escape. He laughed and slapped his leg as he told Boyd about the old jail cellar and the loose rocks in its wall. Nellie shivered in the cold and Boyd dropped his blanket over her shoulders. She smiled up at him in thanks.

"We can't stay here, now. Sheriff Brown will be searching the county from one end to the other with first light," Boyd said. "There's a cabin up on Blackbird knob where we can stay until we figure out what to do."

"Nellie and me was headin' up north. I'm goin' to get me a job workin' fer some farmer an' every thing will be okay then," Henry exclaimed.

"You'll have to be careful, Henry. The sheriff'll expect you to head up north and that's the first place they'll look."

"Yes suh, that's what I figger too, but I'll stay off of the roads an' only travel at night. I reckon I'll make it ifin I take my time an' don' do nothin' stupid," Henry replied.

"How about you, Nellie," Boyd asked. "What are you going to do?"

"I reckon I'll go on up on the mountain with you to that cabin you talked about. I'll figger out what to do after that," she said as she looked across the fire at Boyd. She smiled brightly at the thought. Maybe it was possible to be free after all. Just maybe.

Henry grinned at the two young people, hugged Nellie tightly, solemnly shook Boyd's hand and turned to begin his journey north.

"Henry," Boyd called to him, "here, take this. It isn't much but it'll buy some food to get you started." Boyd pressed a ten dollar gold piece into his hand. Henry held the tiny coin in the palm of his dark, calloused hand and looked at it in awe: He turned it toward the fire and watched it shine in the flickering light. It was the first money he had ever had of his own. As he looked up at Boyd a tear appeared in the corner of his eye, and then he was gone into the darkness.

Nellie and Boyd sat silently beside the fire and listened to Henry's receding footsteps in the dry autumn leaves. For a long moment neither Nellie nor Boyd spoke. Nellie sat very still, knowing that she should never see Henry again. He was someone who had been with her all of her life, and she would miss him.

Boyd quickly kicked the fire apart and scuffed dirt over the glowing embers with the side of his boot. He carefully stomped the dirt into the fire, making sure that it was out. Taking Nellie by the hand, he climbed the ridge behind them. At the crest they could see by the dim glow of the autumn sky, the dark silhouette of Muddy Creek Mountain extending away to the northwest. He could just identify one peak that rose higher than the others surrounding it—Blackbird Knob. It would offer them sanctuary, temporarily at least. It would be a long walk, but he had confidence that they could make it. Boyd could feel Nellie's presence at his elbow, and in the stillness of the autumn night, he could hear her breathe. A great tenderness swelled up in his heart for this woman who had been through so much. More than anything, he had great respect for the manner in which she carried herself. She was not shallow—she was strong, and the depth of her was bottomless.

Boyd took Nellie into his arms and kissed her. She responded immediately and pressed her body against his. They stood on the narrow ridge overlooking the valley and clung to each other as if the world would end. Nellie shivered and from deep within her soul a shuddering sob escaped.

"Oh, Mr. Boyd, I'm sorry. I didn't mean to cry, but everything will be all right now, I just know it," she whispered. "I've lost ever thing I ever had. Mazel's gone, my friends are hung, and now Henry—I won't ever see them again, not never."

"Shush, now. Everything will be okay," he spoke softly into her hair, and, for the first time since he had entered the valley, he knew that it was true—no matter how it turned out between then, everything would be okay. A great burden lifted from his shoulders. It was the kind of relief that comes when a difficult decision is finally made, and you are know that it is right.

He took her hand again and together they made their way down the ridge and walked confidently toward the dark line of the mountain before them.

♪ ♪ ♪ ♪

Charlie Taylor pitched a fork of hay over the wall of the manger as the milk cow thrust her head through the smooth wood of the stanchion and began to eat. He leaned on the fork and absently watched the cow feed. He thought about Boyd; where was he and what was he doing now? That boy had his share of miseries since he arrived in the valley, Charlie thought. And, if he kept messing around with that nigra woman, his troubles were only going to get worse.

He left the barn and walked slowly toward the cabin. A large brown and white striped cat following behind him with its tail held rigidly in the air, a hook at the end. It ran past him and waited impatiently on the porch, rubbing its side against a bannister post. Charlie sat down on the wooden porch steps and looked at his calloused hands. He considered himself a lucky man. He had fought in several bloody battles during the war and had lived, eluding fate by surviving a nasty wound acquired in the Battle of Lewisburg, and now looked forward to a long life with his wife and family here on this beautiful mountain. He wouldn't trade his life for that of any man he knew.

As the sun slid behind the ridge to the west of the valley, the temperature dropped rapidly. He could feel the cool air against his cheek as it drifted down from the mountain sides to pool in the valley bottoms. There would be another heavy frost tonight. He looked toward the garden patch beside the barn; brown stalks of sweet corn stood in ragged rows across the garden, and tomato and sweet pepper plants, browned by earlier frosts, littered the patch. He would clean off the debris in the garden soon, turning the litter under with a spade. It would rot during the long winter and provide nutrients for the crops in the spring.

He heard the boards on the porch creak as Kate joined him on the steps, holding onto his arm and leaning against him. They sat silently for a long time, watching the sun disappear over the mountains.

"'Red sun in the morning, a sailor's warning; Red sun at night, a sailor's delight,' that's what Boyd told me," Kate quoted. "Charlie, where do you suppose Boyd is right now? Do you think that the folks in town will really hang Nellie and Henry? It all seems so senseless. All they want is to be left alone," Kate said. "It makes me shiver every time I think about this slave issue."

"I don't know darlin.' That Boyd is liable to turn up just about anywhere. The sheriff let him out of jail, so I reckon he left town. But, I worry about what he'll do in order to get that girl out of jail. He's just damned fool enough to do something stupid."

"He's a good man, Charlie. You know as well as I do, it's wrong to keep people as slaves, and I think Boyd's about to come to the same conclusion. Besides, I think he's lost his heart to Nellie."

Charlie stood and stretched. "I reckon. But, he's chosen a long row to hoe if he takes up with a nigra woman. I hope he's up to it. I just don't want him to have a harder life than necessary."

"Well, Charlie, sometimes life is hard on those who choose to make the right decision. If there's anything good to come from this war, maybe it will be to abolish slavery."

Charlie looked long and hard at this woman whom he loved more than anything. He had fought for the Confederacy, not to preserve slavery, but because he thought that the South should be in control of its own destiny. It all went against his sense of independence for politicians in the north to tell the south how to live. He shook his head, took his wife's hand and pulled her to her feet, wrapped his hard brown arms around her, and held her tight.

This woman is my life and my conscience, he thought. I wonder where I would be if she hadn't chosen to live with me here on the mountain. In a way, she's in the same situation as Boyd. She chose to live here with me, a social outcast, rather than in a comfortable home near her parents. Why, she could have married any wealthy man she wanted. Instead, she chose me. Well, he grinned to himself, sometimes even a blind hog finds an acorn.

Suddenly, the dogs began raising a ruckus and Charlie looked up to see Boyd and Nellie walking up the path to the cabin. Boyd held her hand and it was obvious to both Charlie and Kate that he had made a decision.

"Hot damn, Sonny. Now you've really gone and done it!" Charlie smiled. "Why don't you two come on in an' sit a spell. Kate, what do you have for these folks to eat?"

↗ ↗ ↗ ↗

Kate and Nellie were in a back bedroom of the Taylor's cabin; Boyd could hear them whispering quietly. Colleen sat on Boyd's lap and looked up at him expectantly. "Tell me again what happened while you were in jail, Boyd," she said innocently.

"Colleen! You know well and good that you're to call him Mr. Houston. Until you're all grown, that's what I want you to do!" Charlie cautioned.

"It's okay, Charlie," Boyd laughed. " There's not much to tell, Colleen, the sheriff just let me out. Said he didn't have enough evidence to hold me" The two older boys sat at the kitchen table and worked on their school lessons. Kate taught all of them at home. Matt looked at Boyd hopefully—he was struggling with his arithmetic and any distraction was welcome. Charlie looked sternly and flicked his finger toward him; Matt hunched quickly over his pad and worked intently with his stub of pencil.

Kate and Nellie rejoined the men in the main room and sat before the blazing fire in the fireplace. Kate had given Nellie one of her dresses and had helped her wash and clean up. She had also cleaned and dressed the gash on her back. Nellie looked radiant in the firelight and Boyd had trouble keeping his eyes off of her. Nellie was ill at ease, though, sitting together with white folks as an equal. She had never experienced that before, and was not comfortable at all. She twisted her hands in her lap before her. She knitted her brow into a frown.

Kate soon rose and began to herd the children toward bed. They complained loudly and Charlie finally rose to intervene.

Nellie looked at Boyd and asked, "What we goin' to do now? We can't stay here. Ifin the sheriff find us here, he'll burn their house down and hang us all from that pole in town."

"I know, Nellie, we'll go up to the cabin on the knob with first light. But we need to get some rest. The climb up on the mountain just about wore us both out," Boyd replied.

Kate and Charlie soon returned and Boyd described how Nellie and Henry escaped from jail. Charlie laughed when Nellie told them about the deputy sleeping through their escape.

Soon, Kate and Charlie drifted off to bed and Nellie and Boyd were left alone before the fire. Nellie sat silently with her head down and Boyd could see tears glistening on her cheeks.

"Nellie, what's the matter?" Boyd asked.

"Nothin's wrong, Mr. Boyd. I jus' keep thinkin' about Mazel an' the others and I wonder how Henry's makin' out 'bout now."

"Oh, you don't have to worry about him. He's a survivor. He'll probably make his way north and find a nice place to live."

"I really hope so," Nellie whispered. "But, that's not all I've been thinkin' 'bout. This is the first time I've ever set down with people and talked like a family. I don't know what to do or how to behave. You don't know what it's like bein' a slave. It's not just doin' the work an' all; it's not havin' a family an' never havin' a mother an' father to take care o' you, an' seein' other folk, white folk, havin' all of them things there just under your nose. Sometimes it's more 'in a body can stand."

"I know, I know, Nellie. You've been through a lot, but that's all over now," Boyd soothed.

"That's the whole point, Mr. Boyd. You don't really know what its like 'til you go through it your own self. Y'all have never known anything but freedom. You don't know, an' you won't ever know," Nellie whispered fiercely. "I thank you for what you've done for me, 'an all;

I might be dead now, like the rest of them, if it weren't for you, but I just don't know what I think any more. I want to be with you, but...

"Shush, now. Don't think about that any more," he whispered into her ear as he placed his fingertips over her lips. He didn't like the way this conversation was going. He took her in his arms again, pressed her tightly against his chest, and they watched the fire burn down to red embers.

♪ ♪ ♪ ♪

Boyd tossed and turned on his bed of old blankets before the fireplace. Finally, dawn crept into the living room and the furniture took shape around him. Kate's old red rooster crowed proudly down by the barn. Boyd stood and worked the stiffness out of his wounds. His rumpled hair stood on end and he absently scratched his stomach. He was deep in thought. He turned with a start and walked outside onto the porch. Charlie's prediction of a heavy frost had been accurate. A white covering of frost lay in the valley bottom like cake frosting in the bottom of a mixing bowl. A distinct frost line ran around the sides of the mountain—frost below, and clear above.

What Nellie had said to him last night weighed on him. What did she mean? Did she want to be with him, or did she want to be free? Free of him, too? He didn't know what their life would be like together, but he was sure he could make it work. He had never known anyone like her. She was so caring and understanding.

He hadn't known many women. Was he really in love with her, or was it just that she happened to be the first to come along? No, he did love her, and he would make her love him, too. It could work out, and he was just the man to see that it did.

He heard the cabin door open behind him. He turned to see Nellie standing in the doorway looking at him with a puzzled face. His heart leapt in his chest.

After breakfast, Charlie and Kate stood on the cabin porch and watched them as they walked briskly up the valley toward the knob. Boyd and Nellie would stay in the cabin for a few days and then make their way across the mountain and down the river to Charleston. As Nellie and Boyd disappeared up the valley, the Taylors began their day.

♪ ♪ ♪ ♪

The early November snow fell as hard, fine granules. It sifted down through the bare branches of the trees and Boyd could hear it strike the dead leaves on the forest floor as a whispering roar. Soon, the frozen ground would be covered. Winter had made its way into the mountains early and the gray sky promised heavy snow and cold weather. Boyd slipped silently through the dim shadows of the forest looking for game. He needed to find something substantial to eat because they were low on food—the staples Kate had given them would soon be exhausted if they didn't have a deer or some other large game to supplement their supplies.

He was lucky. In a small clearing along the side of the mountain he dropped a fat doe with his first shot. Quickly bleeding and field dressing the animal, he began to drag it back to the cabin. He stopped frequently to catch his breath and enjoy the new snow. He had never experienced a major snowstorm before since he had lived on the sea coast down south. The cold, sharp air was invigorating and it drove his blood quickly in his veins as he drew it into his lungs. Here in a sheltered cove on the mountain side, he listened to the chirp and whirr of small, dark birds on the forest floor. He looked out through a break in the trees to see the valley spread below him.

The mountain sloped sharply down to the valley floor. The winter skeletons of countless trees covered the land. All was gray and brown now, such a stark contrast to the brilliant greens of the summer and the vibrant fall colors. The trees on the mountain opposite him marched along the ridge in gray testimony to the coming winter. This, too, was beautiful to his inexperienced eyes. He stood silently, for a long time looking out over the valley. His mind was troubled. He felt a nagging fear deep in his belly: a fear he had not known in battle. He was afraid that something was going very wrong.

Grasping the short length of rope he had tied around the deer's head he began to drag the animal toward the cabin and he was soon sweating profusely under his light jacket. He was within a quarter of a mile of the cabin when he came across tracks in the new snow.

He studied them carefully; they were made by a man wearing a pair of heavy boots. Leaving the deer where it lay, he followed the tracks backward and found that the man had watched the cabin from a clump of bushes beside the stream. Boyd knew the man had stood there for some time because the leaves had been scuffed before the snow fell. He retraced his steps to the point where he had left the deer and followed the tracks up the mountain and found that they led down along the ridge toward the Taylor place.

Boyd returned to the deer and dragged it back to the cabin, strung it up in a nearby tree, and propped the body cavity open with a stick to allow the air to circulate inside and speed the cooling process. Inside the cabin, he quickly told Nellie about the tracks he had discovered.

"I'll stay close, Nellie, but you'll have to learn how to shoot a pistol. You need to be able to protect yourself. It's no telling what that man was up to. It could have been one of the men from the mountain who wanted to use the cabin, but then again, it could have been Troy Jones. Either way, we'd better be ready for the worst."

Nellie stood with her back to the fireplace and stretched her hands behind her feeling for the warmth of the fire. Boyd marveled at how beautiful she was. The light from the oil lamp on the table cast a soft glow on her dark skin and made her eyes seem even bigger than before. The flickering light from the fire outlined her shapely form and highlighted the sharp rise of her breasts.

Boyd smiled to himself, remembering their first night together in the cabin. Nellie had made separate beds for them, one on one side of the room and another in the back corner. She had used an extra blanket to provide some privacy for herself by draping it over a pole suspended across the corner of the room. In this way she had silently informed Boyd that, although she cared deeply for him, she expected him to respect her. Boyd marveled at the dignity that this uncomplicated woman exhibited and respected her all the more for it.

"Do you reckon he'll give us trouble, Mr. Boyd? I mean, what do you reckon he'll do?" Nellie asked with wide eyes.

"I don't really know. If it's Jones, he'll probably try to get even with me. We fought in Lewisburg some weeks back, and I think he was injured. Never you mind. I'll take care of him." Boyd said bravely. Nellie smiled.

Early the next morning Charlie showed up at the cabin. He grinned broadly when he was invited in and saw the bunk in the corner with the blanket screen. "What are you doing up this early in the morning, Charlie?" Boyd laughed. "An' I didn't expect to see you for a few more days."

"Came up to tell you that I seen Troy Jones on the ridge behind my cabin the other evenin'. I follered him down on Snake Run, but lost him in the rhododendron thickets down there. Have you seen anything of him?"

"As a matter of fact, I saw some tracks in the snow. We kinda figured that it was Jones. What do you figure he's up to?" Boyd asked.

"I reckon he wants to get even with you. That's why I'm here—to tell you to watch your back."

"Charlie, we've been talking and have decided that we'll go on to Charleston. Sooner or later the sheriff'll show up looking for us and I can't risk letting Nellie go back to…to where she was before."

"I reckon you're right, Boyd. Kate an' me hate to see you go, but it's prob'ly best. Maybe after the war y'all can make your way back here to visit us."

They spent a pleasant morning talking and just before noon, Charlie said his good-byes and left for his cabin. Boyd became very quiet, knowing that he might never see his friend again. He sat somberly before the fire. Warm, friendly fingers touched him on the back of the neck and then began to massage his shoulders.

"I knows how you feel, Mr. Boyd. I felt the same way when Henry left, and I felt a deep loss when I saw Mazel hangin' there on that pole. It's like a hot iron in your belly that won't go away. But I reckon life has to go on. I feel very sad, but yet, I have never felt so alive as I do now, here with you," Nellie whispered. She wrapped her arms around his neck from behind and hugged him tightly.

＊ ＊ ＊ ＊

Early the next morning, Nellie and Boyd began their walk to Charleston. They left the cabin, carefully leaving a tiny portion of their food for the next occupant, and traveled down the knob, moving the southwest. Soon they would cross the mountaintop. The trail then dropped sharply down to the valley floor and followed the river downstream to Hinton where it joined the New River, and then down to the Kanawha and the river town of Charleston. It was a long, hard walk and would take many days.

Boyd hitched his pack higher on his back and walked swiftly through the thick forest. Nellie followed closely behind, trusting him to lead her to their chosen destination. They walked quietly, enjoying the light snow that fell around them.

"Mr. Boyd, what will Charleston be like? I ain't never been to a big town before."

"I don't rightly know, Nellie. I haven't been there before either, but I guess it'll be like most other cities. Kind of dirty and noisy— lots of people and horses and such. Likely, there'll be a lot of new sights for both of us." Boyd stopped briefly and looked thoughtfully at Nellie. "Don't you think it's about time that you stop calling me 'mister' and just call me 'Boyd'? After all, you're no longer a slave. You're as free as the next person."

"Oh, Mr. Boyd, I cain't do that. It ain't proper."

"Oh, yes you can. It's time," he smiled at her. "You wouldn't want me to call you Miss Nellie, would you?"

"No, I wouldn't," she answered thoughtfully. "But it'll surely seem strange."

They came to a slight rise, wooded with large oak and maple trees, then stepped into a small clearing. The view before them took their breaths away. They were standing on the top of a huge cliff of weathered limestone. The valley, white with snow, stretched to the blue mountains fifteen miles away. The sun, breaking from behind light, fluffy clouds, cast a radiant glow on the land. The river, a green ribbon, wound its way down through the valley. The bare trees and occasional stone outcroppings formed a stark contrast with the dazzling white of the new snow. The entire valley was a study in shades of black and white, with a brilliant canopy of blue sky dotted with cumulus clouds. Boyd automatically reached for Nellie's hand, drawing her close against him.

"Well, isn't this a sweet sight," a coarse voice spoke from the trees behind them. It was Troy Jones.

Boyd and Nellie whirled around to face him. He held a musket loosely in his good hand, and clasped his broken wrist, wrapped with a makeshift splint, against his hip.

"You just put your musket down there on the ground." Jones waved his musket barrel menacingly at Boyd. "I don't want to have to shoot you off this cliff here. At least not until I'm ready to."

Boyd laid his musket at his feet then drew Nellie around behind him, shielding her from Jones. That put her closer to the edge of the cliff. Boyd began to edge closer to Jones.

"Hold it right there, Houston. I've got you just where I want you. You've been a thorn in my side since you got here. Every time I turn around you're there sticking your nose in my business. Well, now I'm going to take care of you. Besides, I've always wanted a nice nigra to carry and fetch for me—especially a nice lookin' woman like this one. I'll even let her do more than carry and fetch," Jones said with a lecherous grin, his voice thick with meaning.

A sudden fury ripped through Boyd's gut. He had to do something, and quick. If Jones took Nellie, her life would be much worse than it had been before with Mr. James. He had to move, and now!

With a scream of anguish and terror, Boyd charged directly toward Jones. A look of surprise, then fright swept across Jones' face as he brought the musket to bear on Boyd. The shock of the musket's blast rocked Boyd, the minnie ball cutting through the shoulder of his jacket, just missing his flesh. He reached Jones in time to knock the barrel of the musket aside and grapple with him as Jones attempted to draw a pistol from his waistband. They struggled, their hands locked on the pistol, falling over the rocks and wind-stunted brush on the mountain top. Sharp rock cut into their skin as they grappled on the frozen ground.

Jones tried to knee Boyd in the groin as they fought for control of the pistol. Boyd deflected the blow and pulled with all his strength attempting to take the gun away from him. Jones howled in pain as his broken wrist was twisted violently. He released his grip on the weapon and scrambled away, looking back toward Boyd. Boyd swung the pistol toward Jones as he crabbed toward the cliff's edge.

"Damn you Houston. You got me again. You would never have beat me if I'd had two good hands," he growled.

Boyd looked around frantically for Nellie. She lay in a bloody heap near the edge of the cliff where she had fallen. She groaned softly. The bullet, meant for Boyd, had struck her instead. Boyd ran to her side while attempting to keep an eye on Jones. A nasty gash was torn through her side, blood pumped steadily from the wound, and Boyd quickly ripped cloth from her skirt-tail and pressed it against the wound. Nellie groaned again, then opened her eyes. A faint smile crossed her lips and she took the cloth from his hands and held it in place.

With a rage that surprised even him, Boyd strode toward Jones who crouched on the rocky ledge.

"Now see here Houston, I didn't mean to hurt her. You heard me; I didn't mean her no harm," Jones blurted.

"Jones, I've had about all of you I plan to take. You've robbed and killed folks in this valley without a second thought. Now it's time you got yours." Boyd stepped threateningly toward him.

"No," Jones pleaded, "Take me down to the sheriff. You can't just kill me in cold blood. I didn't mean to hurt her."

"Oh, yeah? What about old Mr. Cooper? You killed him in cold blood and now I'm going to give you a taste of your own medicine."

Jones staggered backward toward the drop-off, fell onto his back, then scrambled again to his feet. Boyd followed him with a dark, angry look on his face. Jones began to plead again, huge tears streaming down his cheeks.

"Oh God, don't do this. I don't want to die."

Boyd approached him cautiously with the pistol clutched in his hand and placed his other palm against Jones's heaving chest. Jones' heels were almost touching the edge of the cliff. Trees and rocks, five hundred feet below, awaited him. Small pebbles and loose debris cascaded over the edge and hurled away into space.

"Sonny, you sure this is what you want to do?" a familiar voice asked from the trees across the clearing.

Boyd and Jones stood face to face with their eyes locked. Boyd looked at the pitiful man before him, wishing with all his might that this horror would be over once and for all. Death and misery had settled on this valley like a dark cloak. Did he want it to continue? Would Jones' death fix everything? Was it his right to kill Jones in retribution for Pop's death? Was vengeance his?

"I reckon you could just go ahead and get it over with," Charlie commented casually, "but I reckon there's better ways to handle vermin like this. It weren't so long ago that I thought that the way to take care of this kind of situation was by an 'eye for an eye, and a tooth for a tooth,' but after all the blood lettin' in the war, I ain't so sure now. I still 'member the looks on the faces of the men I've killed, 'an I don't ever want to see that look again."

Jones shifted his feet nervously, but stood quietly otherwise, allowing Charlie to talk for him. Boyd grasped Jones's shirt front and shoved him threateningly toward the abyss. Jones' arms windmilled frantically and his eyes widened in horror. Then, just at the last second, Boyd pulled him away from the cliff's edge and threw him roughly to the ground. Jones cowered from him as he rubbed his broken wrist.

"Well now, Sonny, I reckon you made a right good decision there. If you had kilt him, you'd have never forgive yourself." Charlie jerked Jones to his feet and quickly tied his hands and feet with a length of rope he carried in his hunting coat.

"I'll just take him along to the sheriff. With Mom Cooper's and my testimony, I don't reckon that he'll escape the rope," Charlie commented.

Boyd staggered drunkenly away from the gaping void and leaned wearily against a large boulder. His breath came in rasping gasps. Then, Boyd bent over Nellie and carefully examined her wound. It wasn't as bad as he had first feared. The bullet had entered her side just under the skin and exited cleanly causing a nasty, painful wound that bled copiously, but she would recover. Nellie smiled weakly at Boyd and struggled to her feet.

"Well, Sonny, I'm right glad that I decided to follow Jones' tracks when I crossed them on the ridge behind the house. I thought he might be out to get you an' Nellie. What do you reckon to do now?"

"I don't know, Charlie. It doesn't look like Nellie will be able to walk all that way to Charleston."

Charlie disappeared into the forest and returned quickly with his horse. "Here, take my horse. Nellie can ride it down off of the mountain. There's a house just down the river that takes in board-ers. You'll have some trouble getting Nellie in there, but tell ole Howard that I sent you. Him and his wife are good folk. They'll let you stay there until she's well enough to travel on."

Boyd objected strenuously, saying that he had lost one of Charlie's horses already.

"You can pay me for the horse," Charlie suggested.

"You know I don't have any money, Charlie," Boyd objected.

"Oh, yeah? Let me show you somethin'." Charlie stepped again into the forest and returned with a battered knapsack. "I found this back in the woods when I trailed Jones up here." He bent quickly and withdrew a familiar moneybelt. "This look like yourn?"

"Oh, Charlie. It is mine." Boyd exclaimed. He opened it quickly and found several thousand dollars in Union bills and gold coin. Jones watched them sullenly from the ground where he lay.

Boyd counted out his money and handed the remainder to Charlie. "Take this to Mrs. Cooper. Maybe it'll help her get by with-out Pop," Boyd said.

"I'll do that, Sonny, but you've overlooked something." Charlie counted out a generous pile of bills and slipped them into Nellie's hand. "Here, Nellie, you deserve the money as much as anyone."

Nellie stared at the money, her mouth hanging open.

"No, Mr. Taylor, I cain't take that money. Folk'll think I done killed and robbed some poor soul," Nellie objected.

Charlie said, "Nellie, you go ahead now and take the money. Part of it is sure to have come from Mr. James. If anyone deserves it, you do!"

"Oh no, I must'nt," Nellie continued.

"Now, just wait a minute, Nellie," Charlie said. "Do you know how much a slave like you is worth?"

"Well, no, I don't. I ain't never been to a slave auction. I weren't allowed," Nelly frowned, not knowing where he was going with all of this talk.

"The money in your hand is more than enough to buy your freedom. Here's what I suggest. Give me enough to buy you from Mr. James' children: they'll inherit his estate. They'll probably be right happy to have the money anyway and shouldn't ask too many questions. Like my friend used to say, 'somethin is better than nothin.'

That way you'll be free. You an' Boyd won't have to look over your shoulder for the sheriff for the rest of your lives. Boyd," Charlie said, turning toward his friend, "I'll mail her bill-of-sale to you at general delivery in Charleston as soon as I can."

Boyd and Nellie smiled broadly at Charlie. He was a true friend—and smart, too! No one objected.

Boyd paid Charlie for the horse, along with the one the Union soldiers had stolen, a price set ridiculously low by Charlie, and shook his hand solemnly.

"Charlie, I can't tell you how much help you've been to me," Boyd said.

"Well now, Sonny, don't go gettin all soft on me. Just you be sure that you come back this way after all this fightin' is over—an' be sure to bring this young lady with you," Charlie grinned foolishly at Nellie. Despite the pain from her wound, Nellie stood on her tiptoes and kissed Charlie lightly. He flushed deeply, grinning his delight. Charlie took Jones by the arm and began the long walk back to the cabin. Jones stumbled along looking over his shoulder at Boyd and Nellie, a confused look on his face.

Boyd took time to help Nellie bind up her wound, then loaded their meager belongings on the horse and helped her climb on. Taking the reins, Boyd led the horse along the cliff to the trail that led down off of the mountain to the river. Boyd looked back at Nellie and smiled. He didn't know what Charleston would be like, but they would soon find out. Maybe after the war they would return to the coast and try the fishing trade again. They reached the valley floor, found a rough wagon track along the river, and turned downstream.

"Boyd," Nellie called softly, "can we stop for a few minutes?"

Boyd helped her dismount; they stood quietly watching the river roll silently by, and Nellie slid comfortably into his arms. The bright November sun filtered down through the bare white branches of the gigantic sycamores that lined the river's edge and cast mottled patterns on their contrasting skins. Their future together was certain to be difficult, but for this moment it didn't matter.

Afterword

Boyd sat on the elevated front porch of the rooming house and watched the traffic on the muddy city street. Wagons and carriages of all descriptions streamed by—he never tired of watching the activity of this bustling town. Occasionally, elegantly dressed women strolled by on the muddy boardwalk that ran the length of the street and looked curiously at the handsome man sitting on the porch.

A heavy pall of smoke hung perpetually over the city and at times made his eyes water. Just up river from the city, large smoky fires burned day and night as saltbrine, from a natural spring, was boiled down for the salt it contained. As interesting as it was, he had no desire to stay in the city. He missed the open beauty of the mountains and the ocean. He would leave at first opportunity.

Charlie had been good to his word. Nellie's bill-of-sale arrived just as promised. She was free now. Boyd had thought that she would be elated, but she was quiet and thoughtful. While they were in the city, she had attempted to wait on Boyd like a servant, and Boyd would have none of it. And, they had argued for the first time over his name. She still insisted on calling him "Mr. Boyd."

After leaving Charlie on the mountain, they had made their way down the river, along the dark, slick waters of the river. For once Charlie had been wrong. No one would allow Nellie to stay in their homes—not even Howard, Charlie's friend. He had said it was okay for Boyd to stay inside, but Nellie was a nigra and had to stay in the shed in back. Boyd had refused, so they had to travel on, sleeping

237

wherever they could find shelter until they had reached Charleston. Nellie's gunshot wound healed rapidly, leaving a nasty, red scar on her side.

Nellie had insisted on posing as his slave, and only then could they find a boarding house in the city that would take them in. The proprietor had objected when Boyd had insisted on a separate room for Nellie, but eventually shrugged his shoulders and said, "It's your decision, mister. But it looks like a waste of good money to me."

Boyd shifted in his chair. A buggy clattered by on the street, a scraggly, brown dog chased along barking furiously at the horses' heels. The driver swore loudly at the dog.

"Mr. Boyd," Nellie called from the doorway. "We's got to talk. "

"Yes, I know Nellie," Boyd replied softly. "Come on out here and sit with me."

"Oh, no, Mr. Boyd, I must'nt. People will talk."

"Nellie, we don't know another living soul here in Charleston. Why would we possibly care what people say?"

"Yes, suh, I knows what you mean. But, I'm afraid of what they'll do to you if they think we's...you know, friendly" Her voice trailed off.

She walked quietly out beside him and sat gingerly in a large wooden rocking chair. Her face was clouded with concern.

"Mr. Boyd," she began. "They's somethin' I's got to tell you."

"Yes, Nellie, I think I already know what you're about to say," Boyd interrupted sadly.

"Mr. Boyd," she began again, "please let me say what I's got to say, before I loses my nerve." She leaned intently toward him and looked deeply into his eyes. "You 'member when I said that you didn't know what it was like to be another man's slave? Well, you can't know what it's like to finally be free, neither. It's like finally having something that you's looked for all of your life an' when you finally gets it, it make your heart ache somethin' fierce. You feel good and bad all at the same time. But, as much as I care for you, I just have to be free an' on my own. Maybe you can't understand that, but I's just got to!"

Boyd sat quietly, looking at the street before him without seeing. He wanted this woman for his own. He wanted a life with her more than he could say, but he also understood what she was saying. He knew that sometimes you had to let go, no matter how much you wanted not to. He remembered the young dolphin his father and he had captured in their ship's nets when he was a boy. He had wanted to take it home and make a pen for it in the bay in front of their cottage. But, his father had convinced him that if he really loved the dolphin, he must release it to be free to roam the oceans. He had not forgotten the lesson his father had taught him.

He looked with misted eyes at Nellie and said "I understand, Nellie." These words cost him more than all of the sorrow he had experienced in the last year. A large lump rose up in his throat and he continued with difficulty. "I have suspected for some time now, Nellie, that the time would come when I would have to set you free. Not just free from the bonds of slavery, but free from being beholdin' to me as well. Yes, Nellie, you should begin to make your own way. To taste freedom as it is meant to be."

Tears were streaming freely down her lovely cheeks. How could this white man be so understanding, and the others so mean. But, maybe they weren't all bad. Maybe there were others out there like Charlie, and Kate, and Boyd. Maybe she would find them too.

♪ ♪ ♪ ♪

Charlie saddled his horse in the livery behind the boarding house. He tossed the saddle on the horse's back, threw the stirrup up over the saddle horn and tightened the cinch. Then, he tossed his new saddlebags on behind the saddle and tied them down. They were pleasantly heavy with the new gear he had bought in town.

Nellie had found a job in town with a seamstress. She was amazed that her bill-of-sale really did show them all that she was a free woman. She would stay in the boarding house until she could find a permanent room. The owner of the boarding house wasn't very happy, but Nellie had more than enough money to pay for the room, and besides, Boyd had insisted. And, when he wanted to, he could be rather intimidating. It wouldn't be easy, but she was confident that somewhere in this town, there would be a place for her. She was excited about her new-won freedom, but sad, too. Life would be much easier if Mazel was alive, and Mr. Joseph, and Henry. But, no, she would make it on her own, because she had to.

Nellie stepped into the bright shaft of light streaming into the livery barn. It highlighted her shape and made her dark hair sparkle like sunlight on a heavy frost. Boyd's throat tightened and he was afraid he couldn't speak. But, then, words weren't necessary. Nelly came to him and kissed him lightly on his weathered cheek. For the last time, Boyd breathed in the woman smell of her, and felt the firmness of her against his chest. The lump was back in his throat.

Nellie whispered in his ear, "Thank you, Boyd. You've been the best friend I have ever had. I will 'member you for all of my life. And, I will never forget that you given me what all those others took from me—my pride and dignity."

Boyd could only nod his head and smile at her. His eyes said everything to her that needed to be said. He stepped into the saddle and rode the horse out into the bright winter sunlight.

He kicked the spirited animal in the ribs and galloped down the street, sending clods of mud flying behind him. Carriages, dogs, and pedestrians scattered before him. He rode quickly out of town and turned to the east, back toward the coast, back where he belonged.